DiVERSE

DiVERSE

CONVERSATIONS WITH YA AND CHILDREN'S VERSE NOVELISTS

Edited by Linda Weste

BLOOMSBURY ACADEMIC
LONDON • NEW YORK • OXFORD • NEW DELHI • SYDNEY

BLOOMSBURY ACADEMIC
Bloomsbury Publishing Plc
50 Bedford Square, London, WC1B 3DP, UK
1385 Broadway, New York, NY 10018, USA
29 Earlsfort Terrace, Dublin 2, Ireland

BLOOMSBURY, BLOOMSBURY ACADEMIC and the Diana logo are
trademarks of Bloomsbury Publishing Plc

First published in Great Britain 2025

Cover design by Jess Stevens

A catalogue record for this book is available from the British Library.

Library of Congress Cataloging-in-Publication Data
Names: Weste, Linda, editor.
Title: DiVerse : conversations with YA and children's verse novelists / edited by Linda Weste.
Description: London ; New York : Bloomsbury Academic, 2025. |
Includes bibliographical references and index.
Identifiers: LCCN 2024014185 (print) | LCCN 2024014186 (ebook) |
ISBN 9781350455276 (paperback) | ISBN 9781350455269 (hardback) |
ISBN 9781350455290 (ebook) | ISBN 9781350455283 (pdf)
Subjects: LCSH: Young adult literature–Authorship. | Children's stories–Authorship. |
Novels in verse–Authorship. | Narrative poetry–Authorship. | Authors–Interviews. |
Poets–Interviews. | LCGFT: Interviews.
Classification: LCC PN147.5 .D59 2025 (print) | LCC PN147.5 (ebook) |
DDC 808.06/83–dc23/eng/20240719
LC record available at https://lccn.loc.gov/2024014185
LC ebook record available at https://lccn.loc.gov/2024014186

ISBN: HB: 978-1-3504-5526-9
        PB: 978-1-3504-5527-6
        ePDF: 978-1-3504-5528-3
        eBook: 978-1-3504-5529-0

Typeset by Integra Software Services Pvt. Ltd.
Printed and bound in Great Britain

To find out more about our authors and books visit www.bloomsbury.com
and sign up for our newsletters.

CONTENTS

Contents

EDITOR'S BIO

Linda Weste has a PhD in Creative Writing from The University of Melbourne and teaches poetry and poetics. A former reviews editor for *TEXT Journal of Writing and Writing Programs*, she has previously published the edited collections *The Verse Novel: Australia & New Zealand* and *Inside the Verse Novel: Writers on Writing*. Her published articles include "Verse Novel Research and Reception in the Twenty-First Century" and "Country in Representations of Speech and Thought in Australian Contemporary Verse Novels." Her adult-category verse novel set in late Republican Rome, *Nothing Sacred*, was published by Arcadia, the fiction imprint of Australian Scholarly Publishing, and won the Wesley Michel Wright Prize.

PREFACE

Verse novels written for young adults or children have been gaining recognition and visibility within publishing, and among reading audiences, since the 1990s. This conspicuous shift in the reception of verse novels has been accompanied by a growing interest in the genre within literary studies and creative writing. With this book—a collection of interviews that gives sole focus to verse novelists writing diverse stories for children and young adults—the primary aim is to expand knowledge of the unique ways such authors combine narrative and poetic elements to compose their distinctive works. Within an ever-widening field, these interviews chronicle a sample of the verse novels for children and young adults published over the past two decades; a diverse sample, as the title suggests.

Yet *DiVERSE: Conversations with YA and Children's Verse Novelists* has a contextual lens as well as an analytical one, in keeping with its secondary aim—to explore the direction and valence of the genre, as it pivots to be more inclusive—more responsive to the diverse world we live in. It offers hopeful and empowering stories of girls and women, of people identifying as LGBTIQ+, First Nations, Black, People of Color, Asian, or from underrepresented ethnicities and religions. There are stories of resilience: of characters between countries, cultures, identities, and languages. And there are verse novels for young adults and children which offer body- and size-positivity messaging or which affirm the experience of being differently abled or living with a chronic medical condition. This curation reflects an editorial commitment to promoting diverse and equitable representation within publishing. The focus on young adult and children's verse novels is indicative of their enabling role at the forefront of change, as a means by which readers can gain new levels of understanding, acceptance, and inclusion across social divides. Indeed, this book invites a global conversation, by seeking to promote mutual understanding and respect between reading communities worldwide, through a genre that leverages its marginality. Verse novels which embody diverse individual and collective stories, histories, and identities contribute to an inclusive expression of human experience.

DiVERSE: Conversations with YA and Children's Verse Novelists contains interviews with twenty-eight verse novelists whose works were published in either the Children's or Young Adult category. Each author was asked to respond to the same nine questions to enable comparative interview responses. Fifty verse novels published in the period 2003–24 are discussed in the interviews. Several titles straddle the boundary with verse biography, and one is a verse memoir; these works arguably also function as stories, and in reception are regarded as such. With respect to editorial curation, the number of participating writers was contingent on several factors including scope, the extent of all interviews combined, and availability for an interview. There certainly were other verse novelists it would have been apt to include, but who could not participate due to their other commitments. As editor I imposed one research-based caveat: because I research the interplay of poetic and narrative elements, I did not include works of prosimetra or works of versiprosa; these works alternate poetry and prose (in varying extent and duration)—"alternate" rather than "integrate"—poetry and narrative. And in order to enable insights about the genre's reception, the participating verse novelists needed to have commercially published works.

The contributors to *DiVERSE: Conversations with YA and Children's Verse Novelists* are resident in the UK, Australia, the United States of America or United States Island nations, or Europe, and may self-identify as: First Peoples/First Nations/Native; Hawaiian/Pacific Islander; Black/African American/diaspora; Asian/Asian diaspora; Latinx/Hispanic diaspora; white; Arab/Arab diaspora, or mixed race and/or ethnicities. There may be multiple dimensions to how contributors identify. Each contributor may additionally identify, for instance, as living with a disabling or chronic condition, as having an underrepresented religion, or as LGBTQIA+. While the abbreviated terms for the large, diverse population of LGBTQIA+ people have global resonance, across cultures and languages other terms are also in use, and collectively these convey groups, communities, and individuals with different ways of identifying and expressing their specific gender identities, sexualities, or sex characteristics.[1]

Readers may encounter several acronyms in the Introduction preceding the interviews. The acronym "BIPOC" is specific to the United States, intended to make central the experiences of Black and Indigenous peoples and demonstrate solidarity between communities of color.[2] Aside from specific contexts, however, this acronym may be inadequate to convey the positionality of Tribal Nations with sovereign rights and "a political relationship with the US government that does not derive from race or ethnicity."[3] One UK source uses the acronym "BAME" (Black, Asian, and minoritized ethnic) in order to acknowledge the significant and distinct Asian population in the UK, including South Asian ethnicities (Indian, Bangladeshi, and Pakistani, for example) and East Asian ethnicities (Chinese, for example).[4] This acronym is intended only for specific contexts too, with users mindful not to imply homogeneity, and mask the diversity within BAME groups.[5] The UK source also uses the terms "racially minoritized" and "minoritized ethnic" to denote that individuals have been minoritized through social processes of power and domination.[6] "Minoritized ethnic" also reflects the fact that ethnic groups which are statistical minorities in the UK are majorities in the global population.[7]

The verse novelists represented in *DiVERSE: Conversations with YA and Children's Verse Novelists* are esteemed, prominent, and prize-winning—in receipt of some of the most recognized prizes and awards, including the Yoto Carnegie Medal for Writing, the John Newbery Medal, the Randolph Caldecott Medal, the Mildred L. Batchelder Award, the Michael L. Printz Award, the Coretta Scott King Book Award, the Stonewall YA Award, and the Jane Addams Peace Award—a contribution that this book serves to amplify and champion. In addition to their verse novels, the writers are recognized for works published in other genres such as children's picture books, poetry, and novels. A biographical note accompanies each writer's interview and offers a summary of their published works.

In order to situate the conversations with verse novelists in this volume, in the Introduction that follows, as editor I offer an overview of global, anglophone contexts for verse novels (Australia, the UK, and the United States) published from the early 2000s to the present day. These contexts provide a backdrop against which the more personal recounts of writerly processes can be set.

"Reflecting Realities" is a commentary which situates verse novels for YA and Children within broader yet immediate social and cultural contexts. It examines diversity monitoring in books and publishing across Australia, the UK, and the United States, as well as responses to diverse verse novels including the impact of book bans, challenges, or preemptive removals in the United States. "Shifts in the Reception of the Genre" offers further commentary on changes in verse novel discourse and in public reception of the genre—in particular, short courses, podcasts, and arts collaborations. "Negotiations in Verse Novel Poetics" examines ways that the representation of diverse voices, identities, and lived experiences can inform and shape how verse novelists combine poetic and narrative elements. "Widening the Lens of Representation" considers some examples of character representations with intersectional dimensions, and "Linguistic Diversity in the Genre" explores several examples of how diverse storytelling can extend the linguistic strategies employed in verse novels, including translanguaging.

ACKNOWLEDGMENTS

General

I wish to express my deep gratitude, first, to the featured verse novelists—thank you for your contribution and community. For supporting the book's concept and development, thank you to Lucy Brown, Commissioning Editor for Literary Studies and Creative Writing, Dr Aanchal Vij, Editorial Assistant, Bloomsbury (Academic Division) Production Department Kate Clissold-Jones Production Editor (Academic and Professional), Subathra Velayoudam and Dharanivel Baskar from Integra. I also acknowledge the support of the Creative Writing Program at the University of Melbourne. The following people are credited for the photographs of the verse novelists: Shevaun Williams, Tad Souden, Gerald Young, Carter Masegawa, Aris Theotokatos, Lillian Nour Warga, Tiffany Crowder, Lluvia Higuera, Mariette Pathy Allen, Paula Landry, Thomas Sammut, Scott Drexler Photography, Nick Jones, Sulei Watene, Philippe Pereira, Andre Bogard, Celia Hélène, Jessica McCollam, Mariam Shakeel, John Rogers, Tasha Gorel, Carter Hasegawa, Spicy, Anna Hastings, and Tim Andersen.

Acknowledgment of Country

The curation of this book has taken place on the traditional land of the Wurundjeri people of the Kulin Nation. In recognition of the importance of self-determination, and in acknowledgment that their sovereignty was never ceded, I pay my respects to their emerging leaders and their Elders past and present. Aboriginal and Torres Strait Islander peoples are the original custodians of the lands and waterways across the continent now called Australia, with histories of continuous connection dating back more than 60,000 years. I specifically wish to respectfully acknowledge contributing author Kirli Saunders—who identifies as a proud Gunai Woman—and whose story "about a First Nations child, on Gundungurra lands," *Bindi*, is an award-winning verse novel. Saunders received an Order of Australia Medal (OAM) for her contribution to the Arts, in particular, Literature, in 2022, and held the esteemed title of New South Wales (NSW) Aboriginal Woman of the Year in 2020.

The characterization of Aboriginal and Torres Strait Islander peoples, and of Native American and Pacific Islander peoples of settler-colonial jurisdictions of the United States, within *DiVERSE: Conversations with YA and Children's Verse Novelists* is in no way intended to foreclose a fuller acknowledgment of the primacy of First Peoples' stories, sovereignties, and unique relationships to land and waterways. Even as *DiVERSE: Conversations with YA and Children's Verse Novelists* advocates for equity in representation within publishing—its advocacy is in no way intended to suggest that the systemic discrimination perpetuating First Peoples' exclusion can be addressed solely through general equity measures. I offer this caveat mindful of the privilege and presumptuousness implicit in the idea of "redress"—which has no correspondence with the irreparable harm done to First Peoples.

INTRODUCTION

Verse novels for younger readers are flourishing in the twenty-first century for a range of reasons, the most compelling of these being the genre's embrace of diversity. This new generation of verse novels reflects a cultural shift in their commitment to diversity of representation in books for young adults and children. Verse novelists have been writing for younger people since the genre sought out this readership in the 1990s and are well aware of their ability to read fiction with complex and challenging themes— so these qualities are already characteristic of contemporary YA and Children's verse novels published in the past two decades. The embrace of diversity is distinctive for being multi-faceted—an encompassing of diverse storytellers; inflections in how stories are being told; nuances in the representation of story worlds; and characters whose identities intersect dimensions including race, class, gender, sexuality, disability, religion, health, and migratory status. The past two decades have also consolidated the verse novel's contribution as a tool to disrupt normative and stereotyped representations and affirm and support identity development in youth. In the push to publish verse novels that honor and respect all younger people, both the quality of representation and the volume of representation matter. *DiVERSE: Conversations with YA and Children's Verse Novelists* gives a central place to this new generation of verse novels that prioritize inclusive storytelling.

Reflecting Realities

DiVERSE: Conversations with YA and Children's Verse Novelists is informed by data that continues to highlight the lack of diversity in books for young adults and children. This is despite a range of diversity monitoring measures in the UK and the United States, and more recently, Australia, as well as action plans to diversify their respective publishing industries.

Much of the available diversity monitoring data dovetails with the work of organizations that champion cultural change. In North America these include: the US metric enabling transparency about the visibility of women writers and reviewers of color, the VIDA Count; the independent Diversity Review of the CILIP Carnegie and Kate Greenaway Awards, as well as CILIP Action Plans; the initiatives Cave Canem and KidLit in Color—which nurture and amplify diverse voices; and organizations which advocate for equitable representation, such as Inclusive Minds, and We Need Diverse Books (WNDB). In the UK, the disparity of representation is on the agenda of both the Centre for Literacy in Primary Education (CLPE) and Spread the Word. Spread the

Word is a registered charity founded by Bernardine Evaristo and Ruth Borthwick in 1995 with the aim of making British literature more inclusive of all voices. Its initiatives, which include Early Career Bursaries, are for writers underrepresented in publishing who identify as Disabled, LGBTQIA+, Working-class or low-income writers, Black, Asian, and Global Majority.[1]

The UK Centre for Literacy in Primary Education (CLPE) has been collating data on representation for half a decade in its series of *Reflecting Realities* reports. These identify and evaluate representation within children's literature for ages 3–11. Their most recent report *Reflecting Realities: Survey of Ethnic Representation within UK Children's Literature 2022* (published 2023) reflects a continuing upward trend in the percentage of published children's books featuring racially minoritized characters, up from previous data—4 percent in 2017, 7 percent in 2018, 10 percent in 2019, 15 percent in 2020, 20 percent in 2021, to 30 percent in 2022. Similarly the percentage of children's books published in the UK with a main character from a racially minoritized background has shown a gradual increase from 1 percent in 2017, 4 percent in 2018, 5 percent in 2019, 8 percent in 2020, 9 percent in 2021, to 14 percent in 2022.[2] The CLPE monitors the quality of representation as well as the volume of representation and has found "the quality of portrayals of characters from racially minoritized backgrounds varies across and within publishing houses."[3] One response from major corporate publishing houses (Penguin Random House, HarperCollins, Hachette, Simon & Schuster, and Macmillan) has been to contract sensitivity readers. The role of these professionals, according to Lecturer in English at the University of London, Sarah Jilani writing for *The Conversation*, is to "provide editorial feedback on omissions, discontinuity, cliché and credibility issues in a book draft—specifically where they relate to subject matter about people from marginalized groups."[4] A further response has been the rise of specialized diversity imprints.

In Australia, *The First Nations and People of Colour Count* issued in September 2022 provides public data on authorship of books across the publishing spectrum—fiction, nonfiction, poetry, in children's and adult categories. The Chief Investigator, Dr. Natalie Kon-yu from Victoria University, analyzed statistics of the number and diversity of Australian books published in 2018.[5] Of the 245 children's books sampled, 3 percent were by First Nation authors, 11 percent were by authors of color, and 86 percent were by other authors. In the sample of seventy-six Young Adult Books, 3 percent were by First Nation authors, 3 percent were by authors of color, and 95 percent were by other authors. Kon-yu's appraisal of the results noted the underrepresentation of Australian First Nations authors and authors of color within the publishing industry.[6]

In the UK, industry reports have been reporting the underrepresentation of BAME employees and promoting change since 2004 when *The Bookseller* and decibel survey into cultural diversity in publishing, *In Full Colour*, identified an "overwhelmingly white and middle-class" workforce.[7] The Publishers Association's report *UK Publishing Workforce 2020: Diversity, Inclusion and Belonging* found that representation of people from BAME groups had "stalled" and that more needed to be done to recruit, retain, and advance staff from these groups.[8] The Publishers Association's report *UK Publishing Workforce*

2022: Diversity, Inclusion and Belonging culminated in a "new, industry wide 'Inclusivity Action Plan' that comprises of a set of ten commitments for publishing businesses to undertake over the period 2023–2026."[9] In 2023, *An Industry-Wide Statement on The Book & Publishing Industry's Professional Values* endorsed by the Association of Authors' Agents, Booksellers Association, The Publishers Association, and The Society of Authors reaffirmed the commitment to "actively promote and cultivate diversity and inclusion in all its forms."[10] Among the initiatives embraced since 2004, Pride in Publishing is one successful industry intervention—established in 2017 to support LGBTQ+ people who work in publishing, it is now a professional network of more than 150 people "including agents, booksellers and publishers from across the big five publishing houses as well as independent presses and freelancers."[11]

In the United States, Diversity Baseline Surveys by Lee & Low Books provide data for the years 2015 (DBS 1.0; published January 2016),[12] 2019 (DBS 2.0; published January 2020),[13] and 2023 (DBS 3.0; published February 2024).[14] A comparison of the "Industry Overall" across the three Diversity Baseline Surveys shows some change, though overall reflects a publishing industry that identifies as white (79 percent; 76 percent; 72.5 percent), cis women (78 percent; 74 percent; 71.3 percent), heterosexual (88 percent; 81 percent; 68.7 percent), and not disabled (92 percent; 89 percent; 83.5 percent).

Since the 2019 survey, the data set has included the university press workforce and literary agents. Laura M. Jiménez, who provides data analysis for DBS 3.0, reports that "Interns continue to be more diverse than the industry as a whole"[15] and notes some progress in the recruitment of BIPOC entry-level publishing staff, as well as significant changes across other areas. The onus for change, however, rests with those already within the publishing industry, to be enabling, to participate in diversity tracking, and to maintain and further improve representation and inclusion. The responsibility and expectation of effecting change should not fall to diverse interns; however, their unique perspective and particular understanding and expertise about exclusionary practices and policies in publishing will make their viewpoints and experiences important to keep focal as the industry progresses. On the question of why diversity in publishing matters, the Lee & Low DBS 2.0 states:

> The book industry has the power to shape culture in big and small ways. The people behind the books serve as gatekeepers, who can make a huge difference in determining which stories are amplified and which are shut out. If the people who work in publishing are not a diverse group, how can diverse voices truly be represented in its books?[16]

The UK Book Trust has contributed to data by commissioning each of Dr. Melanie Ramdarshan Bold's three reports on the representation of creators of color in children's books; these reports collectively monitor diversity from 2007 to 2021. In the latest report, *Representation of People of Colour among Children's Book Creators in the UK 2022*, creators of color in UK children's publishing were more likely to self-publish or publish with a hybrid publisher than white creators.[17] Some creators noted in their interviews being expected or urged to write about racism or on realistic themes in a limited range of genres. These anecdotes raise concerns about structural inequalities and how writers of color are received and understood. The findings are consistent with those gained from *Re:Thinking Diversity in Publishing*,[18] a UK study of bias in cultural production, specifically trade fiction, written by Dr. Anamik Saha and Dr. Sandra van Lente in 2020. At the Report Launch for *Re:Thinking Diversity in Publishing*, Anamik Saha posed key questions pertaining to the bias experienced by creators of color: "When underrepresented writers are published, are they afforded the same creative freedoms as their white counterparts? To what extent are they able to tell the stories they want to tell, in the way that they want to tell them—including … how they are packaged, promoted, and sold." Dr. Anamik Saha asserts that "assumptions in publishing that present as 'common sense' have racializing dynamics behind them." If marketing targets white middle-class readers as the predominant audience for works, then this impacts on acquisitions, and projected sales may be lower, thus rationalizing the decision for less money to be spent on marketing and PR leading to less visibility and ultimately lower sales—so there is a ripple effect on the publication processes.[19]

In Australia, the baseline data on diversity in the broader Arts industries is the August 2019 report *Shifting the Balance: Cultural Diversity in Leadership within the Australian Arts*. The report was produced by Diversity Arts Australia with BYP Group and Western Sydney University, with funding from the Australian Commission for UNESCO.[20] Cultural background as defined by the Australian Human Rights Commission refers to a person's ethnicity and ancestry, and "According to the Australian Human Rights Commission, 39 percent of the Australian population—more than one in three Australians—have a Culturally and Linguistically Diverse background (CALD)."[21] The literature and publishing sector sampled in *Shifting the Balance* had the highest representation of CALD leaders at 14 percent; however, the sector still underrepresented CALD leaders by 25 percent, and more than one in three literature and publishing organizations (37 percent) had no CALD leaders.[22]

Historically, annual data about the Australian publishing industry was compiled in the Australian Publishing Industry Report, also known as the Benchmark Survey by the Australian Publishers Association.[23] Publishers would submit data on their trading results, as well as their staffing and other expenses. This confidential data was, however, made available only to member publishers, or at cost.[24] In a report on Australian publishing in the years 2019–20 *It's Hard to Be What You Can't See: Diversity within Australian Publishing*, Radhiah Chowdhury argued for transparency on the demographic composition of the industry. Without transparency, Chowdhury further argued, baseline data and realistic diversity targets could not be achieved.[25]

The baseline data became available with *The Australian Publishing Industry Workforce Survey on Diversity and Inclusion*, funded by the University of Melbourne and the Australian Publishers Association. According to Susannah Bowen and Beth Driscoll, authors of *The Australian Publishing Industry Workforce Survey on Diversity and Inclusion Report* published in 2022, the Australian book industry employs a workforce that is concentrated in Sydney and Melbourne, predominantly young and female, especially at the lower levels, and is more likely than the general population to be privately educated and to have a postgraduate degree. Further findings reveal that the Australian publishing industry is largely white, including a high percentage of employees who identify as British. Fewer than 1 percent of publishing professionals identify as First Nations, 10.5 percent identify with a European culture (other than British) compared to an estimated 18 percent of the Australian population, and 8.5 percent of respondents to the survey nominate an Asian cultural identity, compared with 17 percent of the Australian workforce. The industry has high LGBTQ+ representation, 21 percent of respondents, compared to estimates of 11 percent in the Australian population.[26] The Australian Publishers Association released the results, noting "the high level of engagement with the survey indicates a strong desire for greater industry diversity and inclusion." Accordingly, the APA has made diversity and inclusion a strategic industry priority. An APA Diversity & Inclusion Working Group will oversee the implementation of specific policy and programs, and track progress toward a more diverse and inclusive sector.[27]

The disparities in representation are compounded by systemic, structural inequities, and exclusionary practices and policies. In the United States, a resurgence of censorship of young adult and children's books that address racism, gender, politics, and sexual identity has been having an impact on culture, education, students' rights, and freedom of expression, according to The National Coalition Against Censorship, PEN America.[28] In its July 1, 2021, to March 31, 2022 Index,[29] PEN reports that bans in that period had an impact on 537 Young Adult books (47 percent of the unique titles listed) including thirty-two verse novels. An update extends that research to June 30, 2022, representing an entire school year in the United States. The data from PEN America's Index of School Book Bans for the period July 1, 2021, to June 30, 2022, lists 2,532 instances of individual books being banned, affecting 1,648 unique book titles. According to the PEN experts reviewing the data, the bans took place in 138 school districts in thirty-two states, impacting 5,049 schools with a combined enrollment of nearly 4 million students.[30] Forty-nine percent of the banned books' intended readers were young adults, and a further 11 percent were middle grade readers.[31]

The findings by PEN accord with those released by the American Library Association (ALA) for 2021. The American Library Association's Office for Intellectual Freedom (OIF), which has been documenting book challenges for more than two decades, found that the number of reported challenges had more than doubled between 2020 and 2021.[32] Then in 2022, a record 2,571 unique titles were targeted for censorship, a further 38 percent increase from the 1,858 unique titles targeted for censorship in 2021. According to the OIF, "the vast majority [of these titles] were written by or about members of the LGBTQIA+ community and people of color."[33]

During the first half of the 2022–3 school year, the number of book bans increased further by 28 percent. Of the 1,477 books banned in that school year, 30 percent were about race, racism, or included characters of color, while 26 percent of unique titles banned had LGBTQ+ characters or themes.[34] Deborah Caldwell-Stone, director of OIF maintains "These numbers … are evidence of a growing, well-organized, conservative political movement whose goals include removing books addressing race, history, gender identity, sexuality, and reproductive health from America's public libraries and school libraries that do not meet their approval."[35]

Some of the books being banned or challenged or pre-emptively removed are titles that are on the Essential Voices curriculum offered by Perfection Learning in the United States. The Essential Voices Collections encompass a range of K-12 books with Asian/ Asian American, Pacific Islander, Black and African American characters, and at the upper levels representing a variety of ethnicities, religious affiliations, and gender identities. The Essential Voices curriculum is designed to make classroom libraries more diverse and inclusive, so that "Students will see themselves in what they read, developing an understanding and appreciation of themselves as well as others around them."[36]

Among the books being banned or challenged or pre-emptively removed from public libraries and school libraries in the United States are those by Native writers. Debbie Reese, a Nambe Pueblo woman, and co-founder in 2006 of the online site American Indians in Children's Literature (AICL), maintains a separate record of the impact of the bans and challenges on books for all age groups by Native writers, and at the time of writing, the covers of thirty-one books are on display on the AICL site.[37]

Several of the verse novels impacted by bans are discussed by their authors in this collection of interviews, namely *The Black Flamingo* by Dean Atta, Jasmine Warga's *Other Words for Home,* and Aida Salazar's *The Moon Within.* The bans also impact on works cited as significant by interviewees: Jacqueline Woodson's verse memoir, *Brown Girl Dreaming*; verse novels *Clap When You Land* and the multi-award-winning *The Poet X* by Elizabeth Acevedo, the inaugural 2022 Poetry Foundation Young People's Poet Laureate. Young adult verse novels have been particularly impacted by book bans, increasingly so. Past and current titles include K.A. Holt's *Redwood and Ponytail*, Meg Grehan's *The Deepest Breath*, and Joy McCullough's *Blood, Water, Paint.* Young adult verse novels by Ellen Hopkins and by Sonya Sones have been subjected to bans; these writers' respective works remain among the more frequently challenged books.

Contributors to this collection are subject to bans on their books in other genres. Margarita Engle's children's picture book *Drum Dream Girl: How One Girl's Courage Changed Music* illustrated by Rafael López is listed in the PEN America Index[38] as banned in classrooms in several States. In her interview, an undeterred Margarita Engle speaks out against censorship. Indeed, Engle joined two other verse novelists represented in this collection—Reem Faruqi and Aida Salazar—as co-signatories to a letter opposed to the removal of 176 books from Duval County, Florida in January 2022. The letter was sent to the Chairperson, Vice Chairperson and Duval County School Board Members by PEN America, We Need Diverse Books, and seventy authors and illustrators.[39]

PEN America and the ALA are the main organizational representatives acting in defense of intellectual freedom. The OIF has compiled information and data about efforts to censor books in libraries for more than twenty years.[40] The ALA coordinates The Merritt Fund to assist librarians facing discrimination for defending intellectual freedom, and in 2022 launched Unite Against Book Bans, a national initiative to mobilize support for libraries and to oppose censorship.

In conjunction with other ALA platforms including Banned Books Week and the Top Most Challenged Book lists, these initiatives are the means by which, according to Tracie D. Hall, former Executive Director of the American Libraries Association, "libraries convene, empower, and mobilize their campuses and communities."[41] School-based activism includes students and their parents attending school council meetings in protest and calling for the reinstatement of books to libraries and classrooms. These actions have been successful in overturning some banning decisions. Librarian actions, on the other hand, have been stymied in some states by litigation, threatened and actual. Such litigation, Hall maintains, "increasingly positions and compels library workers on and to the frontlines of book banning and censorship challenges."[42]

A "Right to Read Bill" H.R. 2889 put before the 118th US Congress in 2023, seeks to protect access to books for school students, and provide "liability protection to teachers, school librarians, school leaders, paraprofessionals, and other staff for actions that conform with state or local policies regarding the right to read."[43] Citizens opposing book bans successfully sued county officials in Llano County, Texas, "claiming their First and 14th Amendment rights were violated when books—deemed inappropriate by some people in the community and Republican lawmakers—were removed from public libraries or access was restricted."[44] An amendment to the Illinois Library System Act, House Bill 2789 introduced in February 2023, passed both state houses and was approved by Governor JB Pritzker in June. The bill became effective January 1, 2024, and protects the freedom of public libraries to add to their collections without outside limitation.[45] At the time of writing, one of the latest developments is that PEN America, along with other plaintiffs including authors and publisher Penguin Random House, has permission to proceed with their lawsuit against Escambia County School District and the Escambia County School Board for its decision to remove and restrict books from public school libraries.[46]

Shifts in the Reception of the Genre

The reception of young adult and children's verse novels can be gauged to some degree by the extent of current and projected publication. Both boutique and multinational publishers of verse novels have forthcoming titles, and industry reports of book deals reflect projected verse novel publication continuing over the decade. In a *Publishers Weekly* profile of literary agents of middle grade books, agents reported a higher incidence of verse novel projects coming across their desks.[47] Several of these agents specify verse novels in their wish-list. Penny Moore of Aevitas Creative Management notes "an uptick in novels written in verse" for the middle grades, an increase she deems "partially due to the recent success of books like Rajani LaRocca's *Red, White, and Whole* and Lisa Fipps's *Starfish*."[48] Alyssa Eisner Henkin, Founder of Birch Path Literary received "quite a few submissions in poetic verse," and Stefanie Sanchez Von Borstel, Agent and cofounder of Full Circle Literary reports "a similar bump in novel-in-verse projects."[49] Von Borstel attributes the success rate of verse novel submissions as partly due to the fact that "Submissions continue to be polished, thanks to mentorships and programs from organizations like Las Musas, Kweli, LatinxPitch, SCBWI, DiverseVoices, and We Need Diverse Books."[50]

The growing demand for and supply of verse novel-specific courses, seminars, and workshops is a further indicator of improved reception. Of the contributors to *DiVERSE: Conversations with YA and Children's Verse Novelists* who have academic qualifications, seventeen have undertaken a BA or an MFA, in English, Creative Writing, Poetry, or Literature. Highlights Foundation, a US not-for-profit organization, has run various iterations of verse novel courses at Introductory, Crafting, and Revision stages, most recently under the direction of Cordelia Jensen—including two courses featuring a guest verse novelist, to date, Amber McBride,[51] and Andrea Beatriz Arango.[52] Highlights Foundation additionally features nine guest blog posts or podcasts about verse novels with presenters Joy McCullough, Padma Venkatraman, and contributors to this volume, Margarita Engle, Aida Salazar, Rajani LaRocca, Chris Baron, and Cordelia Jensen.[53] A 2023 Highlights Foundation In-person 4-Day/3-Night Workshop and Retreat featured three verse novelist contributors to this volume: Rajani LaRocca, Chris Baron, and Cordelia Jensen.[54] Highlights Foundation in partnership with the Diverse Verse Initiative also provides a scholarship for one diverse writer to attend a virtual verse novel writer workshop.[55] A two-night online mini "Writing Poetry to Empower" was deemed "a great fit" for poets, those who "love poetry," or those "working on a verse novel".[56] The presenters were verse novelist Padma Venkatraman—whose *A Time to Dance* is about a young dancer who must reinvent herself after losing her leg—and Aida Salazar, a contributor to this volume, and author of verse novels *The Moon Within, Land of the Cranes,* and *A Seed in the Sun.*

The introduction of several databases which feature verse novels and diverse books for YA and children further attests to the enhanced reception of the verse novel genre. In 2021, Australia gained a dedicated verse novel database, the Australian Verse Novels Resource; a world-first. Developed by the National Centre for Australian Children's Literature Inc., a registered charity, the database provides synopses and teaching resources for all verse novels for YA and younger readers published in the region.[57] The verse novel *Bindi* by Kirli Saunders, contributor to this volume, Sally Morgan's *Sister Heart,* and *His Father's Eyes* by Ali Cobby Eckermann each receive dual listing in the NCACL Aboriginal and Torres Strait Islander Resource which specifically celebrates children's books by and about Australia's Aboriginal and Torres Strait Islander Peoples.[58] Inclusive literature for younger readers is the focus of the NCACL Cultural Diversity Database which provides a collection of culturally diverse Australian children's books with links to the Australian Curriculum and the Early Years Framework for education professionals.[59]

The shift in the reception of verse novels for young adults and children since 2000 can be viewed as correlative with a succession of high-profile awards. The Chartered Institute of Library and Information Professionals confers the annual British Literary award, the Yoto Carnegie Medal for Writing, upon the author of a book for children or young adults that creates an "outstanding reading experience"[60] and thus, when Irish author Sarah

Crossan's *One*, a verse novel about conjoined twins, won the Medal in 2016, it placed verse novels under a global spotlight. Verse novels for young adults and children began to be captured in the sales data generated by Nielsen Book Research. The Yoto Carnegie Medal for Writing win also paved the way for future verse novel entries. In 2019, three of the eight books shortlisted for the Yoto Carnegie Medal for Writing were verse novels—Jason Reynolds's *Long Way Down*, Kwame Alexander's *Rebound*, and Elizabeth Acevedo's *The Poet X*. The winning 2019 Yoto Carnegie Medal for Writing was awarded to *The Poet X*, by Dominican American, Elizabeth Acevedo. Each of these verse novels became available in the more upmarket literary larger paperback, BC Trade format, as well as hardback. *Long Way Down* also gained a graphic novel version,[61] the first YA verse novel to do so. Verse novelist Yoto Carnegie nominees continued in 2020 and 2021: Dean Atta's *Black Flamingo* in 2020, then Manjeet Mann's *Run, Rebel* and Elizabeth Acevedo's *Clap When You Land* had dual honors as Yoto Carnegie nominees in 2021. The graphic novel adaptation by illustrator Danica Novgorodoff of Jason Reynolds's verse novel *Long Way Down* won the Yoto Kate Greenaway Medal (now the Yoto Carnegie Medal for Illustration) in 2022.[62]

Verse novels for young adults and children now feature in an increasing number of online "top picks" or "best of" selections, recent examples of which include The *Guardian's* "Top 10 verse novels,"[63] *Books for Keeps* "Ten of the Best: Verse Novels,"[64] and *Barnes & Noble* "The Best Novels in Verse to Read Right Now B&N Reads".[65] These "best of" young adult and children's verse novel listings have only begun to proliferate with the rising visibility of verse novels for those age groups. In 2006 by contrast, there was just one "best of" selection listing[66] to be found online (or in print for that matter)—for adult-category verse novels.

A significant shift in reception is that verse novels are starting to be adapted into cross-media format products including podcasts and featuring in arts collaborations. Four verse novelists for young adults and children—K.A. Holt, Rajani LaRocca, Reem Faruqi, and Chris Baron—are guests of the presenter, Melissa Thom, in episodes 10 to 13 of "The Joy of Novels in Verse" for Thom's *The Joyful Learning Podcast*, held during April 2023.[67] The world premiere adaptation of the young adult verse novel *Run, Rebel* by Manjeet Mann—a Pilot Theatre co-production with Mercury Theatre Colchester, Belgrade Theatre Coventry, Derby Theatre, and York Theatre Royal—toured the UK during March–April 2023.[68] The first season of a television series based on *The Crossover* by Kwame Alexander, a verse novel that won the Newbery Medal and Coretta Scott-King Award Honor, was released on IMDb in 2023.[69] Kirli Saunders was one of four celebrated Australian verse novelists who were panelists in a "Verse Novel Poetics" pre-event for Story/Verse Queensland Poetry Festival 2023.[70]

Verse novels arguably gain profile through the appointments of Poets Laureate. Forty-four states in the United States currently have a poet laureate position. Additionally, many cities honor a poet in their community with the title of Poet Laureate. Two participants in this collection served a term as state poet laureate. Cordelia Jensen, author of YA verse novels, *Skyscraping* and *The Way the Light Bends* was Poet Laureate of Perry County, PA in 2006 and 2007, and Ishle Yi Park, author of *Angel and Hannah*, was Poet Laureate of

Queens, NY. Of the eight recipients of the Poetry Foundation Young People's Laureate (formerly Children's Poet Laureate) since its inception in 2006, three writers have published verse novels: Margarita Engle was selected by the Poetry Foundation to serve from 2017 to 2019 as the sixth Young People's Poet Laureate. Other verse novelists who have previously served in laureate positions are Tina Cane, author of *Alma Presses Play*, as Rhode Island state Poet Laureate 2016 to 2021, Jacqueline Woodson, author of verse novel *Locomotion* and verse memoir *Brown Girl Dreaming*, from 2015 to 2017 as Young People's Poet Laureate, Elizabeth Acevedo, writer of the verse novels *The Poet X*, and *Clap When You Land*, also as Young People's Poet Laureate 2022 to 2024, and Joseph Bruchac, author of verse novel *Rez Dogs*, as inaugural poet laureate of Saratoga Springs, NY. In the UK, Sarah Crossan was the Laureate na nÓg (Irish Children's Literature Laureate) from 2018 to 2020.

Negotiations in Verse Novel Poetics

The verse novelists featured in this volume share two fundamental understandings of verse novel poetics: the first of these is that a verse novel has narrative conventions to fulfil: its *narrativity*, that is, the elements that make a story interpretable as a story, namely a story world and a temporal sequence of incidents in connection with characters, mediated from particular perspectives and through acts of utterance or articulation. The second fundamental understanding is that a verse novel has poetic conventions to fulfil: its *poeticity*—which can include any of a range of poetic elements: metaphors, alliteration, types of rhyme, rhythmic-, syllabic-, and visual-patterning, white space which can be read for meaning, and segmentation that can shape and impact meaning at word-level, line-level, stanza-level, and so on. For the verse novelists, these elements are certainly not mere decoration; they inflect and nuance every aspect of their works. Yet nor are the elements always the same, or uniformly applied. The verse novelists utilize a range of poetic forms, and the structures or divisions within their verse novels differ as well, so it requires a good deal of trial and error, and problem-solving. The rigor needed to negotiate the poetic elements in a novel in verse necessitates a knowledge and awareness of formal structures and technical methods.

Of course the choice to represent diverse voices, identities, and lived experiences informs and shapes how verse novelists combine poetic and narrative elements. In her interview, Jasminne Mendez, a Dominican American who lives in Houston, Texas, describes how and why she wrote *Aniana Del Mar Jumps In*, a middle grade verse novel about a twelve-year-old swimmer Aniana diagnosed with Juvenile Arthritis—a story informed by her own experiences of multiple chronic illnesses and disability. Mendez set the story in Galveston, Texas, structured most of the middle section of her verse novel into hurricane categories, and employed a hurricane metaphor to convey Aniana's changing emotions and the physical effects of her Juvenile Arthritis. By extending the use of the metaphor, Mendez could incorporate a range of natural phenomena in the verse novel's imagery and language, which in turn assisted character development.

Rhyme, onomatopoeia, alliteration, metaphor, and simile are among the poetic elements incorporated by First Nations author Kirli Saunders in her verse novel *Bindi*. Saunders explains her choice of poetic techniques: "These techniques bring colour and texture to the story, and make for a more engaging read, especially when read aloud as *Bindi* often is. They also add a melody and lyricism to the story, mimicking a song."[71]

In Mariko Nagai's provisionally titled, forthcoming verse novel, *The Sword of Yesterday*, the protagonist is a Japanese refugee, smuggled then relocated to California as part of the Wakamatsu Tea and Silk Colony. Nagai chose poetic elements to correlate with the historical story world and Japanese traditional forms. As the protagonist "was born as a samurai's daughter of the Aizu Wakamatsu Clan," Nagai chose a poetic form with roots in ninth-century Japanese court poetry, the tanka, though, Nagai specifies "it's more a renga/tanka, each stanza carrying 5-7-5-7-7 syllable structure."[72] Nagai was born in Tokyo, Japan, and has lived in Belgium, England, America, and Japan where she currently resides.

The verse novel *Angel & Hannah* reimagines Shakespeare's *Romeo and Juliet* in its depiction of Hannah, a working-class Korean American teenager from Queens, and Angel, a Puerto Rican boy from Brooklyn who fall in love at a quinceañera in 1990s New York. The verse novel has a cadence based in hip hop, sonnets, and spoken word traditions. Ishle Yi Park "wrote a combination of Petrarchan, Elizabethan, Spenserian and free verse sonnets, and some that were hybrid mixtures of two or more of those styles," though acknowledges in her interview, "When I felt too constricted by the singsong melodies of iambic pentameter, I'd change it up to make it less rhyme-y."[73]

In Holly Thompson's interview about *The Language Inside*, to provide context for why the poems of her bilingual, raised-in-Japan character, Emma, "sometimes incorporate *kanji*—the logographic characters used in Japanese writing," Thompson states: "In those poems, I wanted English-language readers to be able to sense the dimensionality of *kanji*, gain a glimpse of that visual richness, and quickly see how English and other alphabet languages lack that aspect. A person raised in a language like Japanese will inevitably sense a missing dimension in a language like English."[74] Thompson herself has been a long-term resident of Kamakura, Japan, though was born in Massachusetts, in the United States.

The many instructive comments by verse novelists in *DiVERSE: Conversations with YA and Children's Verse Novelists* reveal how they approach the rigorous technical demands of writing a verse novel, and in particular the complex negotiation of narrative and poetic elements with social, linguistic, and cultural knowledges necessary for nuanced representation of diverse voices, identities, and lived experiences.

Widening the Lens of Representation

For the verse novelists featured in *DiVERSE: Conversations with YA and Children's Verse Novelists*, the quality of representation matters. That it matters is evident in their percipient portrayals of characters and story worlds, in their avoidance of stereotypes, and in the broadening of representation beyond traditional norms. Indeed, quality matters because representation can be a radical and powerful act of inclusion. Representation shapes the imaginable. These verse novelists embrace diversity in their featured verse novels—that is, they negotiate dimensions including race, class, gender, sexuality, disability, religion, health, and migratory status—constructing meaning in and through language, in and through poetic and narrative elements, to achieve nuance in their representation of characters and story worlds; the dimensions inflect the stories being told.

For Dean Atta, whose young adult verse novels *The Black Flamingo* and *Only on the Weekends* have Black gay protagonists—it was paramount to tell the sort of story he *wanted to tell*, in *the way he wanted to tell it*. This was important because he "never encountered any books about Black gay characters when [he] was a teenager in the 1990s and early 2000s,"[75] but also because of the need for queer Black, joy stories. In conversation with Jane Link for the blog *bigblackbooks*, Atta states, "We have a lot of tragic stories, and we have a lot of important, necessary stories about the pain and the trauma. But I think the stories about joy and love are equally important and necessary."[76] Atta was named on "The IoS Pink List 2012" as one of the most influential LGBT people in the UK by the Independent.[77]

Kaija Langley's young adult verse novel about grief, family, and change, *The Order of Things*, is set in Boston, MA., and the story centers "on Black working-class families— two single Black parents, two single Black kids [April and Zee]—that each have a non-traditional family structure."[78] Papa Zee is a widower and April's mother, Chantelle, is a single, Army veteran who only dates women. Langley's character choices were intentional. "These characters [Langley explains] and their intersections of race, class, and sexual orientation are not often seen in children's literature, but they exist and deserve to be on the page for young readers."[79]

Each of Aida Salazar's verse novels exemplifies her concern with issues of identity and social justice, but it was her daughter's experience as an Afro-Latina reaching puberty that led Salazar to write *The Moon Within* to create a positive narrative about menstruation for younger readers. The verse novel's protagonist, eleven-year-old Celi, of mixed Black–Puerto Rican–Mexican heritage, is dreading the onset of periods. Her Xicana mother is planning an empowering "moon ceremony"—an ancestral tradition to mark girls' entry into womanhood. Celi is attracted to Iván who is mixed heritage, Black and Mexican, and her best friend, Mar, who is Mexican, is going through transition— from girl to xochihuah, a nonbinary identity.

This intention to portray and positively represent character diversity continues in Lucy Cuthew's YA verse novel *Blood Moon* which extends the representation of young people's bodily autonomy to the upper grades, to address periods, sex, shaming, and online abuse. Chris Baron's Jewish heritage and his personal experiences of fat-shaming and bullying inform *All of Me*, a verse novel about thirteen-year-old Ari who is learning self-acceptance. In *The Magical Imperfect*, themes of mental and physical health are central, with three characters who experience debilitating conditions—depression, anxiety, and severe eczema—in a larger narrative of a supportive multicultural neighborhood in the aftermath of San Francisco's 1989 earthquake.

In historical verse novels, the decision to represent diverse voices, identities, and lived experiences extends to the voiceless, forgotten, or disenfranchised. Stephanie Hemphill pursues stories about historical women and girls of all demographics, knowing full well that "It's easier to ignore a voice you don't hear, a girl not visible on the page."[80] Hemphill is committed to "digging around in the past," so that more diverse, marginalized (and to her mind interesting) people and stories can be discovered and brought to a new readership.[81] Ann E. Burg consulted archaeological artifacts, research, and archives including the Writers Project of America (WPA) Slave Narratives for her historical verse novel *Unbound* about exiled peoples living in the regions of the Dismal Swamp. Helen Frost sourced histories of d/Deaf education, war time, and memoirs by conscientious objectors for her verse novel *All He Knew* about the experiences of an institutionalized deaf boy helped by a Conscientious Objector (CO) in the Second World War.

Human rights, feminism, activism, and agency are central to a number of the featured verse novels. In Melanie Crowder's interview, she discusses her historical verse novel *Audacity*, an inspiring story about labor activist Clara Lemlich. Lemlich was born into a Jewish family who emigrated to New York in 1903 from Russian-occupied territory (now Ukraine). Lemlich began work in the New York textile-manufacturing industry and was instrumental in improving working conditions in the factories on Manhattan's Lower East Side. Lemlich and the International Ladies' Garment Workers' Union led the largest strike by women in American history, the famous Shirtwaist Strike of 1909, famously known as the Uprising of the 20,000. Crowder states: "I couldn't write about life in the sweatshops at the turn of the last century without a mention of the sexual harassment the women faced."[82] *Audacity* earned recognition as a National Jewish Book Award Finalist, and Best Jewish Children's Books of 2015, Tablet Magazine. In Margarita Engle's verse novel *Rima's Rebellion: Courage in a Time of Tyranny*, the focus is on suffragists in Cuba during the 1920s and 1930s, and how women and girls struggled to gain voting rights, overthrow a dictator, overturn a misogynistic divorce law that allowed legal femicide, and gain the right to education for illegitimate children—and while Engle acknowledges, "These are complex situations," she asserts "I truly do respect the modern young reader's ability to understand history."[83]

It is notable furthermore, that these diverse and inclusive verse novels for young readers reflect the importance of social responsibility, that is, of elevating marginalized voices and empowering others, eliminating systemic inequalities, defying stereotypes and restrictive gender norms, and calling out and pushing back at racism and other forms of prejudice. Many of the featured verse novels are notables on the Honor List of the Rise Feminist Book Project.[84] *Rima's Rebellion* features on the 2023 Middle Grade Fiction Honor List alongside Aida Salazar's *A Seed in the Sun* which received additional honors as a Rise Feminist Book Project "Top Ten" for its story of Lula, a young farmworker who meets activist Dolores Huerta and joins the 1965 Delano Grape Strike seeking justice for farmworkers' rights. In previous years, notables include: on the 2022 Middle Grade Fiction category List, Rukhsanna Guidroz's *Samira Surfs*, about an eleven-year-old Rohingya refugee living in Cox's Bazar, Bangladesh, who finds peace and empowerment in a local surf club for girls; on the 2021 Middle Grade Fiction category List, *Land of the Cranes* by Aida Salazar, a story about Betita whose detention by the US government for being undocumented awakens her activism; and Carole Boston Weatherford's *Beauty Mark: A Verse Novel of Marilyn Monroe* in the same year for The Young Adult Fiction category. The Rise Feminist Book Project was formerly The Amelia Bloomer List 2002–19 and in 2016, contributor Marilyn Hilton received a listing for her middle grade verse novel *Full Cicada Moon* about mixed race, Japanese and Black, Mimi, who resists racist and sexist stereotyping to pursue science, and her dream to be an astronaut.

Linguistic Diversity in the Genre

The linguistic diversification within the verse novels featured in *DiVERSE: Conversations with YA and Children's Verse Novelists* constitutes a significant shift for the genre. Certainly, a contributing context is this generation of verse novels' emergence over the past two decades—a period characterized by a multilingual turn, and thus marked by dynamic, evolving, and negotiated uses of language. Linguistic diversification in these verse novels is nonetheless paradoxical, framed by their monolingual contexts—by having been first published in English in Anglophone countries, they are situated within social orders and corresponding social hierarchies that use English as global lingua franca. These verse novels' "familiar norms" are, in their first instantiation, "anglophone norms" encumbered with the assumption of monolingualism.

The conversations with the verse novelists in *DiVERSE* foreground their communicative choices and negotiations with language—including how they navigate monolingual paradigms—as they create diverse characters and stories. Ann E. Burg's verse novel *Serafina's Promise* places eleven-year-old Serafina living with her parents and her grandmother in a mountain village outside of Port-au-Prince, Haiti at the time of the 2010 earthquake. The verse novel includes Haitian Creole phrases, and these are explained in the glossary. Leza Lowitz's verse novel *Up from the Sea* is set mostly in Japan, and accordingly, the initial drafts contained many cultural references and Japanese words and phrases. At each stage of the editing, Lowitz had to decide which words to keep and which to delete. She "ended up leaving only the Japanese words … [that] were essential to convey meaning, important cultural aspects and local history/atmosphere of the story, putting short notes on the pages where these Japanese words appeared."[85]

Thanhhà Lại reflects on writing her verse novel *Inside Out & Back Again* and recalls, "I wanted my poems to read as if they were written in Vietnamese, which (to me) is naturally poetic and concise. Vietnamese has no articles, so for a short time I deleted every 'a', 'an', 'the' from the manuscript. My editor suggested I put them back because, even disguised as Vietnamese, English relies rather strongly on those pesky little words."[86] In answer to what poetic or narrative effects she was hoping to achieve, Lại responds, "One, what it's like to think in Vietnamese, a naturally poetic language. Two, what happens when English mixes into the original voice."[87] Lại was able to further explore these effects in writing *When Clouds Touch Us*, the sequel for *Inside Out & Back Again*. *When Clouds Touch Us* resumes Hà's story one year later. "But the way Hà processes language has changed," Lại explains. In *Inside Out & Back Again* "Hà is thinking exclusively in Vietnamese," whereas in *When Clouds Touch Us*, "Hà knows enough English to at times automatically think in that second language. I wanted to show how the gray avalanche of English has infiltrated her mind. The crisp feel of Vietnamese is still in the poems but weighted at times by the wordiness of English." Lại recalls another linguistic difference in the sequel—"Also, Hà thought in many more similes and metaphors that I eventually deleted to convey how her mind was shifting to a more practical, direct, yet wordy language."[88]

Safia Elhillo made the decision to include Arabic without translation throughout *Home Is Not a Country*. Elhillo, who identifies as Sudanese American, says she was "always thinking a lot about language, often specifically the relationship between English and Arabic" and came to accept—"if that makes the poem less readable to a non-Arabophone reader, that's okay."[89] In Elhillo's early writing she had attempted to transliterate Arabic into English, but came to the conclusion that "it just felt ugly, and it didn't make the sounds in my head, and it wasn't creating any music."[90] To explain her preference for writing in verse, Elhillo states, "Language just feels a lot more malleable in a poem in a way that is much more reflective of what language feels like inside my head; the texture of language before it is spoken."[91] Poetry also offers a release for Elhillo from the stricture of "proper" English and "correct" grammar, and her concerns about fluency. As Elhillo states, "I get to invent my English as one of many 'Englishes."[92]

Jasmine Warga "wanted to honor and exalt the Arabic language"[93] in her middle grade verse novel, *Other Words for Home*, about a young girl called Jude who must leave Syria and is sent to live in the United States with relatives. Jude grapples with the cultural differences and for the first time in her life her identity is referred to as "Middle Eastern." Warga's choice meant "trying to write in a way that captured the cadence, texture, and lyricality of Arabic."[94] Warga states: "I also thought deeply about how I ordered the words on the page as I was trying to mimic the cadence and texture of Arabic in a book that is written in English."[95]

The potential of linguistic diversification within verse novels is at once, valuable, generative, and powerful: valuable—because verse novels gain valence as sites that affirm and sustain minoritized languages and speakers; generative—because the embrace of transnational linguistic repertoires of multilingual language users/speakers, in turn, requires a more complex understanding of the communicative situations in verse novels; and powerful—because they enact inclusion, present an overt challenge to readers' attitudes to language, and disrupt entrenched ideologies that uphold monolingualism as a norm.

In terms of generative possibilities, Warga's comment that verse is "a wonderful space for translanguaging"[96] invites a pathway for inquiry, and creative practice. Translanguaging in verse novels enables a character the ability to think bilingually or in multiple languages and to sample language strategies in thought or speech in ways that suit their communicative situations. The presumption of the textual projection of a stable, unified voice refracts in such a presentation. To assume a character has recourse to any linguistic strategy in their multilingual repertoire—including language skills developed in and informed by prior experience—potentially alters how that character interacts with and perceives the story world of which they are a part. It may alter the rhythms of that character's speech and thought, the mode of their interactions, and the dialogues they have with other characters in the story world. For a verse novelist, achieving the presentation of bilingualism or multilingualism in a character's thought and speech entails cultural knowledge, but also consideration of language production and function, and the cognitive processes behind language use.

Linguistic diversification within verse novels reflects changes within broader poetry over recent decades, both on and off the page, in the growing reception of global poetries. The conventions or familiar norms associated with Slam and Spoken Word, for instance—how a given "page poem" might be recited, or a "stage poem" might be read—have undergone revision. According to Tim Shortis, Co-Director of Poetry By Heart, the design of recitation competitions held in and across UK schools, "has stepped away from some of the poetry recitation legacies of the past … by valuing pupils speaking in their natural voices where earlier modes of recitation had been associated with elocution and the privileging of a Received Pronunciation accent."[97] On the page, just as some poems achieve their poetic and narrative effects by moving verse in the direction of prose, so too, do some verse novels accomplish their effects by moving their poems in the direction of prose. This fluidity continues to be noted in the novel too—whereby prose moves closer to free verse on the page, in adopting loose verse-like lines of variable length. Bernardine Evaristo's *Girl, Woman, Other* is a fitting example of such a novel: it "employs a pro-poetic patterning on the page and non-orthodox punctuation …"; an approach which Evaristo has coined "fusion fiction."[98]

The verse novel continues to innovate, leveraging its marginality as a genre, as these contexts and excerpts suggest. The writers represented in *DiVERSE: Conversations with YA and Children's Verse Novelists* faced the challenges of the verse novel, but importantly, sought ways to enhance and advance it. Collectively their reflections enable greater understanding of the genre's embrace of diverse voices, identities, and lived experiences by revealing how dimensions including racial identity, class, gender, sexuality, disability, religion, health, and migratory status are negotiated in interplay with the verse novel's poetic and narrative elements. Their verse novels counter past erasure and marginalization. By ensuring diverse voices, identities, and lived experiences—vital to an inclusive expression of human experience—these stories in poetry are more responsive to, and celebrate, the diverse world that we live in.

CHAPTER 1
MARGARITA ENGLE

Margarita Engle by Shevaun Williams

There are so many amazing verse novelists. When I was starting out it was a rare form, but now it is common, and young writers are mastering it so beautifully.

Margarita Engle is the Cuban-American author of many verse novels, memoirs, and picture books, including *The Surrender Tree, Enchanted Air, Drum Dream Girl, Dancing Hands, Your Heart, My Sky, A Song of Frutas, Light for All, Rima's Rebellion*, and *Singing with Elephants*. Awards include a Newbery Honor, Pura Belpré, Golden Kite, Walter, Jane Addams, PEN America Literary, and NSK Neustadt, among others. Margarita served as the national 2017–19 Young People's Poet Laureate. Her most recent young adult verse novels include *Wings in the Wild* and *Wild Dreamers*. Recent picture books include *Eloísa's Musical Window and Water Day*. Engle's next verse novel is *Island Creatures*.

Margarita was born in Los Angeles but developed a deep attachment to her mother's homeland during childhood summers with relatives on the island. She studied agronomy and botany along with creative writing, and now lives in central California with her entomologist husband and squirrel-chasing Border Collie. Margarita's website can be found at margaritaengle.com.

Your Heart, My Sky (2021)
Rima's Rebellion (2022)

What ideas or influences did you have in mind when creating this work?

Your Heart, My Sky was inspired by my visits to relatives in Cuba during the 1990s. It was a time called *el período especial en tiempos de paz* (the special period in times of peace) when the Cuban government ordered everyone to make wartime sacrifices in peacetime. Cubans had no choice. The sacrifices were forced by hunger. A sudden loss of Soviet economic support meant food shortages so catastrophic that islanders were close to starving. I wrote *Your Heart, My Sky* as a love story because no matter how terrible the times, people still fall in love. I had written about the decade of hunger while it was happening, for adult readers, in a more journalistic style, as well as in prose fiction. The result shocked me. Essentially, no one in the United States and Latin America cared. Many people simply did not believe me. So now I've decided to try again, with hopes that young readers will be more empathetic. We are living in a time when food could suddenly disappear anywhere on Earth.

How did you approach writing this verse novel? What were the various stages in its development?

Experience was the most important resource. I had to face painful memories. The emotions of that time and place cannot be found in history books, because the lack of freedom of expression forced people to keep their feelings secret in public. Only within family homes could one see the empty refrigerators and hear the true tales of hunger. Only within the family circle could one know if a relative had fled on a raft. I had experienced these things, and now I had to recall the details, transforming them into verse. My goal was to remain hopeful, while telling a true story of decisions made by young Cubans during a time of danger.

Can you recall problem-solving decisions you had to make in the writing process?

I wanted to contrast the impact of hunger for Cubans with the simultaneous development of tourism for foreigners. Tourists attending the Pan American Games in Havana in 1991 feasted at lavish hotel buffets, while local people starved. However, I needed to remain focused on the love story too, so I didn't want to make the style journalistic. Another decision was showing how older people, who had farmed when they were young, could help teenagers rediscover agriculture. I needed to show how the government retained control of food, except when people secretly decided to plant their own seeds.

Which poetic and narrative techniques did you decide to employ, and why?

Your Heart, My Sky is written in free verse with three voices, Liana, Amado, and Paz the singing dog. The dog is actually very important in this story, because he is a link with Cuba's Taíno ancestry, a symbol of hope. For centuries, historians have repeated the colonial Spanish claim that Indigenous Cubans are "extinct." In reality, we survive. At least a third of Cubans (including me) have maternal Indigenous ancestry. In my case, I am traced to a Ciboney woman born in 1550. This proves to me that there is always hope for survival, despite starvation, plagues, and oppression. I chose to use Paz as a matchmaker in the story, as well as a trailing dog who helps Liana and Amado locate scattered sources of wild food.

If there were places in the book where you felt it was best to emphasize the poetic strategies over the narrative strategies, or vice versa—what guided these decisions?

In most of my verse novels I choose emotions as the heart of the story, even when there are historical facts to incorporate. That's why I write in first person and present tense. I want to invite the reader to time travel with me to another era and a place. Historical experiences can be imagined to some extent, but they are only complete when shared by entering a character's mind. How did it feel? What would you do in this situation? This is why I always ask teachers to refrain from analyzing poems. Instead of asking students, "What does the poem mean?" I suggest that they ask, "How did the poem make you feel?" I often discover that they are immensely relieved when I assure them that the same poem means different things to different readers, and can even have varied interpretations on various days, depending on the background of the reader.

What poetic or narrative effects were you hoping to achieve?

Above all, I try to convey hope. I also try to communicate the need for peace. For me, peace is personal. My mother is from the town of Trinidad de Cuba and my father was from Los Angeles. When I was a child, it was normal to travel, visit, and love both countries, both cultures, languages, and extended families. After the Missile Crisis and subsequent travel restriction—which I wrote about in my verse memoir, *Enchanted Air*—it was easier for a US citizen to walk on the moon than to visit a grandmother in Cuba. Hostility between the two nations was like a wall in the ocean, separating two halves of my self. I needed a bridge. Writing has provided that connection. Even after I started visiting relatives again in 1991, I needed poetry as a source of freedom of expression. I can say anything in a poem. No one can stop me. Censors in one country or another might try to ban my books, but I am still free to say what I really mean within the confines of those pages.

What are your thoughts on the verse novel as a form?

Verse novels use the music of beautiful language to retain hope in a story that might otherwise be too sad. In this sense, poetry makes me happy. Poetry offers solace. It is a refuge, a safe place for thoughts and emotions, not only for the writer, but also for the reader. Verse novels are also interactive. Open spaces between stanzas, and after line breaks, are not empty. They resonate like the echoes after ringing a bell. Just as with haiku, those echoes contain both the writer's and the reader's emotions. Our minds rise and meet in midair. This creates a form that is suited to advanced readers as well as reluctant readers. Open spaces on uncrowded pages are visually welcoming. "Come right in," the open spaces seem to say. "This book is friendly. You can read it quickly and easily. You will understand it." At the same time, the book is written for older children, not babies. Hopefully, the subjects will feel challenging enough for preteens and teenagers to know that the writer respects their intellect. My 2022 historical verse novel, *Rima's Rebellion*, is about suffragists in Cuba during the 1920s and '30s. It shows how women and girls struggled to gain voting rights, overthrow a dictator, overturn a misogynistic divorce law that allowed legal femicide, and gain the right to education for illegitimate children. These are complex situations. I truly do respect the modern young reader's ability to understand history.

Have verse novels you have read been influential on this work in some way?

Initially, I was inspired by Marilyn Nelson's biographical verse novel, *Carver,* and by Karen Hesse's multiple-voice verse novel, *Witness.* Since then, I have also felt influenced by many poets who are not specifically verse novelists, including Ada Limón, Dulce María Loynáz, Mary Oliver, and Joy Harjo. There are narrative elements in these poems, even when they are not telling a longer story. I am especially fond of nature poetry, because I am a botanist and agronomist by training, and there is an environmental focus in many of my books, such as *Forest World* and *Silver People. Wild Dreamers* and *Wings in the Wild* are more recent books with an environmental focus.

What have you learnt about writing verse novels from the verse novels you have read?

I've learned humility. There are so many amazing verse novelists. When I was starting out it was a rare form, but now it is common, and young writers are mastering it so beautifully. I have always admired Jacqueline Woodson, Nikki Grimes, and Padma Venkatraman. Now I can add Aída Salazar, Elizabeth Acevedo, Kwame Alexander, Jason Reynolds, and dozens of others.

CHAPTER 2
KIRLI SAUNDERS

Kirli Saunders by Tad Souden

Our old people have told stories through song for all times, and this
audible element felt important for sharing a story about a First Nations child,
on Gundungurra lands.

Kirli Saunders (OAM) is a proud Gunai Woman and award-winning writer, artist, and consultant. An experienced speaker and facilitator advocating for the environment and equality, Kirli was the NSW Aboriginal Woman of the Year 2020. In 2022, she was awarded an Order of Australia Medal for her contribution to the arts, particularly literature. Kirli's books include *The Incredible Freedom Machines* (Scholastic, 2018), *Kindred* (Magabala, 2019), *Bindi* (Magabala, 2020), and *Our Dreaming* (Scholastic, 2022), and have been celebrated by a Prime Minister's Literary Award, Premier's Literary Awards from the States of Queensland, Western Australia, South Australia, and Victoria, as well as Australian Book Industry Awards, the Kate Challis RAKA Award, the Speech

Pathology Book of the Year Award, Australian Book Designers Association Award, and the Children's Book Council of Australia Award. Kirli's solo play *Going Home* was commissioned by Australian Plays Transform (APT) for Merrigong Theatre Company. Her second poetry collection, *Returning* (Magabala, 2023), was supported by Australia Council for the Arts (AUSCO). As an artist, Kirli works in multiple mediums, including painting, printmaking, sculpture, installation, and digital art. Kirli's website can be found at kirlisaunders.com.

Bindi (2020)

What ideas or influences did you have in mind when creating this work?

I love reading my Aunties' and Sisters' works. In the lead-up to writing *Bindi*, I drew a lot of inspiration from celebrated writers like Ali Cobby Eckermann, Dr Jeanine Leane, Tara June Winch, Melissa Lucashenko, Ellen van Neerven, Alison Whittaker, and Nayuka Gorrie.

While I wrote *Bindi*, the 2019–20 bushfires were unfolding all around us on Pop's, Nan's, and Mum's Countries, and the land I was born and raised on too. I was also learning a lot about cultural burning from Traditional Owners on Yuin lands, Jacob Morris, Ado Webster, and Joel Deaves.

The combination of First Nations poetry, and conversations about caring for Country shaped *Bindi* to be a verse novel, written from the perspective of a young girl on Gundungurra lands, who was responding to her own world.

How did you approach writing this verse novel? What were the various stages in its development?

Originally *Bindi* was a long poem. I had written three-quarters of the manuscript as a verse novel, and then re-wrote it in its entirety as the bushfires tore across my Grandmother's, Mother's Grandfathers' Countries, and the land that birthed me. It felt significant to incorporate caring for Country in the context of the bushfires and climate change.

When I create a verse novel or longer form prose piece, I tend to map the story on an arc, and map the character arcs as well. From there, I take creative license, but I can always see the trajectory.

Can you recall problem-solving decisions you had to make in the writing process?

Ensuring there were no loose ends in the manuscript with so many intersecting stories was important. I made sure I highlighted different storylines in different colors on post-it-notes and mapped them ahead of writing. I also had the manuscript proofed by friends who aren't writers; they were honest in their feedback, allowing me to enhance and improve *Bindi*.

Which poetic and narrative techniques did you decide to employ, and why?

Rhyme, rhythm, onomatopoeia, imagery, alliteration, metaphor, and simile. Country is personified as well, as culturally She is our Mother.

I chose techniques that could be replicated by the readership, in middle primary classrooms. These techniques bring color and texture to the story, and make for a more engaging read, especially when read aloud as *Bindi* often is. They also add a melody and lyricism to the story, mimicking a song.

Our old people have told stories through song for all times, and this audible element felt important for sharing a story about a First Nations child, on Gundungurra lands.

If there were places in the book where you felt it was best to emphasize the poetic strategies over the narrative strategies, or vice versa—what guided these decisions?

I'm far more inclined to stress narrative over poeticism. Meaning making is the key priority for younger readers. Poetry is also a medium that's underappreciated and othered from my experience in the classroom, so I wanted to make *Bindi* accessible.

What poetic or narrative effects were you hoping to achieve?

This work is for children, so I experimented a lot with the sound of *Bindi*, hoping it would be read aloud in classrooms or communities collectively to audiences—to mimic the way our First Nations communities share stories orally. There's internal rhyme, rhythm, and onomatopoeia to emphasize our way of storytelling and draw middle grade students into the world of *Bindi* as if they're her classmates along for the journey with her.

First Nations Language, particularly Gundungurra, is interwoven contextually, and there is a wordlist at the back of the book. This also provides a sonic aspect, and a way of forging connection between the reader and the setting of the work (Gundungurra lands, where the language is spoken).

The poems themselves are also typeset to visually entice the reader, drawing on concrete and experimental poetry, with hockey games, horse rides, and bush adventures being brought to life by text mimicking the passage of a ball being passed across a field, a galloping horse scared by lightning or the shape of the land itself being traversed.

The poems also take many forms, including short plays, concrete poems, letters, and free verse.

What are your thoughts on the verse novel as a form?

I loved working in verse. I predominantly write poetry and have shied away from prose in the past. This felt like a sweet transition from poetry to novel and play writing (which I'm working on now).

Have verse novels you have read been influential on this work in some way?

Somewhat, for understanding the ways that other writers have created narrative poetry.

What have you learnt about writing verse novels from the verse novels you have read?

When I won the WA Premier's, Daisy Utemorrah Award for *Bindi* as an unpublished manuscript, I was sent a copy of *Ruby Moonlight* by Ali Cobby Eckermann. I felt like I was given permission to express narrative in a fluid way through poetry. While I read a lot of fiction and poetry, this was my first intentional reading of a verse novel, and Aunty Ali is an expert at her craft, unpacking colonization in poetic verse, where Country is brought to life. It felt like singing with honor for land/Mother Earth, who is central for our work.

CHAPTER 3
CAROLE BOSTON WEATHERFORD

Carole Boston Weatherford by Gerald Young

There is no limit to the subject matter that verse novels can tackle.
The form is ripe for experimentation.

Carole Boston Weatherford joined Fayetteville State University's faculty in 2002 as a Distinguished Visiting Professor in the Department of English. Now a full Professor, Weatherford has eighty books that have garnered scores of national and statewide honors, including the Newbery Honor Medal, the Caldecott Honor Medal, the Coretta Scott King Award, the NAACP Image Award, the BostonGlobe/Horn Book Award, and the North Carolina Award for Literature. Such titles as *Moses: When Harriet Tubman Led Her People to Freedom*, *Becoming Billie Holiday*, and *Birmingham, 1963* mine the past for family stories, fading traditions, and forgotten struggles and span the genres of poetry, nonfiction, biography, and historical fiction.

Weatherford earned a Master of Fine Arts in Creative Writing from the University of North Carolina at Greensboro and holds a Master of Arts in Publications Design from the University of Baltimore. Carole Boston Weatherford's website can be found at cbweatherford.com.

Becoming Billie Holiday (2008)
Beauty Mark (2020)

What ideas or influences did you have in mind when creating this work?

Billie Holiday was my muse long before I realized it or wrote *Becoming Billie Holiday*. However, I have been a diehard fan since age sixteen. Most of all, I wanted to tell her story in a way that would have pleased her.

I was drawn to Marilyn Monroe for several reasons, chief among them her iconic status. I saw young adults rocking Marilyn T-shirts and accessories and decorating their rooms with posters of her. As a child of the 1960s, I could remember hearing about her tragic death. I later learned more about her troubled childhood, marriages, miscarriages, mental illness, and premature demise. To me, Marilyn was not just a movie star; she was a mood and a mystery. Her life was a poem. Though typecast as a blond bombshell, Marilyn was so much more. She was a producer, poet, painter, gardener, avid reader, and, most importantly, the brains behind her brand.

How did you approach writing this verse novel? What were the various stages in its development?

I decided to focus only on Billie Holiday's rise to fame, not her decline and demise—chapters that have been sensationalized ad nauseum. Instead in *Becoming Billie Holiday* I chronicled her childhood and Harlem heyday, culminating with the recording of "Strange Fruit," the anti-lynching ballad that became her signature song.

For *Beauty Mark* I read many biographies of Marilyn—ones that were narrative and others that collected her mementoes. I approached her story chronologically, reading chapters from various references about the same period or episode. Then, I synthesized the information to come up with my own take. I recreated not only her voice but also emotional backdrops for her narrative.

Can you recall problem-solving decisions you had to make in the writing process?

I let Billie tell her own story from first-person point of view. I consulted her discography for song titles evocative of episodes from her life. The song titles became the poem titles. However, the premise was not immediately clear. Only after writing the rest of the manuscript of *Becoming Billie Holiday*, did I arrive at the premise revealed in what is now the first poem. Billie imagines telling her story to the *Time* magazine critic who'd panned her new release, "Strange Fruit."

For *Beauty Mark*, the premise was clear from the start: The story would unfold as a flashback. The first scene shows Marilyn a few months before her death. In a Madison Square Garden dressing room, she is being sewn into her gown to sing "Happy Birthday" to President John Kennedy. During that styling which required Marilyn to stand still for hours—thus the first poem's title, I imagine Marilyn reflecting on how a former foster child born as Norma Jeane rose to worldwide fame.

There was also one poem that I wrote out of sequence—the one where she is committed to a psychiatric hospital. I feared the darkness of going there with her. So, I wrote that poem next to last.

Which poetic and narrative techniques did you decide to employ, and why?

I used repetition quite a bit to mimic song lyrics in *Becoming Billie Holiday*. The book is essentially a series of dramatic monologues. For *Beauty Mark*, I used first-person point of view to allow Marilyn to speak for herself. In life, her voice was often ignored or minimalized by studio executives. It was important to me that she be heard and have agency.

If there were places in the book where you felt it was best to emphasize the poetic strategies over the narrative strategies, or vice versa—what guided these decisions?

To me, Billie's life was a poem. Poetry is also my first literary language. So, story is inseparable from poetry in *Becoming Billie Holiday*.

Among *Beauty Mark*'s most poetic lyrics are: "The Seven Year Itch: Nine Months Hitched"; "The Physics of Ferragamos"; "Miscarriage Blues: Ectopic Pregnancy, 1957"; "Who Is Marilyn Monroe"; and "Late: A Litany of Excuses." The rhyming poem, "The Seven Year Itch," documents the marriage-ending photo shoot which produced the iconic image of her skirt billowing atop a subway grate. That poem is playful but also bluesy. "The Physics of Ferragamos" shows the interplay between her stilettos and her wiggle. The six-line poem, "Miscarriage Blues: Ectopic Pregnancy, 1957" conveys her deep and unrequited maternal yearnings. One of several list poems in *Beauty Mark*, "Who Is Marilyn Monroe?" views her mystique through the lenses of photographers, film directors, history, and finally herself. "Late: A Litany of Excuses" employs repetition to explore her chronic lateness. The book's epilogue is a found poem of headlines and quotes.

What poetic or narrative effects were you hoping to achieve?

I wanted *Becoming Billie Holiday* and *Beauty Mark* to read as if the main characters were speaking or singing directly to the reader. I wanted to create intimacy between the subject and the reader. I approached both texts as one-woman shows.

What are your thoughts on the verse novel as a form?

I love to read and to write verse novels. The form resonates with me as a reader and as a poet. With spare text and distilled emotions, verse novels can pack a more powerful punch than prose. The economy of language can also make verse novels more appealing to reluctant readers who are put off by the dense text in novels. Verse novels are ideal for conveying the power and poignancy of a subject. Further, verse novels allow for experimentation which excites me as a writer. That enabled me to write *You Can Fly: The Tuskegee Airmen* from second-person perspective and to convey the emotional and artistic struggles of Marilyn Monroe in *Beauty Mark*.

Have verse novels you have read been influential on this work in some way?

Long before I wrote for children, I read verse novels by Carole Maso and Vikram Seth and Alexis DeVeaux. *Carver* by Marilyn Nelson re-introduced me to the verse biography. My own *Becoming Billie Holiday* probably had the most influence on *Beauty Mark*. In the twelve years between writing about two iconic female entertainers, I faced mental illness in my own family. That allowed me to take an even deeper dive into Marilyn's life, loves, and losses.

What have you learnt about writing verse novels from the verse novels you have read?

Verse novels are hybrid genre, creating endless literary possibilities. There is no limit to the subject matter than verse novels can tackle. The form is ripe for experimentation. That stimulates me as a writer.

CHAPTER 4
RAJANI LaROCCA

Rajani LaRocca by Carter Masegawa

Verse novels combine the best elements of poetry and narrative to
create a story greater than the sum of its parts ...

Rajani LaRocca was born in Bangalore, India, raised in Kentucky, and now lives in the Boston area, where she practices medicine and writes award-winning books for young people, including *Mirror to Mirror*, and *Red, White, and Whole*, which won a 2022 Newbery Honor, the Walter Dean Myers Award, Golden Kite Award, and New England Book Award. Her other books include *Midsummer's Mayhem* (2019), *Seven Golden Rings* (2020), *Bracelets for Bina's Brothers* (2021), *Much Ado about Baseball* (2021), *Where Three Oceans Meet* (2021), *My Little Golden Book about Kamala Harris* (2021), *The Secret Code Inside You* (2021), *I'll Go and Come Back* (2022), and more. She's always been an omnivorous reader, and now she is an omnivorous writer of fiction and nonfiction, novels and picture books, prose, and poetry. She finds inspiration in her family, her childhood, the natural world, math, science, and just about everywhere she looks. Rajani LaRocca's website can be found at rajanilarocca.com.

Red, White, and Whole (2021)

What ideas or influences did you have in mind when creating this work?

The idea for *Red, White, and Whole* came to me as a metaphor—the metaphor of blood, and all that it means in term of biology, family, and community—so I thought it would be best expressed in verse. I had already read classic verse novels such as Thanhhà Lại's *Inside Out and Back Again*, *Love That Dog* by Sharon Creech, and Katherine Applegate's *Home of the Brave*, and I knew how powerful verse novels could be. But I had never written a verse novel myself—so I read all the verse novels for young people that I could get my hands on, including *The Poet X, Other Words for Home,* and *The Moon Within*—to further immerse myself in the genre. I wanted to write a book that expressed emotion and interiority in the most powerful way possible.

How did you approach writing this verse novel? What were the various stages in its development?

I was busy writing another novel when I came up with the idea for *Red, White, and Whole*, so it became my "Friday night date"—when I would let myself think about this book. I came up with a broad outline and listened to music from 1983 to 1984 to inspire me. Eventually, I wrote a poem that became the "keystone poem"—the poem, that to me, was the heart of what this story is about.

Once I had turned in my other novel, I worked on *Red, White, and Whole* and let the poems flow out of me in whatever order they happened to come to me. I made lists of topics I wanted to cover and drew connections between different themes and metaphors. I knew early in my process how the book would end, and the exact words I would end with. I wrote many "paired poems," in which a concept or phrase I used near the beginning of the book came back and repeated once or twice later in the book … but the meaning had changed, because the character had changed. And eventually, in revision, I figured out the order that the poems should be in. When I was only changing a word here or there, I knew it was time to turn the book in.

Can you recall problem-solving decisions you had to make in the writing process?

I'm a doctor, but I'm not a hematologist/oncologist who treats leukemia. I asked many questions about Acute Myeloid Leukemia, the kind of leukemia that Reha's mother has in the book, to a colleague at my hospital who was practicing in 1983. And I realized that there was an entire part of the book that wouldn't be needed, because scientifically, it wouldn't have happened in 1983. In a way, it was a relief, because it would have made the book that much sadder.

The decisions that made me the most nervous were setting the book in 1983, and the less-than-perfectly-happy ending. I set the book in 1983 because many of the emotions in the book come from my own life growing up as an immigrant in the years before the internet and cell phones … and that was different than growing up today. I also kept the ending, difficult as it was, because sometimes sad things happen to kids, and my hope was that this book could help young readers contend with difficulties in their own lives.

Which poetic and narrative techniques did you decide to employ, and why?

I used a lot of metaphor and imagery—the central metaphor is blood, but there are also metaphors of the night sky and objects (the main character Reha's name means "star" and her mother's name means "full moon"); streams, rivers, and oceans; music and its many layers; mythology and how stories can heal us; and mustard seeds.

I tried to make the text itself musical. And I used repetition to make themes resonate.

If there were places in the book where you felt it was best to emphasize the poetic strategies over the narrative strategies, or vice versa—what guided these decisions?

Some poems were more static, focusing on a particular emotion or moment in time stretched out so the reader could consider it in a deep way. Some poems moved the narrative along more quickly. In revision, I figured out the order of the poems and sometimes added to or subtracted from them to make a "static" poem still move the narrative and to add emotion to a more "narrative" poem.

What poetic or narrative effects were you hoping to achieve?

I was hoping to tell a deeply emotional story in a way that resonates with readers, but also leave enough room on the page so they could imagine and work things out themselves.

What are your thoughts on the verse novel as a form?

Verse novels combine the best elements of poetry and narrative to create a story greater than the sum of its parts, a story that paints a picture that can be viewed again and again in different ways, depending on what the reader brings to it.

Have verse novels you have read been influential on this work in some way?

Absolutely! As I mentioned in my earlier answer, I have loved reading verse novels for children and going on poetic journeys that filled my heart.

What have you learnt about writing verse novels from the verse novels you have read?

I've learned that poetry speaks to our hearts in deep and fundamental ways. Each of us is a poet, just as we are all storytellers. We just need to be brave enough to try to embrace our own poetic voices and share them with the world.

CHAPTER 5
SAFIA ELHILLO

Safia Elhillo by Aris Theotokatos

The novel in verse form … felt like the perfect container for the feeling of being between worlds, countries, cultures, languages.

Safia Elhillo is Sudanese by way of Washington, DC. She is the author of *The January Children* (University of Nebraska Press, 2017), which received the Sillerman First Book Prize for African Poets and an Arab American Book Award, *Girls That Never Die* (One World/Random House, 2022), and the novel in verse *Home Is Not a Country* (Make Me a World/Random House, 2021), which received a California Book Award, a Coretta Scott King Book Award Author Honor, and was longlisted for the National Book Award. With Fatimah Asghar, she is co-editor of the anthology *Halal If You Hear Me* (Haymarket Books, 2019).

Her fellowships include a Cave Canem, a Ruth Lilly and Dorothy Sargent Rosenberg Fellowship from the Poetry Foundation, and a Wallace Stegner Fellowship from Stanford

University. She received the 2015 Brunel International African Poetry Prize and was listed in Forbes Africa's 2018 "30 Under 30." Her work has been translated into several languages and commissioned by Under Armour and the Bavarian State Ballet. Safia Elhillo's website can be found at safia-mafia.com.

Home Is Not a Country (2021)

What ideas or influences did you have in mind when creating this work?

The idea at the heart of *Home Is Not a Country* was originally a single poem, called "Yasmeen," which sprang from an obsession I'd had with the name I was almost given. One of the particulars of my diasporic experience, for a long time, was an obsession with the idea of alternate or parallel selves, who would I be if I had only grown up in the country of my origins, how would I be different, that sort of thing. That other self that could have existed without that rupture. And once I'd finished the one poem, I realized I'd only scratched the surface of everything I wanted to say. So, for this novel, with the little addition of some magic, I wanted to see what kind of story could emerge if I made my main character's alternate self real, and then made them interact.

How did you approach writing this verse novel? What were the various stages in its development?

I was having a conversation with Christopher Myers, who ended up publishing *Home Is Not a Country* through his imprint, and he asked me if I'd ever considered writing a novel. And I was like, "absolutely not!" And it's not about anything like genre purity, or that I'm so particular about only writing poetry, but my default setting is to be terrified of doing anything that I don't already know how to do. Anyway, after I said no, we kept talking, and he asked me what my favorite book of poetry was. I immediately started talking about *Autobiography of Red* by Anne Carson. And he let me finish before telling me: you know that's a novel, right? It's a novel in verse. So, it turned out that I had accidentally been studying the form for years. And that helped demystify it for me and made it feel less like this impossible inaccessible genre.

One of the stories I tell myself is that I don't know how to write narrative. Sensation is my primary sense and my primary way of writing and consuming work as a reader. But when I started thinking of this beloved collection of poetry as a novel in verse, it demystified it; actually, it was a form that I'd accidentally been studying this whole time. So, it was very easy after that to convince me to sit down and try, by changing the assignment from "write a novel" to "write a series of connected poems with a recurring set of characters."

I was still living in Washington, DC at the time, and so were my friends Elizabeth Acevedo and Clint Smith, who I used to co-work a lot with, and we'd read each other's drafts. We did a weeklong local writing retreat together where at 9 every morning, we would report to this little office on the campus of a local university and we would sit in there from 9 to 5 and work on our respective books and at the end of the day, we would each read what we'd written and give each other feedback. That's how the book got finished. So, while it is technically my book, it has so many aunties and uncles. I come from a community that's very generous with their expertise. So, the reason that I wrote narrative is that my community knows about narrative.

Can you recall problem-solving decisions you had to make in the writing process?

As I mentioned, I initially said no when asked to consider writing a novel, because I am so afraid of being bad at something. Here I was, presented with an opportunity to learn a new skill, and at first, I said, no. And then I eventually said yes, and part of what helped change my answer was the reminder that I have never, in my entire poetry-writing life, been in this alone. So much of what I know about poetry, I learned from friends, peers, from that sort of lateral mentorship and community I grew up in as a young poet. I had to remind myself of that community. My friend Elizabeth Acevedo had just published a novel in verse. My partner is a playwright, a narrative writer. I had people I could ask to teach me. I had to ask myself why I was suddenly so embarrassed to ask for help, to ask to be taught, when that was how I'd been taught the whole time. It's always taken a village. So, my friends taught me to write narrative, and in a relatively short amount of time.

Which poetic and narrative techniques did you decide to employ, and why?

Because I'd never written a novel before, it felt important to enter this new form with my existing tools as a poet with me. I feel like I have the firmest grasp on language when I'm writing in verse, so if I was going to learn something new and terrifying, like plot, I wasn't also going to try and learn how to write in full sentences. Language just feels a lot more malleable in a poem in a way that is much more reflective of what language feels like inside my head; the texture of language before it is spoken.

This novel is also written in first person and from the narrator's interior perspective. I wanted to verbalize, through a single point of view, what it feels like to encounter the world. Conventional prose didn't feel right for that, I wanted it to be in little fragments, lowercase, with caesuras to mimic how thoughts can just float across and disappear. Since my narrator is a young person who is obsessed with and tormented by language, I wanted the language itself to be a little tortured. That's where the lowercase, the caesuras, and the bilingualism factor in. It couldn't just be clear, plain, punctuated, capitalized sentences. I wanted it to feel like the kind of language that exists on the tip of your tongue before it comes out.

If there were places in the book where you felt it was best to emphasize the poetic strategies over the narrative strategies, or vice versa—what guided these decisions?

The choice to write the story in verse ultimately comes down to my relationship to verse versus prose. I feel like I am never going to feel fully fluent in English, or in any language, and verse has always been a space for me where the rules of language are mine to set, mine to play with and experiment with and stretch. I feel less at the mercy of external measures of fluency in English, and instead feel the language soften and grow more malleable, able to mutate to accommodate the things I need to say. I don't feel bound by the rules of "proper" English or "correct" grammar. In a poem, I get to invent my English as one of many "Englishes" and set my own grammar. I wanted to be able to tell this story with that set of tools available to me, especially since the medium is new for me. In writing fiction, I wanted to use the form in the way I feel most at home.

There's a bit of untranslated Arabic throughout the book, because I'm always thinking a lot about language, often specifically the relationship between English and Arabic. Earlier in my writing life, in very early poems I was writing, I would try to transliterate the Arabic words into English, but it just felt ugly, and it didn't make the sounds in my head, and it wasn't creating any music. In trying to transport it from one side to the other, I ended up hurting it, so I decided to just leave it intact. I had to accept that if that makes the poem less readable to a non-Arabophone reader, that's okay. I like to think that there are many different versions of a poem available within itself. There's a reading for someone who understands both English and Arabic and has context for my particular intersections and cultural markers. And then there's the version for the reader who only reads and understands English, and I think that version is intended to "work" as well. But I think that's just lower on my list of priorities. All my poems—this novel—are written for a very particular reader, and I only have the bandwidth to care for that reader. My hope is that everyone else is experiencing what it's like to eavesdrop on a very interesting conversation.

What are your thoughts on the verse novel as a form?

The novel in verse form, a hybrid form, felt like the perfect container for the feeling of being between worlds, countries, cultures, languages. In general, I find myself drawn to hybrid forms. The novel in verse is a third space between narrative and lyric. And this is a young adult novel as well, where adolescence is a third space between childhood and adulthood. And the experience described in the book is a third space between a homeland and a host land.

What have you learnt about writing verse novels from the verse novels you have read?

When I re-read *Autobiography of Red* with an eye towards studying it as a novel, it was helpful to see how cause and effect, event—all these ideas that feel more concrete to me than that terrifying word, "plot"—how those elements were being rendered in verse.

CHAPTER 6
JASMINE WARGA

Jasmine Warga by Lillian Nour Warga

When I read verse novels, I am reminded that language is
a place for play and for exploration.

Jasmine Warga is the *New York Times*-best-selling author of middle grade novels *Other Words for Home* and *The Shape of Thunder*. *Other Words for Home* earned multiple awards, including a John Newbery Honor, a Walter Honor for Young Readers, and a Charlotte Huck Honor. *The Shape of Thunder* was a School Library Journal and Bank Street best book of the year, a finalist for the Barnes and Noble Children's and YA Book Award and has been named on several state award reading lists. She is also the author of young adult books, *My Heart and Other Black Holes* and *Here We Are Now*, which have been translated into over twenty different languages. Her latest novel is *A Rover's Story* (2022). Jasmine currently teaches in the MFA program at Vermont College of Fine Arts. Originally from Cincinnati, she now lives in the Chicago area with her family in a house filled with books. Jasmine Warga's website can be found at jasminewarga.com.

Other Words for Home (2019)

What ideas or influences did you have in mind when creating this work?

I've always loved poetry so foremost the poets I frequently read, especially during my high school and college years, influenced my overall approach to poetry. Those poets include Adrienne Rich, Frank O'Hara, Anne Sexton, Sylvia Plath, and Mary Oliver.

Later, when I figured out that I was writing an MG verse novel (it took me a while to figure this out—more on that below!), I referenced several brilliant MG verse novels, looking at them as models. Those books are *Brown Girl Dreaming* by Jacqueline Woodson, *Inside Out and Back Again* by Thanhhà Lại, and *Out of the Dust* by Karen Hesse.

How did you approach writing this verse novel? What were the various stages in its development?

Initially, I did not know the novel needed to be in verse. I had always written in prose, and I assumed this novel would also be in prose. The book originally sold as a prose novel. But as I was going through revision with my editor, I figured out that something wasn't working. I couldn't hear Jude's voice (Jude is the main character of my novel *Other Words for Home*) on the page in the way I wanted to, and I had what I can only describe as a lightbulb moment idea to try to write the book in verse. That decision helped change everything.

Once I decided to write the novel in verse, I scrapped everything I had. I wrote an entirely new draft. But I already had such a deep understanding of the scaffolding of the story that while it was a new draft, it didn't necessarily feel as rough and raw as first drafts usually do. From there, I worked on revising the book with my editor, and it went through the usual steps a book does in the publishing cycle.

Can you recall problem-solving decisions you had to make in the writing process?

Well, my initial problem was that I couldn't hear Jude's voice on the page, and this was solved by breaking the novel out into verse. Later, I encountered the maddening problem that revising a verse novel is particularly hard because when you go in to change something for plot reasons, not only are you messing around with sequential stuff, but you also often blow up a rhythm or cadence you spent hours crafting. I found revising a verse novel to be very difficult!

Which poetic and narrative techniques did you decide to employ, and why?

I leaned heavily on repetition and metaphor. I also thought deeply about how I ordered the words on the page as I was trying to mimic the cadence and texture of Arabic in a book that is written in English.

If there were places in the book where you felt it was best to emphasize the poetic strategies over the narrative strategies, or vice versa—what guided these decisions?

To be honest, I always prioritized the narrative. I was writing a novel in verse, and not to be pedantic, but if you look at the name of the form, there is a reason novel comes first. Of course, I cared deeply about the language being beautiful and moving, but most of all, I wanted the reader to feel immersed in Jude's story. Language was a function to tell the story, not the story itself.

What poetic or narrative effects were you hoping to achieve?

My primary objective was creating a reading experience where the reader felt very close to Jude. I think verse is great at generating a reading experience that is raw and intimate. I also very much wanted to honor and exalt the Arabic language in a book that is written in English—this meant trying to write in a way that captured the cadence, texture, and lyricality of Arabic. Verse, I think, is a wonderful space for translanguaging because you can play with the rules of language, and bend and shape it.

What are your thoughts on the verse novel as a form?

I love the verse novel. I do think of it as separate from poetry though. It sits at the intersection of language artistry (poetry) and storytelling. I love that intersection. For me, it's a very fertile creative ground.

Have verse novels you have read been influential on this work in some way?

Certainly! I mentioned above that I leaned heavily on *Brown Girl Dreaming*, *Inside Out and Back Again*, and *Out of the Dust* when I figured out that I was, indeed, working on a verse novel. I also think Anne Carson's *Autobiography of Red* was very formative for me. I read that novel when I was in college, and it completely opened me up to all the possible forms a story could take.

What have you learnt about writing verse novels from the verse novels you have read?

I've learned just how acrobatic the English language can be. When I read verse novels, I am reminded that language is a place for play and for exploration. I love puzzling over how to put words together in such a way to create a certain emotion or image.

CHAPTER 7
MELANIE CROWDER

Melanie Crowder by Tiffany Crowder

*There are so many reasons to write a novel in free verse—the imagery,
the language, not to mention the freedom …*

Melanie Crowder is an educator, speaker, and the acclaimed author of nine novels for young readers. Her work has received numerous awards and starred reviews and has been featured in publications such as *The Washington Post, The Boston Globe*, and *The Wall Street Journal. Kirkus Reviews* declares that her 2021 historical YA novel, *Mazie*, "deserves a standing ovation" while her 2022 contemporary YA, *Jumper*, "is never less than riveting." Melanie eagerly anticipates the release of two picture books in 2024. Her YA historical novel in verse, *Audacity*, was awarded the Jefferson Cup and Bulletin Blue Ribbon, and was named a National Jewish Book Award finalist. Her middle grade novel, *Three Pennies*, was named a New York Public Library Best Book for Kids. *An Uninterrupted View of the Sky* was a Walden Award finalist. *A Nearer Moon* was declared a Best Book of the Year by *Kirkus Reviews*, the New York Public Library, and Bank Street College. *The Lighthouse between the Worlds* was a Colorado Book Award finalist, while her debut novel, *Parched*, was a Junior Library selection.

A West Coast girl at heart, Melanie lives with her family under the big blue Colorado sky. She holds an MFA in writing and teaches at Vermont College of Fine Arts. Melanie Crowder's website can be found at melaniecrowder.com.

Audacity (2015)

What ideas or influences did you have in mind when creating this work?

Many years ago, I discovered an HBO movie called *Iron Jawed Angels* about the tactics of Alice Paul and Lucy Burns at the climax of the suffrage movement in the United States. It's a story of friendship, courage, and grit. I cried buckets of ugly tears and still list that movie as one of my favorites.

Fast forward several years later: I'm in grad school, trying to push myself outside of my writing comfort zone. Thinking I'll try my hand at nonfiction, I start combing through accounts of women whose work I admire. There are so many places to look—scientists, adventurers, activists. Remembering Alice and Lucy and how deeply their story affected me, I narrow my focus to suffragists active in the early 1900s. Since I'm planning a book for young adults, I want to find someone close to my readers' age. Many suffragists at the time were college-educated women in their mid- to late-twenties, and while their stories are incredibly moving, I know I'm looking for something different. That's when I find my story, in the younger set of suffragists, the less educated, bleakly impoverished immigrant women. To work a twelve-hour day in a dirty, dangerous shop and *then* spend your evening campaigning for women's rights? Astonishing.

Audacity is the story of real-life labor activist Clara Lemlich. Her family escaped the Russian Empire in the wake of murderous pogroms and settled in New York City. Within two weeks, she was at work in a sweatshop on the Lower East Side. Though it meant putting her own dreams aside, she took a stand and changed our world for the better.

When people talk about her, they tend to use the same adjectives: brave, determined, passionate. It's *easy* to be inspired by Clara's story. It's likely that I'd read a sentence or two about her in my US History high school textbook, which covered the plight of immigrants in the early 1900s, the Triangle Shirtwaist factory fire, and the Uprising of 20,000. But none of the extraordinary individuals involved in those dramatic events lived in my mind like Alice Paul and Lucy Burns. What was it about *Iron Jawed Angels* that affected me so deeply?

Through the vehicle of fiction inspired by true events, that movie brought those historical figures to life for me. They were no longer single-line entries in a history textbook. They were no longer just black-and-white photographs. *That's* what I wanted to do for Clara. I wanted to bring her out of those grainy old photos; I wanted to make her story one that my readers would never forget.

How did you approach writing this verse novel? What were the various stages in its development?

I began writing Clara's story as a nonfiction biography, though I didn't get very far. It just didn't work. Clara was intelligent, ambitious, a dreamer, and a *very* intense person. The prose form fell flat—it wasn't *enough* to capture her spirit. And if the writing didn't move *me*, how could I ever expect it to move my readers? So, I set the book aside, but writers never really put things away. Our ideas are always churning in the back of our minds even when we're focused on something else.

When I began experimenting with free verse, I found what I was looking for—a form that amplified Clara's passions, triumphs, and crushing defeats on the page. Once I settled on the right form, the story leapt forward. I could *feel* the character coming to life. Next came timelines, settings spread between three countries, and secondary characters, all tasking me with enough research to fill my calendar for a year.

The verse form has the capacity to hold an abundance of richness in imagery. I set about refining extended metaphors to illuminate the personal sacrifices Clara made in the name of her cause. Then I cultivated poems about birds into an image system that could serve as an echo chamber for her emotions. I loved that part of the process!

Can you recall problem-solving decisions you had to make in the writing process?

Since *Audacity* is fiction inspired by a real person, I needed to read between the lines of historical documents to uncover the living, breathing person. There were certain unmovable dates—the Kishinev Pogrom, Clara's arrival in the USA, the Uprising of the 20,000, the Triangle Factory fire, etc. But in and around those dates, I shifted and moved and reshuffled poems until my head spun. No prose novel I have ever written has required a fraction of the rearranging that this book needed.

I decided early on that the story's arc needed to begin with Clara's early years. For her bravery to mean something, for her selflessness to resonate, readers had to understand all that she came from, all that had shaped her into such an extraordinary individual.

I could have shown this in flashback. But I wanted readers to live through the violent anti-Semitism Clara's community faced, to feel the way she craved and was denied an education, to know why she set herself apart from those around her. Doing that meant I needed to back up, to start at the beginning.

Opening *Audacity* in the Russian Empire during Clara's teen years, however, meant I would have six years to cover in the novel. Some books take place on a single day, or within the span of a week. Six years is a lot. But each one of those years held some part of the whole that I couldn't leave out. Clara's determination is something she grew into, something that solidified inside her until there was no other way forward. I couldn't leave all that *becoming* out of her story.

Writing in verse gave me the freedom to speed up and slow down the timeline as the story demanded. I treated each poem like a snapshot of a scene, staged with historical minutiae, shaded in sensory detail, and tinted by the workings of Clara's mind and heart. Put together, all those little snapshots create a narrative that skips and slows and skips again through time—a little like flipping through pages in a photo album.

Which poetic and narrative techniques did you decide to employ, and why?

There are so many reasons to write a novel in free verse—the imagery, the language, not to mention the freedom to make up your own rules. One of the most unique tools available to the poet is the ability to use spacing and design to convey a character's emotion or state of mind—it's like a second wave of metaphor that hits the reader on a subconscious level. Spacing can be powerful, and it's a tool that prose novelists usually must do without. It can be subtle, like an extra space between letters to slow the reader down, or it can be concrete, words swooping across the page like birds.

I couldn't write about life in the sweatshops at the turn of the last century without a mention of the sexual harassment the women faced. However, since I was not going to dedicate a large portion of the narrative to that trauma, I chose to treat the subject in an abstract, oblique way.

To accomplish this, I used spacing on the page to visually communicate a character attempting to impose order on a situation over which she has no control. I wrote text without punctuation—a run-on, rambling sentence from a character whose voice is normally crisp and sharp. I set those thoughts in a rigid square so different to the rest of the book's flowing, liquid formatting. It's stark, and the moment stands out in a powerful way as a result.

If there were places in the book where you felt it was best to emphasize the poetic strategies over the narrative strategies, or vice versa—what guided these decisions?

Writing *Audacity* was a constant balancing act between maintaining fidelity to the historical record, the needs of the story, and the integrity of the verse form. All three were equally important to me. I viewed the historical markers as the bones making up the structure. Narrative and the demands of story were muscle, stretching and flexing to fill the gaps. And poetry was the story's lifeblood, connecting everything and pumping life through it all.

What poetic or narrative effects were you hoping to achieve?

Verse novels at their best are breathless, intimate encounters with intense, compelling characters. That's what I wished for *Audacity*.

Because the story is set over a hundred years ago, I wanted to write an immersive story in which the historical setting would feel natural. I was mindful of the place this book would hold for many in shaping Clara's legacy; as a result, it demanded my very best work. And I wanted to write the kind of poetry that would feel inevitable as the novel's form.

To accomplish this, I listened to rhythms of antique sewing machines, troves of birdsong, and interviews with Clara herself so I could hear the cadence of her speech.

All of that informed the rhythms of the words on the page. I carefully arranged words to create resonance between vowel and consonant sounds; to build texture and affect mood, to create an atmospheric effect that would complement the content of a given scene. In a verse novel, it's this kind of minutia that, if done well, reads as effortless, flowing text and quickly flipping pages. It's a great deal of work—but so worth it!

What are your thoughts on the verse novel as a form?

When I started writing *Audacity*, it seemed like everywhere I turned there was an article on how the verse novel wasn't really poetry, then another on how verse wasn't an appropriate form for a novel, then back and forth again. At every turn, the author was being asked to defend why *that* story needed to be told in *that* form; to justify their creative choices.

In stark contrast to all those opinions, I love the freedom this form allows. While I'm not a fan of those early articles expounding what a verse novel "should" or "shouldn't" be, I do think there are some books that *want* to be told in verse. There's something about the rhythms of the words on the page, or the tone of the story, or the main character's way of seeing the world—which demands broken lines galloping down the page. When you close one of those gems after savoring the final poem, you're left with a feeling of beautiful inevitability.

Have verse novels you have read been influential on this work in some way?

I always come back to one of the first I encountered: *Heartbeat* by Sharon Creech. The lines are simple, deceptively so, but the emotions running through them are powerful. The rhythm is palpable, and a natural fit for the character's voice. It's an unforgettable classic.

As a reader, I love the almost hypnotic way I sink into these stories. Something about the accelerated pace and the arpeggio-like stanzas carries me through the pages in a delicious blur.

There were relatively few verse novels available when I was writing *Audacity*, though a flurry released around the same time, which is so lovely, I think! Apparently, a whole pack of us were simultaneously holed up in our solitary writing spaces, collectively breaking open this form and offering a beautifully varied collection of stories to the world.

What have you learnt about writing verse novels from the verse novels you have read?

The lesson I am constantly learning, and surely will be for as long as I can hold a pen, is to always reach for simplicity. The most poignant image is often unadorned. The most powerful line is often spare. It can be tempting in the verse novel form to overwrite, to reach for every tool in the poet's toolbox—and there's no harm in that in early drafts. But revising a poem is like carving a piece of wood or a block of stone, cutting, peeling away until only the essential remains.

Though I have written poetry in picture book and short story form since, *Audacity* remains my only verse novel. I can feel another whispering at the edges of my creative consciousness—I can't wait to see that story unfold, and to delight in this form once again.

CHAPTER 8
AIDA SALAZAR

Aida Salazar by Lluvia Higuera

Being able to render both the many tools of poetry and the many tools of story with the same mastery, impulse, and passion really is where the art lies.

Aida Salazar is an award-winning author, arts activist, and translator whose writings for adults and children explore issues of identity and social justice. She is the author of the critically acclaimed middle grade verse novels, *The Moon Within* (International Latino Book Award Winner), *Land of The Cranes* (Américas Award, California Library Association Beatty Award, Northern CA Book Award, NCTE Charlotte Huck Honor, Jane Addams Peace Honor, International Latino Book Award Honor), and *A Seed in the Sun* (NCTE Notable, Jane Addams Children's Book Award Finalist, and ALA Rise: A Feminist Book Project Top Ten).

Her books include the picture book anthology, *In the Spirit of a Dream: 13 Stories of Immigrants of Color* (2021), the biographical picture book *Jovita Wore Pants: The Story of a Freedom Fighter* (2023), the middle grade verse novel, *Ultraviolet* (2024), and the anthology *Calling the Moon: Period Stories by BIPOC Authors* (2023). Aida is a founding member of Las Musas, a Latinx KidLit debut author collective. Her story, "By the Light of the Moon" was adapted into a ballet production by the Sonoma Conservatory of Dance and is the first Xicana-themed ballet in history. She lives with her family of artists in a teal house in Oakland, CA, and her website can be found at aidasalazar.com.

The Moon Within (2019)
Land of the Cranes (2020)
A Seed in the Sun (2022)

What ideas or influences did you have in mind when creating this work?

I have been a poet for most of my writing life. When in graduate school at CalArts, I was introduced to *Autobiography of Red* by Anne Carson and was immensely moved by this hybrid form. It wasn't until I became a mother fifteen years later and was reading many books in tandem with my children, that we read *The Red Pencil* by Andrea Davis Pinkney. This book gave me permission and the inspiration to write a story in verse for children. It was revelatory to be able to bring my poetic training and sensibility to the page while telling a longer story without losing the intimacy of verse. That's when I wrote *The Moon Within*. In terms of story content, however, my daughter was beginning to experience early puberty and because we read so often, we searched for a fictional book about menstruation that would not only give information about puberty but would do it through story. Of course, we only found *Are You There God? It's Me, Margaret* by Judy Blume written in 1971. There were no other books that even remotely mirrored my daughter's experience as an Afro-Latina living in a modern-day San Francisco Bay Area steeped in culture and community. I wrote the book for her, and children like her, to re-write the negative narrative that we have been given about menstruation and to push back on the taboo in children's literature, especially middle grade literature, which is arguably the moment when stories like this are most needed.

How did you approach writing this verse novel? What were the various stages in its development?

I wrote the first fifteen pages over the course of one week. These first pages were all voice and personality. I loved writing them. They felt fresh and so unique to my character, Celi. Then, I attended a local advanced writer's workshop by SCBWI. At this conference, N.H. Senzai gave an excellent workshop on plotting, and she read and provided critique for my first pages. She said that although my writing was lovely, I needed to give it a deeper plot. I took her advice and wrote the synopsis from beginning to end. To my surprise, this process was incredibly thrilling because it was still crafting and profoundly creative. It cemented me forevermore as a plotter because it was still imaginative, I could still dance with my muse, but there was more intention behind it. Then, I didn't touch the novel again until I went away for a solo four-day writing retreat. Armed with my synopsis, I wrote the entire first draft, sans fifteen pages of *The Moon Within* in those four days. When I had a full draft, I queried agents but got more feedback that the novel needed to expand the plot. Clearly, this was my weakness. Luckily, my dear friend, Dianna Perez, a story producer for reality television in Los Angeles, helped me brainstorm and figure out how to expand the story and give it a real arc. With this second edit, I went to the national SCBWI conference and paid for another one-on-one critique. In another stroke of luck, a newer editor at Arthur Levine Books, Nick Thomas, gave me the critique. He almost immediately asked to acquire the book and we did about three different edits. I will always be grateful to Nick for helping push the book to publication with Arthur Levine's imprint at Scholastic.

Can you recall problem-solving decisions you had to make in the writing process?

My biggest question was how to communicate dialogue within the poem. Verse novels require scenes and scenes often require dialogue and people don't usually speak in verse unless they are in a Shakespearean play. Right? It was difficult to negotiate when and how other characters, not my main character, would speak and what their dialogue sounded like in the context of verse. I am still struggling with this when writing my other verse novels. How do we write dialogue naturally without the pretense that the characters are speaking in verse?

Which poetic and narrative techniques did you decide to employ, and why?

I came to this novel by zeroing in on voice. Because I was around so many children both as a home-schooling mother and as an educator, their words, their expressions, their world views were very present in my mind. I listened and tried to mimic their innate musicality but also tried to use other poetic techniques to play with language, re-arrange words, play with placement, and line breaks. The great Puerto Rican writer, Piri Thomas said "every child is born a poet." I tried to communicate this truth through their voices and the inventiveness of their language. For instance, I made up the word "Amifriend" which in Spanglish, is a mash up for friend and amiga.

If there were places in the book where you felt it was best to emphasize the poetic strategies over the narrative strategies, or vice versa—what guided these decisions?

There were several moments where this tension weighed on one side more than the other. It was easy to write poetic reverie. This is my comfort zone. However, sometimes, the narrative had to take center stage because of the necessity of pushing the story forward. It was difficult to accept having to make this sacrifice for me. So, I went back to add poetic layers to the telling. I tried not to leave a poem without some sort of poetic technique present—a metaphor, figurative language, music, anything that would still honor the hybridity of verse novels.

What poetic or narrative effects were you hoping to achieve?

Billy Collins said, "Poetry is the history of the human heart." I was hoping to create a beautiful, sacred, funny, truthful, and moving portrait of one girl's journey through adolescence. By telling it through a very close first-person narrative, I was hoping to show her heart's landscape, to demonstrate a very vulnerable topic and time, with honesty and emotion.

What are your thoughts on the verse novel as a form?

This hybrid form is my favorite, especially when done well. I love telling stories this way perhaps as much as I love reading them. More and more, I find authors underestimate how difficult it is to write verse novels given how popular they are becoming. It is a deeply layered form that cannot be told without a sound knowledge of poetry, or without care and tact. Often, I have seen authors offer economy as their only poetic technique and I feel cheated as a reader. Being able to render both the many tools of poetry and the many tools of story with the same mastery, impulse, and passion really is where the art lies. To do anything short of this is robbing readers of the infinite artful possibilities that are present when telling a story through poetry.

Have verse novels you have read been influential on this work in some way?

I had only really read a handful of verse novels when I wrote *The Moon Within*. As I mentioned, *Autobiography of Red* and *The Red Pencil* were two books that initially inspired me. I read other verse novels such as *Boom Crash Love* by Juan Felipe Herrera and *Under the Mesquite* by Guadalupe Garcia McCall which were remarkably moving and solidified my resolve to write this story in verse. I knew Juan Felipe Herrera as a poet mostly. Seeing him use this form of storytelling so masterfully made me understand how important it was not to abandon oneself as a poet, to be a novelist. In fact, it is the opposite, it is necessary to be a poet first before you attempt to write a verse novel.

What have you learnt about writing verse novels from the verse novels you have read?

I learn something from every verse novel, even if, or especially if it is something I would like to avoid. I have relished writers' works which offer lyricism and beauty not only on the level of the story but also on the level of the line. How do their poems sing? How do they connect and contribute to the greater whole? How deep do they go in showing us the heart of their characters? How and why do writers use poetry to tell this specific story? What poetic techniques are they using? Do they work? I am a demanding reader, perhaps, but I am keenly aware of the heights to which poets can take their words. I read to see all these things on the page and then try to push myself to do my best to deliver a higher form of this art in my work too.

CHAPTER 9
CORDELIA JENSEN

Cordelia Jensen by Mariette Pathy Allen

*I think the verse novel form is one of the most exciting
and experimental forms out there.*

Cordelia Jensen graduated with an MFA in Writing for Children and Young Adults from Vermont College of Fine Arts in 2012. Cordelia's verse novels are *Skyscraping* (Philomel/Penguin), *The Way the Light Bends* (Philomel/Penguin), *Every Shiny Thing* (Amulet/Abrams) co-authored with Laurie Morrison, and a forthcoming MG novel in verse *Lilac and the Switchback* (Holiday House, 2025). *Skyscraping* was named an American Library Association's 2016 Best Book for Young Adults, a Los Angeles Public Library's Best Book for Teens and a 2016 NCTE Children's Notable Verse Novel. *Every Shiny Thing* was nominated for the South Carolina Junior Book Award. Cordelia has taught creative writing in a variety of settings: Bryn Mawr College, Germantown Friends School, and The Writing Barn. She currently teaches for The Highlights Foundation. She also runs a local kids' literary journal called the *Mt. Airy Musers*. Cordelia is represented by Liza Fleissig of the LRA agency, and her website can be found at cordeliajensen.com.

Skyscraping (2015)
The Way the Light Bends (2018)

What ideas or influences did you have in mind when creating this work?

Skyscraping originally began as a memoir in verse, based on poems I wrote about my family of origin. Upon suggestion from an advisor in my MFA program at Vermont College of Fine Arts, I fictionalized it as a story. Even so, the story was highly informed by my own past, so I knew the emotional world of the characters intimately. When I was writing this book, I was also reading MG/YA verse novels for the first time and felt inspired by the "in-betweenness" of the genre. Although I have a background in writing poetry, I always preferred to read stories and narrative poetry. After years of failing to tell my story in a poetry chapbook, it was refreshing to find this hybrid form combining poetry and story; it was the only way to tell *Skyscraping*.

The idea for *The Way the Light Bends* was initially inspired by a news story I heard on NPR on the history of Central Park, specifically on Seneca Village. That, combined with an article I had written years ago for a Twins magazine on "virtual twins." What was most compelling to me, though, about writing this story as a verse novel was the fact that the main character is an artist; so, I thought more about the visual component of the form even more than I had in *Skyscraping*. With more attention to sculpting the white space, playing with word design and punctuation, I tried to represent the creativity of Linc's inner world.

How did you approach writing this verse novel? What were the various stages in its development?

For Skyscraping, the story began with a series of family poems I had written through college years and in my young adult life (some of which still appear in the book). Once I decided to fictionalize the story, the first poems I wrote revolved around astronomy. Once I chose celestial imagery as the image system for the book, I traced Mira's emotional arc through this imagery. I then wrote a loose outline for the story and proceeded to move linearly through the story. However, the story went through considerable developmental edits with my editor Liza Kaplan.

For *The Way the Light Bends*, I wrote around fifty exploratory poems in Linc's voice, trialing poetic devices and exploring the background of her family and her past. After this stage, I wrote a detailed outline, which, of course, went through changes after I drafted the story. This book sold on proposal, so the process was quite different than with *Skyscraping*, a story I worked on for years before it even sold. One version of *The Way the Light Bends* was in dual perspective and Holly had her own point of view in the book. Her point of view was written entirely in poems with traditional styles and structures such as the sestina, sonnet, and villanelle. I loved writing these and they really helped me get to know Holly. Ultimately, however, my editor and I agreed that the story was really Linc's.

Can you recall problem-solving decisions you had to make in the writing process?

In *Skyscraping*, the biggest challenge was creating more story tension. In the first version Mira (formerly named Lia) found out every family secret at once in the fall section of the book. My editor Liza encouraged me to space out these reveals, creating mini story arcs for each season of the book, therefore elevating tension. She also had me limit the cast size (one character became a room!) in order for the story to focus more on the family. Having too many sub-plots in a verse novel can be a challenge for the author since you are working with a more limited word count. Liza also had me create a more obvious emotional arc for each season, so, in fall, Mira moves from feelings of excitement to anger; in winter, from anger to fear; in spring, from fear to hope; and in summer, from hope to grief. Although we, as actual people, don't necessarily move through emotions this explicitly, when fictional characters do, the reader can access their emotion intensely. Also, Liza had me change everyone's name! I had a lot of trouble separating my personal story from the fictional one and in the original version the names were much closer to the actual real people's names. This simple switch was transformative. In *The Way the Light Bends*, the biggest challenge was the story construction. Since this work is entirely fictionalized it always felt like it could go in many directions, and it took a few different turns. But I always knew I wanted to tell a story about insecurity and confidence and about sisters who were disconnected, reconnecting. Sticking to these two themes guided my choices along the way.

Which poetic and narrative techniques did you decide to employ, and why?

I think the emphasis on figurative language is my favorite thing about poetry and it is probably what I do best as a writer. Thinking about emotion and interaction and dynamics through metaphor really excites me. For *Skyscraping*, I kept an *Astronomy for Dummies* book by my side and for *The Way the Light Bends*, my mother (a photographer) taught me some techniques. I also watched videos and kept a print-out of photography words by my side. Whenever I was stuck, I turned to these resources (for both books) and picked a scientific fact or photography technique to inspire me and help me find my way out.

I also think a lot about where to break the line. I love thinking about where to break the line, as it can change the meaning of a poem, surprise the reader, or emphasize one emotion or the other. In addition, I like to consider enjambment versus end-stopped lines and the mood these choices can create on a character level. For every poetic device there is to consider, there is also a character's voice to consider! This is absolutely what I love best about the form.

If there were places in the book where you felt it was best to emphasize the poetic strategies over the narrative strategies, or vice versa—what guided these decisions?

I always say verse novels need to be poetic overall, but one individual page of a verse novel might be a poem and another page might be something more like broken prose, giving the reader information or passing time. So, for both books, I tried to strike a balance and tell a story poetically. In *Skyscraping*, for example, the interview sections with the father are not poems but they give the reader a better sense of the Dad's voice and show (rather than tell) how Mira and her father relate differently throughout the course of the year. This is all shown through dialogue, which is more of a narrative technique than a poetry technique. There are a few concrete poems in *Skyscraping*—they are in the spring section when Mira finds out her father only has thirty days to live. They are in this section because time has become so precious. I felt like it would make sense that the painstaking precision of concrete poems might reflect this mindfulness. Therefore, this poetic device was emphasized over the story. Some of the summer poems come from poems I wrote very soon after my actual father died in 1994. Grieving can feel surreal and shocking, and I think these poems speak to that, and emphasize that, over moving the story forward. For me, writing in verse, I always need to be reminded that my characters need to act, and not just stand around thinking and feeling. This is something I have learned to do on the job!

In *The Way the Light Bends*, I had the challenge of trying to show a photo essay through poems. For these poems, I emphasized the poetry over the story, while still attempting to connect Linc's project to her own life and experiences. There are other places, like in the moments where Linc writes her essay for art school, where I needed to give the reader information and emphasize action that the story "overtook" the poetry.

What poetic or narrative effects were you hoping to achieve?

In *The Way the Light Bends*, I wanted to focus on sculpting space and playing with word design. For an abstract and artistic thinker like Linc, it seemed authentic to her character that she would use more word and punctuation play, for example. In both *The Way the Light Bends* and *Skyscraping*, I focused on imagery to delve deeply into metaphorical thinking about character dynamics and emotion.

What are your thoughts on the verse novel as a form?

I think the verse novel form is one of the most exciting and experimental forms out there. I really appreciate being able to use the array of tools from the poet's toolbox to create a character's voice, something you might not do as much in a traditional poetry collection. I also think the challenge of plotting verse novels—stringing a plot together from a series of moments—offers structural flexibility.

Have verse novels you have read been influential on this work in some way?

Thanhhà Lại's *Inside Out and Back Again* was influential for me while writing *Skyscraping*, in terms of imagery and thinking of extending metaphors throughout the course of the book and tracing the main character's journey over the course of a year.

What have you learnt about writing verse novels from the verse novels you have read?

So much! I have learnt that they work best when you use white space and line breaks to reflect the emotional world of your main character, that you should use different poetic tools depending on who your main character is and where their passions lie, that interpolating verse with other forms (prose, letters, emails, text, etc.) can help round out storytelling and aid in secondary character development and that verse novels are a good choice for authors interested in working with nontraditional plots and structures.

CHAPTER 10
THANHHÀ LẠI

Thanhhà Lại by Paula Landry

The fewer words used—the better the emotional depth.

Thanhhà Lại is the #1 *New York Times*-best-selling author of *Inside Out & Back Again*, her debut novel in verse, which won both a National Book Award and a Newbery Honor. The sequel, *When Clouds Touch Us*, was published in May 2023, and was a 2023 Boston Globe–Horn Book Award Honor Book. Thanhhà also wrote the acclaimed *Listen, Slowly*, the award-winning YA debut *Butterfly Yellow*, and the picture book *Hundred Years of Happiness*.

Thanhhà was born in Việt Nam and now lives in New York with her family. In 2005 she started a charity called Việt Kids Inc. Her website can be found at thanhhalai.com.

Inside Out & Back Again (2011)
When Clouds Touch Us (2023)

What ideas or influences did you have in mind when creating this work?

Inside Out & Back Again is the story of ten-year-old Hà who must leave the only home she has known, Saigon, and flee Việt Nam with her mother and brothers. Hà's family arrive in Alabama as refugees of the Việt Nam War. I wanted to show how hard it is to resettle. It's one thing to flee war in panic. That's like an earthquake, sending a body into automatic flight mode. But the slow process of rebuilding: acquiring a new language, house, life—that requires the reconfiguration of every atom in your body.

When Clouds Touch Us picks up a year after *Inside Out & Back Again*. After two years in Alabama, Hà now speaks passable English and has enough friends to no longer eat lunch in the bathroom. But shock surges through Hà when her mother announces they must move again for a better job. Starting over in Texas proves daunting. Hà navigates three schools during sixth grade and walks the hallways alone.

As I visit schools to talk about *When Clouds Touch Us*, I realize students identify even more with Hà. Readers don't have to be immigrants or refugees to see themselves in this story about reclaiming a sense of self in a new school, home, world.

How did you approach writing this verse novel? What were the various stages in its development?

First, I spent fifteen years writing a novel that spanned four thousand years and had fifty characters. Once I allowed myself to abandon that mess, I was exhausted so decided to write about myself—thus no research. I wrote a draft in two months of a much more condensed story, which became *Inside Out & Back Again*. But that easy effort would not have been possible without the previous fifteen years of anguish.

I knew I needed to keep the sequel *When Clouds Touch Us* in the same verse novel format. But the way Hà processes language has changed. In *Inside Out & Back Again*, Hà is thinking exclusively in Vietnamese. In *When Clouds Touch Us*, Hà knows enough English to at times automatically think in that second language. I wanted to show how the gray avalanche of English has infiltrated her mind. The crisp feel of Vietnamese is still in the poems but weighted at times by the wordiness of English.

Can you recall problem-solving decisions you had to make in the writing process?

I wanted my poems to read as if they were written in Vietnamese, which (to me) is naturally poetic and concise. Vietnamese has no articles, so, for a short time I deleted every "a," "an," "the" from the *Inside Out & Back Again* manuscript. My editor suggested I put them back because, even disguised as Vietnamese, English relies rather strongly on those pesky little words.

Also, Hà thought in many more similes and metaphors that I eventually deleted to convey how her mind was shifting to a more practical, direct, yet wordy language.

Which poetic and narrative techniques did you decide to employ, and why?

I used as few words as possible, and I called upon an object, metaphor, or mood to convey a feeling without naming it. In addition to keeping the voice, I advanced story by also providing dates at the end of each poem. In *Inside Out & Back Again*, the dates matched actual history that was important to the story. In the sequel, *When Clouds Touch Us*, the dates evolved to seem like journal entries.

If there were places in the book where you felt it was best to emphasize the poetic strategies over the narrative strategies, or vice versa — what guided these decisions?

I never had to choose between the two. Both were interwoven into each poem.

What poetic or narrative effects were you hoping to achieve?

One, what it's like to think in Vietnamese, a naturally poetic language. Two, what happens when English mixes into the original voice. Three, I wanted readers to be fully engaged with Hà's emotions without spelling out those emotions for them. In *Inside Out and Back Again* in the poem "Wet & Crying," I conveyed Hà was distraught about leaving Saigon by describing her cutting into her first papaya. That simple symbolism encapsulated her emotions without me having to create a scene where she packs, cries, clings to her bed, refuses to go, etc.

What are your thoughts on the verse novel as a form?

I grew up hearing my mother quote by memory from *The Tale of Kiều*, an epic poem that showcases the melodic flow of Vietnamese. My mother speaks only Vietnamese, so she helps keep poetry in my mind. I would read a verse novel over a prose novel any day. And for me, the form only makes sense if the character is thinking in Vietnamese. I do understand this is the last reason other writers use verse novels.

Have verse novels you have read been influential on this work in some way?

For decades I have been reading the great epic poem *The Tale of Kiều* in Vietnamese and am in awe of Nguyễn Du's magic for conveying the world in two lines. I shredded apart *The Tale of Kiều*, trying to understand how Nguyễn Du said so much in six-syllable and eight-syllable couplets. But it must be read in Vietnamese. There's no way to do it justice in a translation.

After writing *Inside Out & Back Again* and *When Clouds Touch Us,* I realized that my ongoing project of deciphering Nguyễn Du's every word has crept poetry into my being.

What have you learnt about writing verse novels from the verse novels you have read?

I love the craft of saying something without saying it, of using images to hint at emotions—thus activating readers' curiosity to engage and immerse into the text. And the fewer words used—the better the emotional depth.

CHAPTER 11
DEAN ATTA

Dean Atta by Thomas Sammut

I think verse novels work especially well when written in first-person present tense with the protagonist as the narrator ...

Dean Atta was born in London, of Greek Cypriot and Jamaican descent. He is a Malika's Poetry Kitchen member, National Poetry Day ambassador, and LGBT+ History Month patron. Dean's poems have been highly commended by the Forward Prizes for Poetry and shortlisted for the Bridport Poetry Prize and Oxford Brookes International Poetry Competition. His books have been praised by Bernardine Evaristo, Benjamin Zephaniah, and Malorie Blackman.

Dean's debut poetry collection was shortlisted for the Polari First Book Prize and his novel in verse, *The Black Flamingo* (Hodder Children's Books, 2019), won the Stonewall Book Award and was shortlisted for the CILIP Carnegie Medal, Jhalak Prize, Los Angeles Times Book Prize, and Waterstones Children's Book Award. Dean's second novel in verse, *Only on the Weekends* (Hodder Children's Books), was published in spring 2022, and this was followed by his second poetry collection, *There Is (Still) Love Here* (Nine Arches Press, 2022), and his memoir, *Person Unlimited: An Ode to My Black Queer Body* (Canongate, 2024).

The Black Flamingo (2019)
Only on the Weekends (2022)

What ideas or influences did you have in mind when creating this work?

I've been writing and performing poetry since I was a teenager and since then it has been the way I feel I can best express myself. At school I was introduced to the works of Black British poets such as Benjamin Zephaniah and John Agard, and later through my own research I took inspiration from African American poets such as Gil Scott-Heron and Maya Angelou. I was inspired to write young adult verse novels more recently after reading books in this form by authors such as Elizabeth Acevedo and Jason Reynolds. Both of my young adult verse novels, *The Black Flamingo* and *Only on the Weekend* have Black gay protagonists. This was especially important to me because I never encountered any books about Black gay characters when I was a teenager in the 1990s and early 2000s. My work explores the intersection of being Black and gay.

How did you approach writing this verse novel? What were the various stages in its development?

My novels are written in first-person present tense with the protagonist as narrator. Once I've come up with a protagonist and a basic idea for a story, an early stage of my process is to write lots of poems in the voice of the protagonist, even if those poems won't have a place in the published book. This helps me get to know them before I decide how their story will play out. I will write key moments of the story, in the form of individual poems, to establish tone of voice, vocabulary, the cultural references, and imagery I'll be using throughout the book. Then I write more and more individual poems and build up my narrative ideas from there. At some point I'll fully plot the story but that hasn't been my starting point with either of the two verse novels I've written. My starting point is always getting to know my protagonist, their desires, their fears, and flaws, so that whatever situation I put them in I'll know how they'll act and react.

Can you recall problem-solving decisions you had to make in the writing process?

There is a jigsaw-puzzle-like nature to the early stages of my writing process once I have many key moments written that need to be connected. I must be willing to let go of some moments if they don't serve the story I've decided to tell. When working with an editor, it helps to have another opinion on the direction of the story and the amount of detail needed for any given plot point. I often write a lot more than I need for moments that particularly excite me; however, sometimes the level of detail I give those moments isn't always needed from a storytelling and pacing perspective. Most of the problems in the writing process are solved by my editor suggesting cuts to the text. The cuts they suggest usually bring about more clarity and greater focus to the story.

Which poetic and narrative techniques did you decide to employ, and why?

I employ repetition to show desires and preoccupations of the narrator. In *The Black Flamingo* the phrase "fight or flight" is repeated throughout the book at pivotal moments for Michael. Feathers and wings also appear in different ways throughout the story, flamingos too—flamingo facts, flamingo sightings, flamingos' dreams and daydreams, and Michael's drag alter ego The Black Flamingo. But this flamingo repetition is not simply repetition, it's also the central metaphor of the whole book. I employ many other metaphors and similes in this story but the metaphor of the (black) flamingo is the beating heart of the story.

In both *The Black Flamingo* and *Only on the Weekends* I use stand-alone poems that are not narrative led, to give the reader some pause for thought and reflection and to allow for further insight into the heart and mind of the protagonist. In the design of the book these stand-alone poems are set apart from the narration with a background image to show they are written in a notebook or on a mobile phone.

Text message communication, group chats, and emojis are used in both my books to show communication happening between characters using mobile phones. Rather than have the narrator tell the reader about these conversations, the reader is shown the mobile phone exchanges happening, including when a character is *Typing … * and then *Stops Typing*. This aims to convey the anticipation and hesitation of this style of communication.

"Show don't tell" is a rule I try to employ across both books; however, exposition is sometimes required or preferable when something needs to be made totally clear and not left open for interpretation.

If there were places in the book where you felt it was best to emphasize the poetic strategies over the narrative strategies, or vice versa—what guided these decisions?

Stand-alone poems were times when I emphasized the poetic strategies over the narrative. I wanted the books to have a reason why they were written in verse. *The Black Flamingo* is written in verse because Michael writes poetry in the back of his school exercise books and eventually performs a poem at an open mic night at university, not long before his first drag performance in which he also performs a poem. *Only on the Weekends* is written in verse because Mackintosh loves listening to his late mother's record collection and he pays close attention to the song lyrics, hoping to feel closer to his mother. Towards the end of the story Mackintosh discovers a poem his mother wrote to him before she died. In this way, poetry was always a part of Mackintosh's story, even before he knew it.

The prologues of my books place the emphasis on the narrative to locate the reader and set them up with the information they needed to enter the story with a sense of anticipation, and they also set up some foreshadowing of what is to come.

What poetic or narrative effects were you hoping to achieve?

My hope with *The Black Flamingo* was for part of the book to be readable in isolation and still make sense to a reader without the rest of the story, and therefore this book has more stand-alone poems. *The Black Flamingo* covers the childhood of Michael from the age of six to nineteen, and in the prologue, Michael also retells the story of the first year of his life as told to him by his mum. With such a time span, it had to be told episodically with big leaps forward in time rather than a continuous single narrative.

On the other hand, with *Only on the Weekends* I tell a story over a much shorter time frame of eighteen months and therefore I wanted to focus on a single narrative of a love triangle and needed fewer stand-alone poems and even fewer big leaps forward in time.

What are your thoughts on the verse novel as a form?

I think verse novels work especially well when written in first-person present tense with the protagonist as the narrator, as they allow the reader direct access to the heart and mind of the protagonist. Being so close to the protagonists allows an author to elicit a greater amount of empathy from their reader.

Verse novels can do interesting things with typography, such as how Kwame Alexander's *The Crossover* uses typography to show the movement and energy of a basketball game.

Verse novels can very successfully use dual narrators, such as how Elizabeth Acevedo's *Clap When You Land* has one narrator speak in two-line stanzas and the other in three-line stanzas.

The freedom and versatility of the verse form afford the author of a verse novel many more possibilities when it comes to design, stanza breaks, line breaks, and how they choose to use negative space.

Something you see in the design of many verse novels is the white page with black text suddenly becoming a black page with white text; this is often done for dramatic effect at an important part of a story. Readers are quite used to seeing a white page with black text but when you see a black page with white text it feels somehow much more confrontational and as a reader you know the use of all that black ink must mean something.

Have verse novels you have read been influential on this work in some way?

The verse novels I have read have given me the permission and a template to write verse novels of my own. Elizabeth Acevedo's *The Poet X* in particular won me over to the idea of writing in this form. It has a reason to be a verse novel because the protagonist is a poet, it has a clear voice, it has dramas and dilemmas, secrets and lies, regrets and redemption.

I modeled *The Black Flamingo* after *The Poet X* in many ways and I was delighted upon the publication of *The Black Flamingo* to be invited to be on a panel alongside Elizabeth Acevedo at the Edinburgh International Book Festival and to be able to thank her personally for the great influence her book had on my work.

What have you learnt about writing verse novels from the verse novels you have read?

I have learnt that there are very few rules to writing a verse novel, besides the rules you set for yourself.

If you know what rules and conventions you want to set up for yourself as a writer, your editors and readers will quickly pick up on what those rules and conventions are and expect you to continue to follow them. Whenever you break one of your own rules or conventions, your editor or reader will look for a meaning behind this break from your norm.

Whether it's a rule about punctuation, capitalization, line breaks, stanza breaks, you should know what your rules and conventions are and stick to them unless breaking them is done in keeping with some significant shift in the story.

CHAPTER 12
LUCY CUTHEW

Lucy Cuthew copyright Lucy Cuthew

I've read a lot of verse novels and enjoy how
many different ways they are approached.

Lucy Cuthew is a Lecturer in the MA in Writing for Young People at Bath Spa University. She is the author of more than thirty books for children, including picture books and nonfiction. Her verse novel, *Blood Moon* (Walker Books), was shortlisted for the Wales Book of the Year Award, and nominated for the Carnegie Medal 2020, shortlisted for the Bath Children's Novel Award, Highly Commended in the Bath Spa/United Agents Prize, shortlisted for the Amazing Book Awards 2021, and listed in the Kirkus Reviews Best Books of 2020, and The Reading Agency's Best Books of the Year. *Blood Moon* was also selected for National Poetry Day, and for the USBBY 2021 Outstanding International Books List. Lucy lives near Cardiff, Wales, regularly speaks on the BBC about children's books and current affairs, and runs creative writing workshops in secondary schools.

Blood Moon (2020)

What ideas or influences did you have in mind when creating this work?

I loved poetry right from early childhood—one of my favorite books was *Under the Bed* by Michael Rosen, illustrated by Quentin Blake. It was short and each poem was no more than two pages, but each told a story and did something playful with language at the same time, and I adored it. As a teenager I rediscovered poetry while studying Dylan Thomas and began writing my own again.

Later, when I was writing *Blood Moon* during an MA in Creative Writing, I was thinking about how poetry is so often a vehicle for expressing something difficult. I read *One* by Sarah Crossan and I especially loved how it could be read in the same way you would watch a film—in one immersive, consuming sitting. I then read the verse novels of Jason Reynolds and Kwame Alexander, among others, seeing the different techniques they had used to approach the form.

I knew that *Blood Moon* was a story for a YA audience, and I read YA widely—some authors whose work I admire and was thinking about include Meg Rosoff, E. Lockhart, Tanya Landman, Jennifer Niven, John Green, Lucy Christopher, and particularly Louise O'Neill, whose novel *Only Ever Yours* was a big influence on me.

I was also doing some research for an MA in Writing for Young People, into twists— which are always the stories that most delight me. *We Were Liars* by E. Lockhart is a tight, spare novel which plays with an unreliable narrator, weaves fairy tale into the narrative and has a big twist. I am very interested in the mechanics of twists in narrative fiction and film. I looked at films like *Shutter Island*, *Sixth Sense*, *Fight Club*, and *Memento*, and though all of these are psychological thrillers, I used some of the aspects of this research to orchestrate the light twist at the end of *Blood Moon*.

Lastly, I was interested in shame at the time. I had heard Jon Ronson talking to Adam Buxton on the *Adam Buxton* Podcast[1] about his book *So You've Been Publicly Shamed* which got me thinking about what it would be like for a teenager to go viral. This research took me to the work of American academic, Brené Brown[2] on the mechanics of shame—which was invaluable for understanding how it manifests, and how someone can recover from it.

How did you approach writing this verse novel? What were the various stages in its development?

I began *Blood Moon* with the creative writing prompt "She sells seashells by the seashore." I wasn't sure what I was going to write, but out came this strong voice, a teenager, walking to school and crushing on a boy over the street, and walking with him, and then getting her period. I think the period came because I was writing in verse. I find that writing with the rhythm in my head serves to lay down train tracks a little ahead of my consciousness, stopping me from thinking, and letting me just write what comes up. It is a way of connecting with truth, and in the case of *Blood Moon*, that truth was talking about periods, which are still a taboo topic. I have wondered whether this is the case for other verse novelists—whether there is a quality to writing poetry which makes it easier to write about something taboo. Poetry is frequently employed to address a difficult topic—death, grief, separation, tragedy, trauma—or to explore something intense—love, the visceral experience of the natural world. I believe this is because it is such an intense form of literature—the condensing of language mirrors and magnifies the intensity of the subject. However, as a writer, I think there is another level at play to expressing something that is difficult to talk about. It is sparer than prose, the way that rhetorical devices—metaphor, simile—are more automatic and natural in verse, but for me anyway, it is also the inner voice anticipating the sound the language will make which enables me to find my way into a state of flow and tell the story from my imagination's heart.

Can you recall problem-solving decisions you had to make in the writing process?

From a technical point of view, I spent some time working out how best to lay out the document so that I could edit it. It was roughly 300 pages long, and I wanted to be able to jump around between sections. I write in Microsoft Word, so I used the headings function to create a list in the navigation pane with the titles of each poem. I also wanted to set out the verse myself, because the lay-out was so intrinsic to how I heard/saw the story. I considered writing it in InDesign, which I use as an editor, but I found that too fiddly for moving large chunks of text around when I was still editing the structure of the story. In the end I used Word, and where I couldn't make it look how I wanted, I added a note for the typesetter.

I found working on *Blood Moon* rather like constructing a building—I found that I could move poems around easily to change the structure and shape, needing only minimal tweaking for plot consistency. However, this also meant that I spend a lot of time moving things around—I changed the order of events often, trying it out to see what worked best. This became quite frustrating in Word, and I wished that I'd used Scrivener, which enables you to move parts around very easily. I have since tried writing in Scrivener but haven't found it works for me.

At one point in the editing, I printed the whole book out four pages to a sheet of A4 and cut it up into poems and stapled them together. I then laid out the story into three horizontal sections so that I could physically see the shape it was taking—where it was weighty, where it was sparse. When I did this, I was able to see the surpluses, and I wanted the novel to be tight, on point and as spare as possible without feeling stark.

Which poetic and narrative techniques did you decide to employ, and why?

I was primarily focused on the rhythm in which I was writing. This was important for me because I wanted the story to unfold quickly and pull the reader in, playing with the pace to make it feel engaging, addictive even. I wanted it to be a book that a reader wouldn't be able to put down. I used rhyme, internal rhyme, assonance and sibilance and a consistent tum-ti-tum beat to create the sounds I wanted the reader to hear when they read the story. There were times when I was worried that I didn't know whether I was writing in a set form—iambic pentameter for example—and I started to try and work it out, but in the end, knowing this didn't improve the quality of the work, and so I let it be more fluid and unstructured, more natural. I considered including highly structured poems—I thought about writing the love scene as a sonnet for example, but in the end, I didn't use any formal poetic structures like that. Instead, I used a loose rhythm, and broke with that rhythm or rhyme in places where I wanted to disrupt the flow—to show a character's state of mind or to mirror an interruption in the plot, to shock, pull the reader up short. I also used the two sides of the page for the dialogue between two characters—so the main character on the right, as it would appear in text/ WhatsApp/messenger and the person she is with on the left. I then used the middle of the page when the two characters' ideas or feelings were in alignment—I used this for a romantic scene and a scene where the two best friends made up after a fight.

Ever since I learned about stichomythia as an undergraduate, I have wanted to use it. I love the idea of two characters' dialogue mingling to form alternate lines of verse. I used this to show how the main character was very close and attuned to her best friend, then later I dropped it in their dialogue when they were arguing, and not understanding one another. I also used it to show the main character growing closer to the romantic interest.

If there were places in the book where you felt it was best to emphasize the poetic strategies over the narrative strategies, or vice versa—what guided these decisions?

This was a big battle for me, but I tried to always stay true to the narrative. First and foremost, I would remind myself, a verse novel is a novel. In the case of *Blood Moon*, I had the additional crucial rule to not be boring, because this is a novel for teenagers. Don't be boring is probably one of the most important mantras for YA writers. I found this a helpful guide, because in my writing in general, like many writers, I am probably prone to indulge and do something overly elaborate, because I like playing with rhetorical devices. In a few lines which I changed in favor of narrative, I still hear the echo of the poetic thing I took out. Occasionally when I do readings, I pop them back in—they sound nice, they rhyme, there is a neat pun or a pleasing bit of alliteration that gives it a nice ring, but overall, I tried to prioritize plot, not poetry.

What poetic or narrative effects were you hoping to achieve?

I wanted to use verse to tell a contemporary story about something considered slightly smutty, taboo, or inappropriate, with the devices used by the most venerated writers in literature. I studied poetry at school and university, and so rarely read something which spoke to my heart. I wanted to use the form to be playful, to speak to young adults today, and to talk about something which is difficult to talk about.

What are your thoughts on the verse novel as a form?

I think verse novels are an engaging and innovative form for exploring story and language. They are often issue-based, but rarely heavy-handed. They are, instead, most commonly an engaging and joyful way of engaging with a story, an issue, a world.

Having come from a publishing background, I was aware that a verse novel might not be considered a very commercial book, and that I might therefore struggle to get it published. Since writing it, and around the time I was still working on it (roughly 2018) there was a rise in the number of verse novels published, which I think changed the perception of them as a niche for YA, in the UK anyway. I think in the US and Australia they were already well established. Since *Blood Moon* was published, I have discovered that many readers specifically like verse novels and seek them out—others have come to *Blood Moon* through interest in the theme, but a large number have specifically engaged with it owing to the form.

A couple of social media posts I've been tagged in have stated something to the effect of "I liked the story, but I wish it had been written in prose". I found that an interesting avenue to think about, because without the verse, there would have been no story—I think poetry can be a means of tapping into the subconscious; meditative, and therefore able to unearth deep truths.

Have verse novels you have read been influential on this work in some way?

One by Sarah Crossan was certainly an influence on *Blood Moon*. I read that before I wrote it. Since then, I've read a lot of verse novels and enjoy how many different ways they are approached.

What have you learnt about writing verse novels from the verse novels you have read?

I recently read *The Girl and the Goddess* by Nikita Gill, and I think she is doing something interesting and different in that book. Her poetry is extraordinarily beautiful, moving through space and time, telling a story over a longer time frame. Louisa Reid's *Gloves Off* switches between the voices of a mother and a daughter. The styles of their voices were very well-defined, and the poems took on different shapes. Jason Reynolds's *Long Way Down* made me think more deeply about form and structure. It is told entirely in an elevator as a boy goes down six floors of a building on his way to kill his brother's murderer. On each floor he is joined by a ghost who converses with him, adding a new dimension to the moral dilemma he faces.

CHAPTER 13
RUKHSANNA GUIDROZ

Rukhsanna Guidroz by Scott Drexler Photography

*As a verse novel author, the challenge is how to show in a few words
what your characters are thinking and feeling without stating it.*

Rukhsanna Guidroz is the author of the middle grade novel in verse, *Samira Surfs*, published by Kokila/Penguin Random House in 2021. Her verse novel was a Publishers Weekly Best Books for 2021, a Center for the Study of Multicultural Literature Best Books, also for 2021, and was chosen for the 2021 Society of Illustrators Original Art show selection. It was a NCTE Notable Poetry Books and Verse Novels for 2022. Rukhsanna also wrote the picture book *Leila in Saffron*, published by Salaam Reads/ Simon & Schuster in 2019. This book was a Choose to Read Ohio "Floyd's Pick" honor title, Pennsylvania Young Reader's Choice Award Master List, Ohioana Book Award Finalist, Picture This Recommendation List, and a Choose to Read Ohio Booklist Selection. Her first picture book, *Mina vs. The Monsoon*, was published by Yali Books in 2018 and was a Kirkus Best Picture Book.

Rukhsanna juggles multiple cultures. She was born in England, and her parents are Indian and Chinese. While London and Paris have been her home, she decided to settle in the Hawaiian Islands after working as a journalist and news producer in Hong Kong. These days, when she's not writing or teaching, you'll find her surfing with her husband and two sons. Her website can be found at rukhsannaguidroz.com.

Samira Surfs (2021)

What ideas or influences did you have in mind when creating this work?

The idea to write *Samira Surfs* first came to me when I read an article in *The Surfer's Journal*. The article was about a girl called Nasima Akter. Nasima was part of a group of young teens who surfed in Cox's Bazar, Bangladesh. I was immediately struck by the story. A surprisingly large number of people in the world cannot swim. Surfing takes even more courage. However, what filled me with awe was the determination of these girls to cross a boundary that few dare to approach. In Bangladesh, it is taboo for girls to be in the water, never mind surfing. Girls stay close to home in this primarily conservative Muslim nation and marry young. I grew up in a part–Muslim household. While my family is liberal, I am familiar with Muslim values and traditions. After digging deeper into the article, I found out that Nasima was Rohingya. Rohingya is an ethnic group from Myanmar, formerly known as Burma. This predominantly Muslim population has suffered years of persecution, discrimination, and violent acts at the hands of Myanmar authorities. To save their lives, many fled their homeland and settled in neighboring countries, including Bangladesh. I was moved by their circumstances, history, and resilience. A story was already taking shape in my mind. I spent the next two years in deep research, gathering information I read in reports by aid agencies and refugee organizations. After consulting with experts in the refugee crisis, I was better able to piece together the social and political backbone of the story. I also interviewed Rohingya refugees to understand who Rohingya are as a people. Photos in *The Surfer's Journal* article and other images I found online were a constant source of inspiration—the expressions on the girls' faces, the colors of the water, and scenes of their daily lives. I could hear the voices of their concerned parents, rebuking them for entering the water. My own journey of learning to surf on Maui provided me with details that made it onto the page. I know the joy and tears that come with learning the sport. If I needed inspiration or clarity when writing the story, I headed to the surf to experience the physical sensations of my toes in the sand or the moment I lie down on my surfboard. I revisited all the valuable lessons I have learned, and still learn each time I paddle out.

How did you approach writing this verse novel? What were the various stages in its development?

Writing this novel was a long process. It's hard to overstate how creating and editing a story requires time and patience. I started *Samira Surfs* as a short picture book, and from there, I expanded the narrative layer by layer. It is essential to fill out characters' traits to make them believable and fully rounded. Personalities dictate a character's actions and dialogue. Once their traits are worked out, the plotline is easier to develop. For example, Khaled, the main character's brother, is creative. He keeps a notebook that he uses to record his innermost thoughts. I asked myself several questions about this aspect of Khaled. How would he feel if he lost his notebook? What would that do to his emotional stability? Since this item is so meaningful to Khaled, it would surely be devastating for him to misplace it. The reader knows some of the notebook's contents and understands its value to Khaled. I created a thread where Samira unwittingly loses his notebook. Khaled feels lost and frustrated without it and then rejoices and regains his emotional well-being when it's back in his possession. Of course, it is essential to have a resolution for each exciting action or theme that you introduce to ensure your reader is engaged and satisfied at the end of the story.

After writing each draft, I would send my work to my editor for comments. Her gentle nudges helped me develop the story from a picture book to a children's novel. Initially, I had a very rough outline for the plot because I prefer to leave room for creativity. Ideas don't always appear on demand for me. My editor was respectful of my writing process and allowed me the space to explore as I went along.

Can you recall problem-solving decisions you had to make in the writing process?

In my original draft, Samira makes friends with a group of Bengali girls. But it came about too quickly, and the friendship wasn't earned. I realized that I had to revise the relevant episodes to ensure this relationship had more authenticity and credibility. Samira needed to work her way into a tightly-knit group of friends. The girls are all Bengali (apart from one girl), and the arrival of the Rohingya refugees has put a strain on their already fragile economic situation. Why would they welcome her? Samira and her family represented a threat to their lives in terms of jobs and resources. I decided to make Maya, one of the Bengali girls, kind and open to making friends with Samira. Maya is eager to have Samira teach her to swim, and she eventually becomes Samira's pathway into the sisterhood. Nadia, on the other hand, is guarded and insecure and mistrusts Samira. She feels threatened by her appearance on the beach and in their social group. These opposing elements went back and forth in the narrative. I created a more complex and realistic relationship between the girls by adding these scenes to the narrative. I had to create, track, develop, and resolve each thread I added as the story unfolded. Once Maya introduces Samira to Nadia, and Nadia realizes Samira is not competing with her, she lets her guard down and befriends her over time. When Nadia accepts her, the sisterhood is sealed, and Samira is finally accepted.

Which poetic and narrative techniques did you decide to employ, and why?

I use a combination of poetic techniques in *Samira Surfs*, and one of my favorites is repetition. It is simple, easy to use, and effective because it reflects how an eleven-year-old might think. In the poem "All of Me," Samira feels sad and isolated. Life is tough, and she wonders if it is because of her identity.

Reading my work aloud is always helpful, no matter what I write. I also record my stories and listen back to them. Another idea is to ask someone else to read your work. It is surprising how much you can learn by doing this.

I use flashbacks to fill in the historical and political context of *Samira Surfs*. This context is important because it lets the reader know what the characters have lived through and what events have shaped the individual personalities. But most readers dislike backstory. If the flashback is relevant and flows with the story, readers are left informed, feeling closer to the characters, and more compassionate to their situation. As I write, I like to ask myself, will my reader care?

If there were places in the book where you felt it was best to emphasize the poetic strategies over the narrative strategies, or vice versa—what guided these decisions?

Verse novels have a rhythm and beat that is fun to create as an author. In the poem, "A New Language," Khaled shows Samira a surf magazine, and as they flip through the pages, a wave of enthusiasm rises in Samira. She takes in images of waves, surfer girls, and surfboards. After setting the scene, I show Samira learning the names of some surfing maneuvers. My idea was to create a beat that was fast and dynamic. It reflects Samira's mounting joy and enthusiasm as she is introduced to words of a language she wants to learn.

In the poem "Before and After," I wanted to slow down the story and draw the reader even closer. It is a pivotal moment in the story. Samira has finally learned to surf and feels the joy of her achievement. She has overcome obstacles in her life, taken significant risks, and continued to push boundaries. She is elated when she can ride waves at last and be with her friends on the water. Samira describes her life before surfing and after surfing. The word "and" represents a separation of the chapters of her life. That separation becomes a point of reference for her. The white space on this line forces the reader to slow down, almost pausing before reading the following line.

Other places where I emphasize poetic strategy are in the poems towards to end of the novel, in "Inside Out" and "Gone." Samira uses a metaphor of the banks of a collapsing river. She has felt the weight of her secret reading and surfing for several months. Now her lies have been exposed. Her goal is to maintain everything she has claimed for herself. But that weight is too much. Samira likens it to the banks of a river that are about to give way. Even as she realizes she must surrender and acknowledge defeat, she still looks for a lifeline. Perhaps Khaled can help. Even Baba. But nothing will change Mama's mind. She will not allow Samira to surf, and neither will Baba. The banks collapse, Samira is swept away, and no branch can save her.

What poetic or narrative effects were you hoping to achieve?

Word choice, syntax, and narrative structure are deliberate and calculated. To maximize the effect with as few words as possible, especially in a verse novel, is part of an author's job. When writing my novel, I wanted to create poems that would have a visceral impact on the reader. They know Samira's challenges—lying to her parents, keeping secrets, loving a forbidden sport. My intention was to create physical sensations in my readers' bodies as they read. In the poem "Numbers to Nothing," Khaled's cell phone battery dies, and the family can no longer call home. If my reader felt disappointed and let down, just like my characters, then I did my job.

What are your thoughts on the verse novel as a form?

I write sparsely, and my thinking comes in short, compact spurts, so this novel form naturally suits me. It is an excellent way of getting inside the protagonist's head and showing how they feel about the world around them. The intimate and emotional qualities of the first-person point of view allow the reader to feel like they are involved in the story because they are standing in the main character's shoes. But this also prevents the reader from having an omniscient perspective. As a verse novel author, the challenge is how to show in a few words what your characters are thinking and feeling without stating it. That's where practice, research, and reading across genres come into play. I use the word "play" intentionally. Sometimes it's helpful to see writing as an exercise and not an end goal. Reading stories from different genres, categories, formats, and for different ages is all valuable for fine-tuning your craft.

Have verse novels you have read been influential on this work in some way?

The first verse novel I read was *Inside Out and Back Again* by Thanhhà Lại. The free verse form felt powerful and liberating. I had to find more to read. That search led me to many other works, including *Garvey's Choice* by Nikki Grimes, *The Crossover* by Kwame Alexander, and *Home Is Not a Country* by Safia Elhillo. These books resonated with me, and I began to see how writing in verse and from the first-person point of view could be an exciting way to share a story with a reader. I was curious to know if I, too, could write one. When I found the right story, I discussed the idea with my editor. She was on the same page as me. I started the novel's first line and ended up with *Samira Surfs*.

What have you learnt about writing verse novels from the verse novels you have read?

While many verse novelists use the same techniques, their stories are unique, and techniques vary, making each book feel different. It's easy to overthink sometimes.

Following my instinct has always worked for me, and, even if I must edit my work several times over (most authors do), I find that my voice begins to settle down and find the right pitch. It takes practice and reading other people's work, but it ultimately comes down to the author finding their way to tell their story because no one else can tell it.

CHAPTER 14
MARIKO NAGAI

Mariko Nagai by Nick Jones

I am in for a lifetime of apprenticeship with this form. Each book is different, and each book is more difficult to write.

Having grown up in Europe and America, Mariko Nagai studied English with a specialization in poetry at the New York University where she was the Erich Maria Remarque Fellow. She has received the Pushcart Prizes both in poetry and fiction (nominated five times in total) and has received fellowships from the Rockefeller Foundation Bellagio Center, UNESCO-Aschberg Bursaries for the Arts, Akademie Schloss Solitude, Yaddo, and Hawthornden International Writers Retreat, to name a few. Her works have appeared in Pushcart Prize anthologies, *Best Pushcart Poetry of the Last 30 Years*, *New Letters*, *The Gettysburg Review*, *Southern Review*, *Asia Literary Review*, *Drunken Boat*, *Prairie Schooner*, amongst others. She is the author of *Histories of Bodies: Poems* (Red Hen Press, 2007), *Georgic: Stories* (BkMk Press/University of Missouri Kansas City, 2010), *Dust of Eden: A Novel* (Albert Whitman & Co, 2014), *Irradiated Cities* (winner of 2015 NOS Award, Les Figues, 2017), *Under the Broken Sky* (Christy Ottaviano Books, 2019), *Body of Empire* (Tarpaulin Sky Press, 2024), and *Imaginary Death* (punctum press, forthcoming 2025). A third verse novel, provisionally-titled *The Sword of Yesterday*, is forthcoming 2025 from Christy Ottaviano Books, an imprint of Little, Brown Books for Young Readers, a division of Hachette Book Group. Her work has been translated into Vietnamese, French, Chinese, Romanian, Bulgarian, and German. She currently lives in Tokyo and is Professor of Creative Writing and Japanese Literature at Temple University Japan Campus. Her website can be found at mariko-nagai.com.

Dust of Eden (2014)
Under the Broken Sky (2019)
The Sword of Yesterday (2025)

What ideas or influences did you have in mind when creating this work?

I'm a voracious reader of history books—when I have a question, I read everything and anything I can get my hands on about a period, including newspapers and cookbooks (cookbooks and etiquette books are an amazing window into an era), and whenever I come across interesting facts, I make a mental note. Maybe I'm like a squirrel with ideas—I gather, gather, gather ideas and eventually, things start to connect in my head, and something magical happens. I see a vision, a snapshot of a moment I know is from a future work. A girl carrying a pot of a rose plant in the sandstorm (*Dust of Eden*); a girl sitting on the road, getting her hair shorn off (*Under the Broken Sky);* a girl in a dress with a Japanese sword, moving with it in the moonlit night (*The Sword of Yesterday*); a girl floating in the sea, looking at the sky, thinking, "I want to live," (work-in-progress); a girl in a kimono with a dog in one arm and a sword in another, facing a man (work-in-progress) a girl crawling out of a dark cave (work-in-progress). I am now seeing a girl and a cat on a canoe with an old person wrapped in a blanket, navigating through a stormy sea at night. This was how I was feeling as I navigated the pandemic with a new kitten I found on the street when Tokyo went into a soft lockdown, and with my mother who was dying from cancer. I imagined all of us as a fleet out there in the dark stormy sea, each on their individual canoes, each trying to navigate through the pandemic months; in my mind I imagined us calling to each other for reassurance once in a while, for worry, for love, and we respond, telling them we were doing okay, or we were drowning, or we had to let someone go—but we were, each in each, navigating through that dark time. Maybe, many years later, this snapshot will come in focus as a plot emerges.

How did you approach writing this verse novel? What were the various stages in its development?

Under the Broken Sky was a long journey in making. It started out as a prose novel, with many more characters and covered a longer time span and geographical areas. The tone seemed more like young adult than middle grade—there were graphic depictions of violence, dead, dying, and trauma. The manuscript went through many many revisions— each revision changing the story in such a drastic way—and if you were to compare the first draft to the published version, the only thing that remains is a protagonist (different name, same gender, and age) who had to evacuate from the little village she grew up in

Manchuria. Throughout multiple revisions, here was a mother who played a major role and then disappeared, two teachers who played significant roles and had to disappear, there was a failed mass-suicide scene, there was a rape scene, and on and on and on. At one point, a version started with the protagonist as a middle-aged woman on a tour bus, first time back to China, to look for her little sister she lost during the war—and ended with seeing a middle-aged woman in the crowd that looked exactly like her mother; pretty much covering half a century or so. In another version, the protagonist was an old woman telling her secret to a nursing home staff: that she sold her little sister so she could come back to Japan. When I discovered where the true starting point was, I also discovered the true ending: starting with the protagonist's birthday, right before the evacuation, and ending on the repatriation ship to Japan a year later. I learned how to write a verse novel by revising—How do you stay true to the demand of poetry while also to the demand of prose fiction? How do you create a poem that can stand on its own while maintaining a narrative arc and character development? How do you deal with time movement? I'm still learning—I fear that I am going to have a lifelong apprenticeship, always learning, always discovering.

Can you recall problem-solving decisions you had to make in the writing process?

Every book demands a completely different problem-solving decision. In *Dust of Eden*, one of the preoccupations I had was: how to cover four years in a very limited space, while maintaining a middle grade voice? Putting dates as section headings helped. In *Under the Broken Sky*, the challenge was: how to choose which moment to start, and which moment to end at? That was one of the hardest decisions to make, because I wanted to cover half a century of this girl's life. I knew her life inside out, and I wanted to put that all in one book, which I know doesn't work in a middle grade. In this book, I learned to let go; ninety-eight percent of what I knew about the protagonist had to be thrown away, and I just worked with that one important year of her life. In the forthcoming verse novel, *The Sword of Yesterday*, I knew I wanted to write in a traditional form—so my challenge was more on a language level than on a character level. It was like riding a horse—I had to have complete mastery over the language so that the form didn't dictate the diction. Every book poses a different set of questions and challenges.

Which poetic and narrative techniques did you decide to employ, and why?

Both *Dust of Eden* and *Under the Broken Sky* are written in free verse for many reasons, but one is because of its setting and the character. Both of these characters are either bilingual or bicultural—or, hybrid in terms of cultures and languages they grew up in: Mina is a sansei (third-generation Japanese American) who grew up in a household where the grandfather only speaks Japanese (someone who came to America and had married late in his life), the father writes for the Japanese-American newspaper in English, and the mother speaks perfect Japanese but a "broken" English (I always saw her as having grown up in Japan and came to the US to marry in the traditional arranged marriage fashion) and though she is not a proficient speaker of Japanese, she understands it completely. She is the product of both the American culture (outside) and the Japanese culture (inside). This is also the case with Natsu in *Under the Broken Sky*: Natsu's father and mother were the state-sponsored colonists to Manchuria, and though Natsu was born in Japan, she doesn't remember anything about Japan, though that's the only language she speaks. She didn't really have contact with the Chinese (Japanese and Chinese did not occupy the same space during the time Manchuria as a country existed) so her Chinese language skill was minimal. So in both books, using free verse as the narrative vehicle made sense because the free verse form offers prose-like rhythm while also having to rely heavily on internal rhymes, line breaks, and white space.

In *The Sword of Yesterday*, the protagonist is one of the first Japanese immigrants in the US—though to call her an immigrant is wrong. She was a refugee from Japan, smuggled out and settled in California as part of the Wakamatsu Tea and Silk Colony, a failed experiment in resettling. Because she was born as a samurai's daughter of the Aizu Wakamatsu Clan, the poetic form I utilized was a tanka format—though it's more a renga/tanka, each stanza carrying 5-7-5-7-7 syllable structure. In a book I am working on right now, where a girl goes on a vengeance trip, I wanted to emulate the traditional journey format of Basho and Issa, so it is written in haibun (prose and haiku) diary form.

If there were places in the book where you felt it was best to emphasize the poetic strategies over the narrative strategies, or vice versa—what guided these decisions?

When I teach haibun, I often use the analogy of watching a musical. There are moments of heightened emotions, when time stands still, and emotions are fully experienced. I think that's where, for me, the poems switch from narrative to lyrical. Time stops. We submerge ourselves in an emotion (or emotions) of that moment. Time, lines, structural, sonic patterns, all of that can be reshuffled and abstracted in a lyrical moment. It must have a sense of inevitability. Not forced. Inevitability. The sense of "yes, because A and B happened, there is no other feeling except for C to happen." Then time starts up again when we go back to the narrative form. The feeling—for all its complexities—are embodied in that lyrical moment.

What poetic or narrative effects were you hoping to achieve?

Each poetic choice I make within a text also must somehow fit into the fictional storytelling. I know this is a cliché, but each story must find its own form, its own ways of best encapsulating the narrative not just in language, but in form and shape and pace. So as I mentioned earlier, free verse, choka, tanka, haibun—each of these choices nod toward the cultural setting of the story (i.e., Japan) and are a conscious choice I make on the macro level, and the same can be said about the micro decisions I make—or the story makes for me: a poem's relationship to the preceding and proceeding poems have to make sense. I use sonic techniques to convey certain unsaid feelings (harsh consonants and one to two syllables to convey speeding of the emotion; open vowels and sonorous words to convey relaxed mood), and this can play with or against the words on the page. So, the protagonist (and the narrator of the story) might tell you that she is feeling one way, but the erratic sonic pattern of the poem conveys otherwise (a bit like the successful picture books where the text on the page is at odds with or enriched by the illustration). Another thing I want to stress is that as as a poet/writer, I never want to dumb down my books. One of my favorite professors in college, Rosanna Warren, told me, "Books are patient, they will wait for you until you are ready to understand them," and I agree. Sometimes we are not ready for the book, but it will wait for you until you are. Sometimes, we read the book, then reread it some years later, and we get another layer of understanding. That's the kind of book I want to write—books that beg to be read again and again, offering different journeys with each reading.

What are your thoughts on the verse novel as a form?

Because I am a poet by training and practice, I can always tell when someone is trained primarily in fiction—the poem in each page doesn't stand on its own. It is part of the whole, not the individual making the whole. These poems fall flat in terms of line breaks, word choices, phonetic music. When I read verse novels, I want to savor each page, and I also want to see character develop over the pages; I want to see the fragments connected. Verse novels are often promoted as a means by which to engage reluctant readers, but truly phenomenal verse novelists are rare, and I can only think of a handful of writers today who fit these descriptions. Me? I'm still a novice.

Have verse novels you have read been influential on this work in some way?

I think every middle grade or Young Adult verse novel can trace its lineage to *Out of the Dust* by Karen Hesse for the possibility of how we can tell a story through verse. I remember the first time coming across it. I was living in New York, working as an intern in a children's book publishing house, just dipping my toes into the amazing world of children's books. It was still an innocent time for children's books, I think. Barnes and Noble and Borders were affecting the sales, and there were massive layoffs in the Kidlit publishing world, but books were getting more diverse. Young Adult was beginning to emerge as an age category. Books like the Harry Potter series and His Dark Material series were really revolutionizing the book industry. I don't remember who introduced me to *Out of the Dust*—I think it was Christy Ottaviano, who I was interning for and who is now my editor, who thought I would like it because of my degree in Creative Writing in poetry. I remember going to St Mark's Bookstore, which was down the street from my apartment back then (and which closed its door a couple of years ago, to the huge disappointment of the neighborhood) and seeing this beautiful quiet cover: the forget-me-not blue cover with an inset of a picture of a girl staring at the camera (a Dorothea

Lange photo), and when I opened the book, seeing pages and pages of poems. I knew then that this is the kind of book I wanted to write—and more than twenty years later, this is the kind of the book I still want to write: a story that touches and moves the heart, that pushes the boundary of form and language; a story that you can read when you are twelve, twenty-four, thirty-five, forty, and it grows with you, offering different perspectives with each read. There are other books I admire that are not verse novels, but lyrical prose: Cynthia Ryland's *Missing May*, Kate DiCamillo's *Because of Winn-Dixie*, to name a few.

What have you learnt about writing verse novels from the verse novels you have read?

That I am in for a lifetime of apprenticeship with this form. Each book is different, and each book is more difficult to write. From reading? Just like anything else in life, there are good ones and there are bad ones, and there are, in rare cases, phenomenal ones, and all of them had a journey to make in order to get published.

CHAPTER 15
ISHLE YI PARK

Ishle Yi Park by Sulei Watene

I happen to love the verse novel as a form—it's not easy, but it's engaging, and suited to adventurous and brave writers.

Ishle Yi Park aka LANI has been awarded the Sister of Fire Award from the Women of Color Resource Center in California, a Poet Laureate title for the Borough of Queens, New York, a Certificate of Merit from John C. Liu at City Hall, New York, and her birthday, May 24, was made "Ishle Yi Park" day in Queens, New York. Park has also been the recipient of music, poetry, and fiction writing grants from NYFA (The New York Foundation for the Arts), the Serpent Source Foundation, and the Jerome Foundation. Park's first book of poetry and fiction, *The Temperature of This Water* (Kaya Press), was the recipient of literary awards including the Pen America Beyond Margins Award for Outstanding Writers of Color, and the Member's Choice Award of the Asian American Writers' Workshop and is taught in Asian American Literature classes in colleges across the country. Her work has been published, featured, and anthologized in *The New York Times, The SF Weekly, New York Newsday, The NY Post, The Boston Review, Daily News, Tribes Magazine, Lotus Magazine, KoreAm, Ploughshares, Barrow Street, Many Mountains Moving, Echoes Upon Echoes: New Korean American Writings* (Asian American Writers Workshop), Elaine Kim and Laura Hyun Kang (Eds.) (Temple University Press, 2003), *Can't Stop Won't Stop: A History of the Hip-Hop Generation* by Jeff Chang and D.J. Kool Herc (Picador, 2007), *Words in Your Face: A Guided Tour Through Twenty Years of the New York City Poetry Slam* by Cristin O'Keefe Aptowicz (Soft Skull, 2007), *Afro Asia: Revolutionary Political and Cultural Connections between African Americans and Asian Americans* by Fred Ho and Bill V. Mullen (Eds.), (Duke University Press, 2008), *Century of the Tiger: One Hundred Years of Korean Culture in America 1903–2003* (Manoa 14, 2) by Jenny Ryun Foster, Heinz Insu Fenkl, et al. (University of Hawaii Press, 2003), and *Rise: A Pop History of Asian America from the Nineties to Now* by Jeff Yang, Phil Yu, et al. (Harper, 2022). *Angel & Hannah*, a novel in verse (One World Penguin Random House, 2021), received praise from *Publishers Weekly, Kirkus Reviews*, and *The APA Smithsonian*. Park has been an Artist-in-Residence, a Judge for the Youth Speaks National Slam, enjoyed writing residences at New Pacific Studio (New Zealand), the Saltonstall Foundation (Ithaca, New York), and the Blue Mountain Center (New York), served as the Arts-in-Education Director of the Asian American Writers' Workshop, and taught creative writing at all levels. She has organized readings and benefits to raise awareness about Korean Reunification, to support women in situations of domestic violence, to help victims of natural disasters, and to support the greening of our planet. Park currently works as a writing mentor and coach to emerging writers.

Angel & Hannah (2021)

What ideas or influences did you have in mind when creating this work?

Angel & Hannah was greatly influenced by Pablo Neruda's *Cien Sonetos de Amor* (*100 Love Sonnets*), a beautiful poetic tribute to his then-wife Matilde. The book is divided into four parts, which represent the four stages of the day: morning, afternoon, evening, and night. When I first began this novel, I was at the end of a tumultuous, heartfelt, and passionate ten-year relationship, and wanted to mark this experience and remember it, recreate it through art. So, I poured the heart and soul of my first love story into this story. Many elements, however, are fictionalized, and I changed the timeline of the relationship from a decade to one year, and divided my book into four seasons: spring, summer, winter, and fall.

Shakespeare's classic love story *Romeo and Juliet*, of course, was in my mind and heart while writing this novel. I knew there would inevitably be comparisons to those two timeless lovers and the similar struggles they faced with their families, so I went out of my way to pay tribute to this tragic romance in my book, in my own way. I wanted *Angel & Hannah* to be a classic story of young passionate love, with ties to the classic love stories of our times (*Romeo and Juliet*, the Book of Songs from the Bible), as well as to classic '90s hip hop and soul music, which was the backdrop of Angel & Hannah's love affair.

I was watching Joy Harjo's Masterclass on Poetry recently, and in one video, she spoke of mapping out your poetry ancestors—how all of us have a lineage of poets, musicians, and artists that we can name and trace who have helped us in our spiritual and artistic development. A friend of mine said that the "Acknowledgments" section of *Angel & Hannah* read like its own poem to her, and I realized that it is—it is actually a poem of gratitude that maps out my own poetic and artistic ancestral map. It names every major writer, singer, artist, activist, comedian, family member, lover and friend who has been not only influential, but instrumental in my life and creative development—all of the influences that have in some way or another shaped the language, content, musicality, and style of *Angel & Hannah*.

In terms of ideas, it was simple. I was following Toni Morrison's advice to "write the book you want to read." I was craving to read a novel where the main character is a sensual, many-layered young Asian American woman exploring her sexuality and emotions in the bloom of young love. Most of the literature I had read either ignored or excluded Asian American women completely, or sexualized and exoticized us, so we are rarely truly viewed and seen for the complex human beings and souls we are. We are often Othered, marginalized, stereotyped, or tokenized completely, in literature. So for once, I wanted a main character to be someone very relatable to me, whose story I could identify with—a working-class Korean American teenager from Queens.

How did you approach writing this verse novel? What were the various stages in its development?

This novel came to me in a dream. I saw the arc of the story, our "shero" and her beloved, and the blossoming of their love in seasons … as soon as I woke, I drew it like a book with flapping pages, with the seasons sketched above, and with each sonnet—poem capturing a moment of love, struggle, pain, or beauty in their shared lives.

In the beginning, I approached this story as a simple chapbook—a collection of twenty-five poems about a young couple in love. My idea was to tell the story of their inter-racial love affair in one year, in a movement of four seasons—spring, summer, winter, fall—where you could see and feel the growth and evolution of first love.

So, *Angel & Hannah* debuted as a chapbook, and I had a reading from it at the Asian American Writers' Workshop in New York, where I sold out of my handmade limited-edition copies.

One of these chapbooks found its way into the hands of Kamilah Forbes, who is currently the director of the legendary Apollo Theatre in Harlem, New York. At the time, I had known Kamilah through Stan Lathan and Def Poetry Jam, of which I was a touring cast member.

Kamilah loved the sonnets about Angel and Hannah and asked me if I might be interested in turning the collection of poems into a theatrical solo show for the New York Theatre Hip Hop Festival, which she happened to be co-producing that year, and I agreed. Under Kamilah's direction, I found new life in the characters, got deeper into their histories, and wrote more sonnets to give more context about their lives.

I also chose to work with DJ Reborn, my dear friend and touring cast member of Def Poetry Jam, and she ended up becoming the musical choreographer and DJ for the *Angel & Hannah* show. DJ Reborn is now Lauryn Hill's tour DJ. She brilliantly and seamlessly wove the perfect melodies, hip-hop classics and songs between the sonnets, creating a lovely dance and interplay between sonnets and songs, poet, and DJ. We performed two sold-out shows one weekend and it was a thrilling experience and received great reviews.

I ended up expanding *Angel & Hannah* into a longer body of work when I was a graduate student at New York University's Graduate School of Arts & Sciences, in the Creative Writing Program. My thesis advisor was the poet Kimiko Hahn, and she was very thoughtful and encouraging as a teacher and mentor and helped me map out and visualize the overall story arc better, and structure it with a stronger skeleton.

I learned to place my poems on the floor, on the walls, and all around me—to play with groupings and imagery and motifs … it was great fun, and led to new ways of structuring, ordering, and envisioning the poems in *Angel & Hannah*.

I also had extended time to focus on *Angel & Hannah* at the Saltonstall Writing Residency in Ithaca, New York, and at the Blue Mountain Center in upstate New York. My time at both artist residencies was crucial to the development and completion of this work, because as a single working-class woman or color, I often had to sacrifice my writing time because I was too busy performing, working, and hustling to make ends meet, pay rent and pay bills.

After being buried in my laptop for years while I was working three jobs and living a humble off-grid lifestyle in Hawaii, my sonnets were miraculously re-discovered and loved by two editors from Random House who happened to be taking a writing workshop in New York with my dear friend and old roommate Bushra Rehman, a talented South Asian poet, writer, and teacher. They resurrected *Angel & Hannah*, and after I signed a contract, I started working with editor Nicole Counts to refine, deepen, and expand the story.

I came back to *Angel & Hannah* with a fresh eye and years of life experience to make the book wiser, more seasoned, and mature … so it was completed in Hawaii, at night while my children were sleeping.

Can you recall problem-solving decisions you had to make in the writing process?

During the writing of this story, the size of the work expanded and contracted multiple times, like an accordion. One challenge I constantly faced was deciding how many poems were enough to tell the whole story, how many poems were too many, and how many were not enough.

Which poetic and narrative techniques did you decide to employ, and why?

I decided to employ a combination of sonnets, hip hop bars, and free verse into this book, because I wanted it to read like an extended song of sorts—a dream in rhymes through space and time. I appreciate the musicality of sonnets and hip-hop bars, and wanted to specifically juxtapose the two so that readers could see and feel the similarities between the forms, old and new, classic and modern, as well as appreciate the differences in style, subject matter, and voice.

The free verse poems started coming through when I was writing in the voice of Hannah's ancestor: her deceased *halmoni* (grandmother). Somehow, she refused to be confined to the boxy structures of sonnets—it felt like a jail to her, and she spoke and wrote herself as she wanted, breaking free of any forms I tried to impose. So, if you notice, most of the free verse poems in the book are when Hannah's family are involved.

Also, there was trauma to be dealt with as well—generational, historical, ancestral trauma, both spoken and unspoken. Trauma does not like to fit into boxes or confined spaces. It needs to tumble over, stumble, stomp, spill, make itself known as it must. So certain parts of the book that speak to or about various traumas employ free verse— trauma needs to release itself in its own way to heal. So, it does.

In terms of sonnets, I wrote a combination of Petrarchan, Elizabethan, Spenserian, and free verse sonnets, and some that were hybrid mixtures of two or more of those styles. This helped to keep things interesting, challenging and fun for me. When I felt too constricted by the singsong melodies of iambic pentameter, I'd change it up to make it less rhyme-y.

It was also a fascinating challenge for me to see if this classic, time-honored traditional form could hold such a modern-day love with all its grit and grittiness and be an effective sacred container—it worked surprisingly well.

Combining all these forms in this book was my way of paying homage and giving respect to these various poetic forms and poets who used them brilliantly over time. My way of dancing with and singing to the poets of the past and the present, on the page.

If there were places in the book where you felt it was best to emphasize the poetic strategies over the narrative strategies, or vice versa—what guided these decisions?

Some poems and sonnets came as pure gifts. Divinely channeled, flowing easily from dream-state to paper, whole and complete as they are. With minor edits along the way, of course. But the heart of them was present and beating from the start, and the core of them were captured in that first writing.

Others, took months, even years. Many were discarded, not up to par. Some had to serve to move the story forward, develop characters, and had technical uses in the novel underneath the story. I had to have a mixture of both, to make the whole book work.

Pure instinct guided these decisions: a combination of my heart, my mind, and my *naʻau*, or *piko*, as people say here in Hawaii.

What poetic or narrative effects were you hoping to achieve?

Honestly, I just wanted to transport the reader into a quiet space where she could immerse herself and get lost in the intimate world of these two lovers, and perhaps, in the reading, get lost in love in general.

When you put down a good book and go into a dreamy state, feelings expand past the book and seep into your consciousness on some level. I wanted each poem to be a small gift that was like a globe, showing one side, whether attractive or unappealing, heavy, or light, of this young couple's lives, hopefully giving the reader insights and/or compassion into their harsh and challenging reality. Perhaps you can imagine each poem as a small flame, illuminating Angel & Hannah's passion, their conflicts, their secrets, and their dreams. And in the end, it's a book filled with tiny flames that you can turn towards, open, and warm yourself with its truth, get burned by its fire, passion, or despair, or sit by the light of the hope inside the character you're reading about. You want to spark a light in the reader's heart, to get her to imagine or feel something, or dream it, with love.

What are your thoughts on the verse novel as a form?

I happen to love the verse novel as a form—it's not easy, but it's engaging, and suited to adventurous and brave writers. The verse novel gives you structure—a solid spine and skeleton; it gives you a definite shape, and you simply must fill it in with as much music, jazz, life, pain, soul, heart, and love as you can.

Having the challenge and the adventure of rhyming couplets, Elizabethan, Petrarchan and Spenserian sonnet forms gave me something to look forward to, so I was engaging and continually entertaining myself and trying new things lyrically. It kept it fun.

There were of course, times when I was exhausted, annoyed, and fed up with the strict little boxes I'd confined myself to, and that was when I'd break into the long-sentenced tornadoes that you see sometimes in the novel, or I'd fragment a poem into tiny, bite-sized bits like the Jail & Godless sonnets, in order to tap into a different, sparser feeling.

However, somehow, I felt the fourteen- and sixteen-line sonnets and hip-hop bars very appropriate for our heroes and how they lived—the city of New York is laid out like a boxy grid in some places, and I felt that the tight structure of most of the poems symbolically represented and reflected our young couple's entrapment in the confines of the harsh city and their realities, in a way.

The balance of freedom and structure kept me coming back. I could wander, and always come back home to the heart of the love affair, with these sonnets and hip-hop verses as support.

Have verse novels you have read been influential on this work in some way?

One novel written in poetic form which I absolutely love, is called *Autobiography of Red*, by Anne Carson. It's about a little boy monster with wings and his relationship with his mother and the world around him. On the surface, it may look like it has absolutely nothing to do with this verse novel, but reading it opened a door in me as to what is possible, and how it is possible to play with poetry beautifully, even while in the novel form.

Carson's imagery, her sentences, and her use of space is stunning. Quiet beauty and sharp observations everywhere. I loved it, how it felt to read those lines and that strange, yet very familiar story of motherlove turned legend. I also wanted to make something as simple and pure as first love feel epic for the reader, because that is how it is when one experiences love for the first time. It's captivating, enthralling, magical, transformative—pure poetry.

Certain hip hop albums, like Nas' Illmatic, and the classic Black Star album, read like verse novels to me, in their lyricism, storytelling, drama, and adventure.

What have you learnt about writing verse novels from the verse novels you have read?

A verse novel takes you on a very special journey of words, rhythm, and story that is very much like traveling down a river. There will always be a current to guide you through the deep waters, and it feels fluid and quite magical.

Jimmy and Rita, by Kim Addonizio, is a beautiful example of a verse novel love story that is absolutely beautiful, raw, and heart-wrenching. I found this incredible book and loved it, slept with it by my bedside for a while, and then, years later, was fortunate enough to take actual writing workshops from Ms. Addonizio in the Bay Area where we were both living at the time. Truly a gift of a book, and a woman writer.

Her book taught me to take time, and focus on details, sharp details that bring the story and scene to vivid life. San Francisco is such a strong energy in the book it almost becomes its own character, and I strove to make the early '90s New York vibrant with music, flavors, scents and sounds as well, to bring people back to that time with a touch of nostalgia.

Thomas and Beulah by Rita Dove is also an exceptionally moving and profound verse novel for me. Both books really laid a foundation and provided a map for *Angel & Hannah*, because they captured a couple's epic romance through a sequence of poems which ultimately creates one long story, or love-song, and that was my intention as well. When I found these books, I felt I had found two vital keys to a secret door to a room only I wanted to explore—a room filled with stories of a young working-class couple, made timeless through love and rhymes. I love how each poem stands on its own in merit and strength, and at the same time weaves together with the others to create a timeline and an intimate look into the lovers' lives against the backdrop of their historical eras.

CHAPTER 16
JION SHEIBANI

Jion Sheibani by Philippe Pereira

… the verse novel is a great form for an outsider voice.

Jion Sheibani is British-Iranian and grew up in Brighton. She is a self-taught illustrator and studied English literature at Oxford University. One of her very first jobs was as an intern to Green Party MP Caroline Lucas in The European Parliament. Jion was a teacher at the Paris Institute of Political Studies and ENSAE before opening her own language school in Paris.

Jion's highly illustrated new young fiction series, *The Worries*, is published by Penguin Books Puffin imprint, and *The Silver Chain*, her debut YA verse novel, was published by Hot Key Books in 2022.

Jion's website can be found at jionsheibani.com.

The Silver Chain (2022)

What ideas or influences did you have in mind when creating this work?

Like most writers, I feel like everything is an influence! Music is very important to my writing, even for stories that aren't explicitly about music: classical, R&B, folk, jazz … I'll listen to anything and soak up lyrics, rhythms, mood. I play the violin and piano too and sometimes when I'm feeling stuck it can help loosen something up, as can drawing. Reading poets who are brilliantly playful like Carol Ann Duffy helps me to be experimental in my writing. I am also very influenced by psychoanalysis: dreams are usually the starting point of anything I write.

How did you approach writing this verse novel? What were the various stages in its development?

I'd played around with a verse novel for some time, but it was so messy I decided to start afresh. When I did, I wrote about sixty poems in one big burst, and these were the pillars of the story from beginning to end. I didn't realize that at the time of course. I just had this bunch of very intense emotional moments that I then had to thread together. It wasn't an easy process to find the story I wanted to tell but it helped to have these important points mapped out. It meant I didn't want to give up on the story like I had before. I would read these poems and really care for the character and think, "no I can't give up on her now!"

In the new verse novel that I'm currently working on, I find this to be a good starting point: write the bits that make me most care about the character, the most confessional, intimate voice possible. That gives me a lot to work from. It feels a bit like starting at the end and working my way backwards. I used to think I'd get to know my character as the story went on, but I now realize that I need to know these very deep, important things early on, otherwise I won't have a story at all.

Can you recall problem-solving decisions you had to make in the writing process?

I suppose one challenge was ensuring this very delicate space for readers to see between the lines: building rich enough relationships in few words is what's so difficult about verse novels. But it's also what makes them special.

Another difficulty was a very practical one in terms of space on the page: lines I didn't want to break but had to because they were too long. There was a concrete poem I had to completely transform because it wouldn't fit the page, even when reducing the font size. Then there were overly ambitious things where I wanted a poem to swirl in the middle of an illustration but from a design perspective, it was a nightmare. Sometimes I just had to keep things simple! And keep my designer sane …

Which poetic and narrative techniques did you decide to employ, and why?

I really enjoyed doing the concrete poems. As I was also illustrating the story, I loved the idea of illustrating with words too. I suppose all poems are illustrations in a sense because their visual arrangement on the page is so important.

The poem where Azadeh performs Vaughan Williams's The Lark Ascending, I knew had to be in rhyming couplets—because George Meredith's poem The Lark Ascending is. This is the poem that influenced the Vaughan Williams's composition and gives my verse novel its title. Meredith describes the lark's silver chain of sound which I think is such a lovely metaphor for music and poetry.

I also enjoyed using the ghazal form (rather loosely, mind. Persian poets will probably be turning in their graves!) It felt like an important way to show Azadeh connecting with her heritage and trying to reach her father.

It was fun to play around with poems—both with and without form—and to think about text messages and even hashtags as poetic forms we use daily. I love the energy and wit in the way teenagers communicate: the exchanges between Azadeh and her friends really helped carry the story along and change up the pace when necessary.

If there were places in the book where you felt it was best to emphasize the poetic strategies over the narrative strategies, or vice versa—what guided these decisions?

It's quite hard to say because it's often a very instinctive thing. I suppose those poetic moments were usually more reflective or emotionally important in understanding Azadeh and the characters around her. They were almost always internal moments, either Azadeh questioning something or confessing something very intimate. I do enjoy this push and pull of the poetic and narrative. Sometimes poetry can be thought of as a bit static or slow and I liked having to get back to pushing the story along, not being too contemplative or elliptical.

What poetic or narrative effects were you hoping to achieve?

I'm not sure I really hoped to achieve anything other than finishing the book! Of course, I did hope to convey the effect that music has on us, while also realizing that it was always only ever going to be an approximation. It was often very frustrating to try to capture a piece of music with words. It felt like trying to paint with mud or something. But I hope I caught some glimmer of it at least.

What are your thoughts on the verse novel as a form?

It's incredibly liberating, accessible, creative and it's great news for the future of poetry. I think we've all been intimidated by poetry for far too long—and I've done a literature degree! I love the idea that teens across the world, from all kinds of backgrounds, are hooked on this form. It's perfect for our times, where communication is snappier and more succinct than ever. It can also be re-read which is a wonderful idea. I never have time to re-read prose novels, but I can with verse novels and poems, and I love that. It's something we do constantly as children with our picture books and then suddenly, we stop. Re-reading is such a comforting thing.

Have verse novels you have read been influential on this work in some way?

Yes, *The Weight of Water* by Sarah Crossan, the first verse novel I read. It was so fresh and inspiring and made me want to sit down and write immediately. The form lent itself brilliantly to the foreign voice of the character. It made me realize that the verse novel is a great form for an outsider voice.

I also admire the writing of Elizabeth Acevedo, Kwame Alexander, David Elliot, and Manjeet Mann—all hugely talented verse novel writers.

There are also prose novels that are incredibly poetic and feel like they could be verse novels if arranged differently. I'm thinking of Patricia Lockwood's *No One Is Talking about This* which is just extraordinary. It will probably influence everything I write from now on!

What have you learnt about writing verse novels from the verse novels you have read?

To constantly remind myself that I'm writing in verse and not broken up prose! Not that everything must be a self-contained poem necessarily but that I must constantly justify the verse form.

To remember that I must work doubly hard at developing relationships.

To let sounds and rhythm lead me to the emotional heart of the story.

Finally, I have learnt to have fun with it all. The best verse novels have made me cry and laugh too. This form has the potential to give you an emotional rollercoaster ride!

CHAPTER 17
KAIJA LANGLEY

Kaija Langley by Andre Bogard

... all the elements of good story—voice, characterization, plot and subplots, setting, emotional resonance—in concise evocative language.

Kaija Langley was born in Northern NJ and raised on a healthy diet of library books, music and theater performances, and visits to the family farm in rural North Carolina. Langley is the author of the award-winning debut picture book, *When Langston Dances*, which received a Black Caucus ALA Youth Literary Award and was a finalist for the New England Book Award and NAACP Image Award for Outstanding Literary Work for Children. Her debut middle grade novel, *The Order of Things*, from Nancy Paulsen Books, is a Junior Library Guild Gold Selection and has received three "starred" reviews. A second picture book, *A Century for Caroline*, with Denene Millner Books, is scheduled for Spring 2025.

Kaija loves long road trips, dancing wherever music moves her, and adventures near and far with her Beloved. She splits her time between Cambridge, MA and Los Angeles, CA. Kaija's website can be found at kaijalangley.com and she is on Instagram and X under the handle @mizzkalwrites71.

The Order of Things (2023)

What ideas or influences did you have in mind when creating this work?

Years before I began *The Order of Things*, I knew I wanted to write a story about a young person's grief. I had someone very close to me die young, when we were both still young, and the memory and feeling of that loss never really goes away. It didn't help that at that time children were more "seen than heard" broadly speaking. I didn't have the language to share my emotions or a trusted adult to help me navigate my feelings, and I wanted that for young readers today.

How did you approach writing this verse novel? What were the various stages in its development?

It wasn't my intention for *The Order of Things* to be a verse novel. I tried writing it for almost six months in prose, but it wasn't working. When April's voice finally came to me clearly, it was in verse.

In terms of process, I created a very loose outline initially where each poem was about three sentences long. In that brevity I captured character, action, emotion that I would later fully flesh out in subsequent drafts.

From initial draft to published book, I revised the novel about eight times. Adding clarity, tightening language, nailing character motivations, removing superfluous characters and plot threads. Each draft became closer to the story the world can now read.

Can you recall problem-solving decisions you had to make in the writing process?

Yes! The biggest problem to solve was the relationship between April and her mother, Chantelle. April loves playing the drums. Chantelle adores quiet. There's tension in that alone, but I had to work through several drafts to get that relationship right for the reader's sake.

This story is for young readers after all and I didn't want to send the wrong message, especially in a book about sudden loss and grief. I needed to find a way for Chantelle to still be an ally for her daughter's desire, even if it set her nerves on edge. The solution was partially to have other characters rallying around April until Chantelle could also join in as a cheerleader.

Which poetic and narrative techniques did you decide to employ, and why?

The joy and challenge of verse novels is the language must move the narrative forward while capturing all the other elements of story with very few words. In a story this emotional, I felt it needed to be in a first-person point of view. A reader needs to feel what April is feeling, as she feels it, both the highs and lows.

In terms of poetry, the stanzas are varying lengths—mostly four or five lines, some as few as one, others as many as six—to either allow a reader to linger in a moment or move forward quickly if the emotions are heavy. Very few stanzas employ rhyme.

If there were places in the book where you felt it was best to emphasize the poetic strategies over the narrative strategies, or vice versa—what guided these decisions?

In Part II of the story, after April's best friend, Zee, dies, I relied more heavily on the poetry of the language to navigate the reader through the heavy emotions of a sudden loss.

What poetic or narrative effects were you hoping to achieve?

I was hoping that a reader of any age could feel a wide range of emotions reading this story—excited, confused, sad, hopeful—and I believe I've achieved that goal.

What are your thoughts on the verse novel as a form?

I think verse novels for young readers have become very popular in recent years for good reason. The form has an immediacy that prose doesn't and thrusts a reader into a story without all the extra details, backstory, and character development that a traditional novel requires in the early chapters.

It's also more accessible reading, meaning a reader can complete most verse novels from start to finish in a few hours, not a few days or weeks. And if done well, the novel can be satisfying and linger long after the book is done.

Have verse novels you have read been influential on this work in some way?

I fell in love with several verse novels by other children's authors of color, including *The Crossover* by Kwame Alexander, *Inside Out and Back Again* by Thanhhà Lại, and *The Poet X* by Elizabeth Acevedo. There were others as well, but these three texts were so dynamic in their use of language, emotion, and story arc that I return to them often for reading pleasure as well as craft.

What have you learnt about writing verse novels from the verse novels you have read?

They are powerful, remarkable, unforgettable if done well. And doing it well is no easy feat. An author must capture all the elements of good story—voice, characterization, plot, and subplots, setting, emotional resonance—in concise evocative language that's about half of the words used in a prose novel.

CHAPTER 18
ANN E. BURG

Ann E. Burg by Celia Hélène

*Verse novels cut to the core of the story with a minimum
of words and maximum of emotion.*

Ann E. Burg was born in Brooklyn, New York, and has been writing since early childhood. Believing in the power of poetry to cut to the heart of the matter, Ann's most recent books are middle grade verse novels, and include *Force of Nature: A Novel of Rachel Carson*, published in 2024. She is drawn to stories of the disenfranchised and voiceless, and finds inspiration in little-known, or too-soon-forgotten, historical incidents. Her books have won numerous awards and appear on several school reading lists.

A teacher for ten years, Ann is interested in the challenges children face and strives to engage readers in stories which will broaden their world view and prepare them for a global society. She and her family live in Rhinebeck, New York. Her website can be found at annburg.com.

All the Broken Pieces (2009)
Serafina's Promise (2013)
Unbound (2016)

What ideas or influences did you have in mind when creating this work?

I really didn't have any specific ideas when I started *Unbound*. As often happens, I was researching another possible story, when I stumbled across an NPR interview with the archaeologist, Dr. Daniel Sayers. Dr. Sayers was collecting artifacts in the Great Dismal Swamp, a marshy region between Norfolk, Virginia, and Elizabeth City, North Carolina. For hundreds of years, Dr. Sayers noted, the Dismal Swamp had been a hideaway for Native Americans escaping the encroachment of Europeans. Years later, he went on to explain, the swamp was also a place of refuge for the formerly enslaved. I had often read stories of enslaved people escaping north but knew nothing of those who lived in such proximity to the plantations they were escaping.

Dr. Sayers talked about the tiny artifacts that he was collecting—a bead, a particle of gunflint, a chip of pottery. At first, I was amazed to think that such small objects could tell so large a story. But the more I thought about Dr. Sayer's discoveries, the more I wondered about the stories the artifacts couldn't tell. Maybe we'd learn about an inhabitant's diet, how they hunted or built their homes, but the newly discovered artifacts would never reveal what each brave inhabitant had endured, what terrible experiences had pushed them so deep into the wilderness.

I am always moved by stories of the voiceless or forgotten and I wanted to learn more. An invaluable resource was *Slavery's Exiles: The Story of the American Maroons*, by Dr. Sylviane A. Diouf.[1] Her extensive research helped me navigate the swamp and imagine what life for these exiles must have been like. Living in the swamp meant dealing with bobcats, brown bears, snakes, and an assortment of biting bugs. In addition to my research material, I brought to the swamp my own fear of things that creep and crawl.

How did you approach writing this verse novel? What were the various stages in its development?

The first step was further research. I read most everything I could find about the Great Dismal Swamp and its inhabitants. I've already mentioned Dr. Diouf's informative book, but one book leads to another and then another. I also read the Writers Project of America (WPA) Slave Narratives, a collection of first-person accounts collected between 1936 and 1938. Although I recognized the limitations of first-person narratives (and I was aware that the formerly enslaved were talking to interviewers who might well have looked like their oppressors), still I was moved by the indisputable truth that enslaved people were cruelly separated from their families, forced into servitude, and denied their basic human rights. No work of fiction could ever adequately capture the daily indignities and harrowing experiences endured by the enslaved but reading and listening to voices long gone compelled me to offer some recognition of their suffering. In each archived voice, there was an absolute and unblemished dignity which I hoped to honor.

As I researched, a coterie of characters began to assemble in my mind—wraithlike figures who followed me through the day, posing questions, suggesting paths I might explore. As always happens when I research, one or more of these characters eventually delineates herself—or himself—from the crowd and speaks a few words that start me on my journey.

In the case of *Unbound*, it was Grace's voice I heard most vividly. And the first scene in my mind, was the button scene at the end of the book. I could see so clearly Grace and Brooklyn plucking strands of hair and wrapping them around the button—a recast artifact that in my novel was consciously buried to remind the world that these two beings existed and didn't belong to anyone but themselves. Grace presented that scene to me, and my job as author was to find a way to get her there.

Can you recall problem-solving decisions you had to make in the writing process?

One problem I had when writing *Unbound* was something that often pops up when writing historical fiction. Technologies and attitudes change, societal norms shift, but the human heart remains the same. I want what I write to be authentic but I'm aware that what is acceptable in one century may be off-putting and outright objectionable in another. My job is to find the link to feelings and emotions which are universal and not subject to the whims of time. I must note immoral and illegitimate bias without recreating it. I must acknowledge the boundaries of yesterday while respecting the sensibilities—and hopefully, the ever-evolving wisdom of today.

There is a scene in *Unbound* where the adults are deciding whether to go North or to find their way into the swamp. Mama mentions that Grace could pass as white and perhaps enjoy the kind of life denied to the enslaved. Since Grace has matured greatly since the opening pages, I wanted it to be Grace who determines her fate. In my original draft, Grace gave her opinion and set the family's plan in motion. Sylviane pointed out that while children worked as hard as adults, there were limits to what they could say aloud and restrictions to their power within the family structure. Grace had already experienced the rigid boundaries of the Big House. I struggled to find a way to portray an authentic scene that would speak to contemporary readers while acknowledging the reality of a child's place in the nineteenth century. I wanted to give Grace the opportunity to highlight the ruthless absurdity of slavery.

I finally opted to let Grace speak through an interior monologue in which she could explore what passing as a white person might mean. While it is Mama who makes the final decision to keep her family together, the reader has the satisfaction of knowing that Grace would have made the same decision. The interior dialog made it possible for me to create an authentic scene without robbing Grace of her power or her ability to give voice to the ludicrous notion of slavery.

Which poetic and narrative techniques did you decide to employ, and why?

This is a harder question because most poetic modalities evident in my writing are not usually employed consciously. I was lucky enough to have a mother who sang constantly, who read to me, and who herself wrote poetry. It seems that I have always grown up with words and rhythms marching about in my mind! I remember, when I was very young and was dazzled for the first time by the beauty and power of words. I was at church, at that wooly age when grown-up gibberish had just begun to break into patterns that I could understand and think about. "Our hearts are on fire," people in the pews sang. Though I was young, I was still old enough to know that hearts couldn't really be on fire and was amazed that so few words could capture so large a feeling. I know this doesn't really answer the question, except to say that a fascination and love for the limitless meaning of words somehow built a depository in my brain that I am lucky enough to unconsciously access when I write. Of course, I do use a thesaurus when a word or thought may be just outside my grasp. Word lists wiggle me closer and sometimes suggest a better way of expression. Poetry is not a very precise science, but I prefer it that way because it always leaves room for unexpected inspiration!

Narrative techniques are more deliberate and are the combination of lessons gleaned from a lifetime of reading as well as from teachers, professors, and my extraordinary editor. A story moves through a character's choices and decisions. A story stalls when the author's will gets in the way!

If there were places in the book where you felt it was best to emphasize the poetic strategies over the narrative strategies, or vice versa—what guided these decisions?

When I write something and it doesn't work, either poetically or narratively, I reread and ponder, ponder, and rewrite. I guess I do a lot of pondering, rereading, and rewriting. It's important that I don't sacrifice the poetic voice for the narrative one or vice versa. Sometimes it seems impossible, but I've found that there is always a way around an awkward sentence or concept … a new way … a different word or action. Sometimes grabbing a snack (or throwing clothes in the laundry) helps—it doesn't really matter what I do after I push myself away from my desk. It's the distraction itself which releases my obsessive control and resets the internal metronome. Sometimes the moment I'm standing, a solution lilts by in the voice of another character, a knock at the door or the wind whistling through a tightly closed window.

What poetic or narrative effects were you hoping to achieve?

Ever since that Sunday morning so long ago when I first heard the words "my heart is on fire," in everything I've written, I've tried to find simple words for big feelings, small stories that tell big truths. Whether a single poem, a picture book, or a verse novel, I've tried to reduce large numbers (millions lost, thousands suffering, hundreds hidden) to the smallest common denominator. The stories I create, the words I use are simply the covering for the fragile filaments of human emotion and experience. If I can create a connection that lights a spark, then I've achieved my goal. We are all in this journey together is a popular expression. And though that is true, some of us are traveling in sleek style, while others of us are barely holding on to our ragged rafts. Wouldn't it be wonderful if we could stretch across the divide? Stories give us that opportunity. Poetry transcends barriers.

What are your thoughts on the verse novel as a form?

I am drawn to the verse novel because it strips a story of extraneous elements. A clock is always ticking somewhere in the background, but we don't always need to hear it. Sometimes when we are deep, deep in thought, we won't hear the clock until we drift back into consciousness. The verse novel seems to allow many more opportunities to wander deeply before bumping into narrative boundaries and hearing that age-old clock ticking away.

I mention the clock because after I wrote my first verse novel, *All the Broken Pieces*, one of the editors to whom I submitted it asked if I could rewrite the novel in a more traditional way. By that, she explained, she wanted me to include lengthy character descriptions and a division by chapters. I did what this editor asked and started my story with the sound of a clock ticking in Matt's bedroom. The editor rejected my rewrite. I was glad. The voice of my protagonist, so clear in the verse novel, was buried in extraneous details that had little to do with Matt or the story he so desperately needed to tell.

When I visit schools, the most consistent question I'm asked is why I choose to write in verse. This is usually followed by a lively discussion about my connection to the characters and my desire to get to the heart of the matter without the intrusion of too many unnecessary details. Many of the students write poetry and we talk about the power of limited words to express deep feelings. As far as a whole novel written in verse, many like the white space because it gives them a chance to think about what they've read. Some confess that they like verse novels because "even if the book is thick you don't have to read so much." We bounce that around for awhile and discover that even with a minimum of words, we can write or read a deeply satisfying story. And then, after most of us have decided that the verse novel is a wonderful opportunity to explore deep topics without getting bogged down, there is always the student, whom I call, "the closer". After everything is explained and described and shared, he (mostly he's speaking here) invariably asks "will you ever write a real book, like you know, a chapter book?"

You can't please everyone I guess, but I'm happy that the publishing world is open to the hybrid form and that most readers are too.

Have verse novels you have read been influential on this work in some way?

The first verse novel I read was *Out of the Dust* by Karen Hesse, an extraordinary writer. I was moved by both the personal story of Billy Jo and her family and the whole depiction of Oklahoma during the depression. Verse novels cut to the core of the story with a minimum of words and maximum of emotion. I've read lots of verse novels since then and one of my favorite writers of the verse novel is Margarita Engle. Like Karen Hesse, Margarita captures large emotions and important stories with a whisper of words. Karen Hesse and Margarita Engle inspire me to reach for the stars that they've already shined!

What have you learnt about writing verse novels from the verse novels you have read?

In the beginning of my writing, I thought verse novels would be like comparing a charcoal sketch to a vibrant multi-colored painting. But I was wrong. When it's successful, the verse novel is as dynamic and dazzling as any more traditional rendering.

CHAPTER 19
MARILYN HILTON

Marilyn Hilton by Jessica McCollam

The difference between ... [verse novels] and writing in traditional prose is like the difference between a catamaran skimming across a lake and a cargo ship plowing through heavy seas.

Marilyn Copley Hilton is an American novelist and poet. Her debut middle grade novel, *Found Things* (Atheneum, 2014), received the Sue Alexander Award in 2010. Her middle grade verse novel, *Full Cicada Moon* (Dial, 2015), received the Asian/Pacific American Award for Literature (2016) and the Arnold Adoff Poetry Award for New Voices (2016); was a Jane Addams Children's Book Award Honor Book (2016), a California Book Award finalist (2016), and a Cybils Awards finalist (2016); was selected for the Amelia Bloomer List (2015), the Booklist Editors' Choice list (2015), and the Junior Library Guild (2015); was named a Kirkus Best Book (2015), an *Air & Space Magazine*'s Best Children's Book of the Year (2015), and an Amazon Teachers' pick (2021); and has appeared on several state reading lists. Hilton's short fiction and poems have appeared in various literary journals, such as *Chariton Review*, *The Nebraska Review*, and *Mid-American Review*, and her poetry has been nominated for the Pushcart Prize. She holds an MA in English/Creative Writing and a BA in Japanese. A former longtime technical writer and editor in the software industry, Hilton now writes full time. Her website can be found at marilynhilton.com.

Full Cicada Moon (2015)

What ideas or influences did you have in mind when creating this work?

The germ of this book sprouted while I was writing another manuscript. (Isn't that often the case?) I had been thinking about the characters in the stories I'd written, and they all looked like me. I am Caucasian and grew up in a middle-class family in New England. My husband and children are mixed race (their preferred term), and I'd begun to feel that not writing main characters like them was ignoring their unique lives and, in a sense, betraying them and my love for them. So, *Full Cicada Moon* began as a gift to my children, who at the time had no books that starred characters with their unique racial makeup (Black, Japanese, Caucasian) to read. Then the question arose: did I, a white writer, have the right to tell this story? With encouragement from my family, cohorts, and professionals in the industry, the character of Mimi Yoshiko Oliver and her story began to form.

I decided she needed to be isolated in a place and time where and when her story could be best told. I had spent a good deal of my childhood in the 1960s in rural New Hampshire and knew the people and culture intimately. At that time the area was nearly 100 percent white, despite that it was a college town, so I had my setting. (Much has changed since then, and now those areas have a far more diverse population.)

I knew this story needed to be set in the past. I wanted Mimi to represent change, and so what better year than 1969 to set the story in? There was political and cultural change and upheaval, the hippie movement, war protests, the civil rights movement, the sexual revolution, the dawning of the women's and gay rights movements. And there was the United States space program and first moon walk.

I had the protagonist, the setting, and the time, and so Mimi's story grew. This girl of big dreams, who had moved from diverse California to a small Vermont town where she and her family looked like no one else there, and who dreamed of becoming an astronaut at a time when the very idea of a woman in space brought ridicule, would bring immense change to her community. She would do it with conviction, cleverness, bravery, and tenacity, encouraged by the hardships and fortitude of her loving parents. All within the structure of a year of full moons and under the canopy of the space program.

Shortly before I began to write this book, I'd read two historical middle grade verse novels, *Dust of Eden* by Mariko Nagai, and *Out of the Dust* by Karen Hesse. I was intrigued by the form. Though I had published poems in literary journals and my master's thesis had been comprised predominantly of poetry, I had no idea how to write a novel in verse. But I had written enough novel manuscripts (and my debut novel had recently released) and, knowing that the best way to learn is to do, I began writing Mimi's story in verse. The first poem came to me while sitting in commuter traffic on my way home from work one afternoon in December. At the first stoplight, I scribbled it out on a sticky note, which to this day is in my project notebook. The story continued to come quickly to me, and though I hadn't committed to delivering the manuscript as a verse novel, I continued writing in that form. After I'd finished about a quarter of the first draft, verse fit perfectly for the story, and so it stayed.

How did you approach writing this verse novel? What were the various stages in its development?

I wrote the first draft in about four months, which is extremely fast for me, as I usually need time for ideas and layers to develop. But because I already knew the setting so well, I didn't need to create one and then allow myself time to inhabit it. However, I did need to include cultural and historical references to place Mimi firmly in 1969 without overwhelming readers with facts (and thus making the novel sound like a history textbook). The references needed to occur organically, so, as all historical novelists know, only a small percentage of their research ends up in the novel. I would write and then stop to do research, spending hours reading period magazines, watching videos, and listening to interviews and news reports to be able to mention a perfume Mimi would smell, a store where Stacey bought her dress, a record album the girls listened to, particular national and global events and when, and exactly when and how the moon landing and moon walk occurred, and so on. Though I remember watching the moon walk on television as a child, memory can be deceptive, so I needed to watch it again. Thank goodness for libraries, bookstores, the internet, eBay, and YouTube!

As for the Japanese cultural references and vocabulary, my bachelor's degree is in Japanese, and I'd studied the tea ceremony (*chadō* or *sadō*) for three years—one year intensively in Kyoto—and continued to stay connected to the culture. I had the manuscript read for overall authenticity as I worked on the manuscript.

Also, I wanted days of the week, moon phases, and weather conditions to be historically accurate. The calendar and moon phases were easy to research, but information about weather conditions in central Vermont in 1969 was patchy online. Here's where I used some poetic license: my great-grandmother, who had lived in central New Hampshire, kept a daily diary all her life. At the top of each page, she recorded the temperature and weather conditions. So, I used her entries of central New Hampshire whenever the story referred to the weather in central Vermont. I'm still moved by the thought that my great-grandmother had no idea that decades later her daily practice would become essential to a novel.

As I wrote the book, I noted each poem in a spreadsheet, which included the poem's title, the content, date, weather, moon phase, any historical event that took place on or around that date, and anything else that was pertinent to the story (for example, the date a pop song was released).

After my editor read the manuscript, she asked me to rearrange a few poems and fill in some gaps with new poems. We also decided to remove a few poems that didn't serve the story.

Can you recall problem-solving decisions you had to make in the writing process?

In addition to what's noted earlier, deciding on the protagonist's name took much time and thought. Names are important, as they need to serve multiple purposes by conveying meaning, history, and potential. Mimi had several names before I arrived at just the right one for this character.

Titles are also extremely important to me, as they need to convey the essence of the story. For *Full Cicada Moon*, I wanted to incorporate the moon phases, Mimi's awareness of them, and the notion of her coming into fullness over the course of one year. Also, Mimi, named by her mother after the sound of the cicada, emerges in her fullness after a time of growth beneath the surface—like brood cicadas, and like bulbs planted deep in the Vermont soil to bloom in spring—when her time comes. After I wrote a long list of possible titles, the perfect one presented itself.

Which poetic and narrative techniques did you decide to employ, and why?

I decided to tell the story in first-person point of view and present tense because I wanted readers to experience the story as Mimi did. The metaphors of the moon phases, growth underground (hidden from view), and flying/soaring as a means of attaining goals were used throughout.

I found that enjambment was effective in creating more than one meaning of a line of action or thought.

While writing the first draft, I discovered that, though each poem was either a scene or sequel, sometimes it took three poems to complete a full scene, much like the arc of the overall story, with a beginning, middle, and end.

I'm always more interested in exploring a character and what makes them who they are. But a novel must be more than that, and Mimi's story had to be more than a collection of poems. Mimi's appearance and her newness in the community wasn't conflict, so I had to create some for her. Years after quitting piano lessons as a child, recently I've taken up the practice again, and am seeing a profound connection between music and storytelling. Halfway through Bach's Prelude in C Major, I thought I must be reading the notes wrong because the music sounded so disjointed—just awful! But when I played for my teacher, she murmured, "Here's the discord ... and the resolution," and I understood that storytelling, like music, needs conflict and tension, if only to make us feel comfortable again after the discomfort. The reconciliation is as peaceful as the tension is disturbing. For Mimi's story, I decided to have her see the gender inequality at school and resolve it by making others aware of it as well. She effects this change through her awareness of nonviolent resistance.

The best stories, I believe, have a circular narrative, with the end dovetailing in the beginning and vice versa. Mimi begins the story by dreaming of soaring, and in the end, she flies in an airplane, a step in her big dream of becoming an astronaut. Like the story, I wanted individual poems to be circular, and used this technique in poems such as "The A Group," "Stacey's Birthday," and "Secrets."

I also wanted to emphasize the metaphors of the moon coming into fullness each month (as does Mimi by the end of the year) and inner life and growth, as described by brood cicadas, winter bulbs, and the people of Vermont. In this story, Mimi discovers that people—including herself—are often different from what they appear to be.

If there were places in the book where you felt it was best to emphasize the poetic strategies over the narrative strategies, or vice versa—what guided these decisions?

How to format dialogue was a bit challenging. After *Full Cicada Moon* was published, some verse novels were using italics instead of quotation marks. Italics give a different tone to the narrative, creating distance between the character and reader. Yet, this formatting feels "poetic." Though quoted dialogue draws the story and the characters closer to the surface, it breaks through that poetic veil. But for *Full Cicada Moon*, I felt that using quotation marks was the right decision. In my future verse novel manuscripts, whether to use italics or quotation marks has been determined by the story.

What poetic or narrative effects were you hoping to achieve?

I wanted readers to experience what Mimi was experiencing, and in her mind and heart. The verse form helped achieve that, because by nature it establishes an intimacy between the character and reader that narrative prose sometimes can block or constrain. For example, I didn't have to think about stage direction when writing the poems, and transitions were indicated by the space between poems.

Poem shapes also expressed mood, tone, or atmosphere. The words in the poem "Snowfall" are placed on the page in a narrow column to reflect the snow drifting downward. Other poems, such as "Winter" and "Bad Dreams" are haiku-like in expressing snapshot moments through sounds, images, and similes.

What are your thoughts on the verse novel as a form?

There's a freedom in writing verse novels. The difference between them and writing in traditional prose is like the difference between a catamaran skimming across a lake and a cargo ship plowing through heavy seas.

Since writing *Full Cicada Moon*, I've read several more verse novels and have written three. I'm always more interested in a character than in the plot (which makes plotting a challenge for me), and the verse novel is an excellent form for getting quickly into a character's mind and heart. From there, the story develops.

Unfortunately, verse novels aren't as popular among adult readers because those readers tend to shy away from poetry, which they may have read (or been forced to read) and it was dense and difficult to understand. The verse novels I've read are so different. On one level they're a quick read, and on the other they're deep and rich. There's a visual metaphor of a book as a glacier; verse novels are like that—you can read what's visible above the surface, but the subtext, the deeper layers, is what's submerged. That subtext, written invisibly between the lines, between the poems, and in the margins, is what keeps me thinking about the story long after I've finished reading the book.

Though teens and middle grade readers are more likely than adults to read verse novels, in general, middle grade books are chosen by adults (teachers, librarians, parents) for children to read. Though there are hundreds of adult champions of verse novels, until more become comfortable with this genre, fewer readers will have access to these wonderful books.

Have verse novels you have read been influential on this work in some way?

I've read several more verse novels, mostly for middle grade and young adult readers, and prefer writing in this genre. In addition to verse novels by Mariko Nagai and Karen Hesse, those by Ellen Hopkins, Andrea Davis Pinkney, Laura Shovan, Jeannine Atkins, A.L. Sonnichsen, and Jason Reynolds are a few that come to mind which have influenced my study and work. But there are many more.

What have you learnt about writing verse novels from the verse novels you have read?

Just as there's no one way to write a poem, there's no one way to write a verse novel. Each writer has their voice and their unique style in which they interpret and express the genre.

Stories find their form in which to be told. The writer simply needs to listen and experiment and trust their creative instincts. It's important for the poet-writer to observe the world outside and inside oneself, listen to its poetry, and write what one hears. The best poetry is wordless, if that makes sense, creating unobstructed and intimate connections among our shared humanity and to the divine. This is what I've found in the verse novels that have influenced me most profoundly.

CHAPTER 20
REEM FARUQI

Reem Faruqi by Mariam Shakeel

… each novel in verse that I read inspires my thinking in some way and how I write.

When Reem Faruqi taught second grade, her favorite time was "Read Aloud" time. Now, her favorite time at home is reading with her daughters. Reem Faruqi is the award-winning author of *Lailah's Lunchbox*, a picture book based on her own experiences as a young Muslim girl immigrating to the United States. Of Pakistani origin, Reem moved to Peachtree City, Georgia, from Abu Dhabi, the United Arab Emirates, when she was thirteen years old. She's also the author of three middle grade novels in verse, *Unsettled* (HarperCollins 2021), *Golden Girl* (HarperCollins 2022), *Call Me Adnan* (HarperCollins 2023), chapter book *Anisa's International Day* (HarperCollins 2022), and picture books *Amira's Picture Day* (Holiday House 2021), *I Can Help* (Eerdmans 2021), *Milloo's Mind* (HarperCollins 2023), *Swimming toward a Dream* (Page Street Kids 2023), many of which received starred reviews. Reem seasonally works as a photographer at ReemFaruqi Photography and currently works as a Scheduler for the Islamic Speakers Bureau of Atlanta. She loves to doodle, write, and take photos. Currently, she lives with her husband and four daughters in Atlanta. Her website can be found at reemfaruqi.com.

Unsettled (2021)
Golden Girl (2022)
Call Me Adnan (2023)

What ideas or influences did you have in mind when creating this work?

I get ideas for my novels in verse from things that happened in real life. Those experiences usually inspire me to create a story.

Like Nurah in my story *Unsettled*, I immigrated to Peachtree, Georgia. Unlike Nurah, I moved from Abu Dhabi, the United Arab Emirates, whereas Nurah moves from my country of origin, Pakistan. Since this experience was like mine, it felt natural to write what I knew. I also wanted to write about my immigrant experience that felt true to me.

For *Golden Girl*, I covered the theme of kleptomania because I knew someone close to me who battled with it. I was on the other side of the story, like my main character Aafiyah's best friend Zaina, and I still remember the shock, betrayal, and pain when my things went missing. There were so many complex emotions!

In *Call Me Adnan*, a tragedy happens within Adnan's family. My grandmother's family experienced a similar tragedy and I wanted to explore the themes of grief and found verse a great medium to do so.

I usually weave these real-life experiences into my stories and find those are the stories I enjoy writing most and that they resonate the most with readers too.

How did you approach writing this verse novel? What were the various stages in its development?

Initially my story *Unsettled* was in prose, and when I sent an early excerpt to my agent at that time, she said that it read like a novel in verse—and was that what I had intended? I hadn't. I didn't even know that was an option for me. It didn't click that I could write a novel in verse. It was almost as if I needed permission to write in verse. I discovered novels in verse and loved how they covered so much with so few words. I felt refreshed reading them. I checked out many more novels in verse from the library and really immersed myself in them. I eagerly made the swap from prose to verse and never looked back.

I was a picture book author first, so I got used to trying to tell a story in fewer words. Writing a middle grade novel felt intimidating for me, so a novel in verse felt much more do-able to me.

I took the clunky prose and chopped it up into verse and I loved how the words breathed and the story shone more.

For my story *Unsettled*, verse felt fitting because when you reluctantly move continents, you feel a little broken at first (or for a while!), sort of like how my character Nurah felt when she first moved. The broken nature of the lines in this novel in verse reflects Nurah's experience. To me, novels in verse are bits of broken lines that come together beautifully.

For my story, *Golden Girl*, my character Aafiyah struggles with kleptomania and as a result, the choices she makes are emotionally charged and she deals with a lot of guilt. I found the white space gives the reader time to reflect and that I add more emotions into my verse novel than I may normally do for a prose one. For example, Aafiyah likens her tears to shame in the poem titled "Weird But True Fact #23."

I also loved creating a fast-paced plot and found using fewer words for verse made the story flow smoothly, and quicker.

Can you recall problem-solving decisions you had to make in the writing process?

For my story, *Call Me Adnan*, my character Adnan is dealing with a huge family tragedy. The character Adnan was inspired by my younger brother who is a person who uses fewer words. Thus, when I worked on Adnan's story, I had to remember that this character was not a talkative person, but rather a reflective, quieter one. This helped shape his verse differently than my characters from *Unsettled* and *Golden Girl*, Nurah and Aafiyah. Adnan's language was less flowery, and more to the point. His words may read as slightly simpler, but they still pack an emotional punch. Adnan is also a character who loves to win at table tennis no matter what: as the poem titled "The Beginning" conveys when Adnan asserts that he doesn't ever lose.

When editing *Call Me Adnan*, it was tempting to want to add more to the verse, but I wanted to stay true to the character and nature of Adnan.

On a side note, I would also recommend authors have an outline for their novels in verse. It is challenging to come up with, but with an outline, you won't get lost in the verse, and you will keep the story moving.

Which poetic and narrative techniques did you decide to employ, and why?

I love to include lists in my novels in verse. I find that lists can be playful. For instance, in *Golden Girl*, in the poem "Places I've Been" the names of ten countries are listed one under another in a single column, and this gives additional back-story about the second-generation immigrant experience of the character Aafiyah.

Another technique I try to use is to keep the verse simple in emotionally charged scenes. In *Unsettled*, for example, when Nurah's mother miscarries, I chose to keep the words in the poem "Baby Sizes" sparse to let the reader register the emotion of the situation. Nurah absorbs the shock of her mother's miscarriage by talking about the baby's size, which was the size of a raspberry.

In *Golden Girl*, Aafiyah faces major consequences when her mother discovers that she has been taking things. She reflects on her mother's anger comparing it to notes in a tune she's never heard before.

In *Call Me Adnan*, after a devastating family tragedy happens, Adnan reflects on "bad stuff" as a ball you don't see coming, that spins right by you.

If there were places in the book where you felt it was best to emphasize the poetic strategies over the narrative strategies, or vice versa—what guided these decisions?

I think with a novel in verse, it gets tricky to balance the poetic verses with plot. But above all, when writing a novel in verse, one must remember it is a novel, so try to have a clear beginning, a middle, and an end. I try to outline the story and then have fun with the poetry. Yes, there can be a few parts in the book where my character makes a comment about something small and I can describe it as poetically as possible, but overall, the story or plot trajectory must stay in motion and move toward a clear end.

What poetic or narrative effects were you hoping to achieve?

With my novels in verse, I don't want my story to lag but rather to immerse the reader wholly and take them through an emotional and lyrical journey. I want my books to be un-put-down-able! I was so glad when BookPage gave *Golden Girl* a starred review. They thought Aafiyah's story was told in carefully chosen words, skillfully imagined and absorbing.

What are your thoughts on the verse novel as a form?

Verse is visually and emotionally appealing. I love playing with the words, like making the word "big" in bigger font, and the word "fade" in faded font. I think that part is so playful.

In *Call Me Adnan*, in the poem "My Trick Now That I'm Twelve" Adnan describes his table tennis technique of adding a touch of spin to the ball, and at that point in the poem I space several words apart to convey the ball spinning to the opposite side of the table tennis table.

I am also a huge fan of the white space in the verse novel which I think allows readers to take a breather and really process the emotions from the stories. I think with verse you can also delve deeper into character emotions. In *Unsettled*, in the poem "Inside" I chose to highlight the way Nurah processes anger as water simmering, and her anger as a tea kettle reaching boiling point.

Have verse novels you have read been influential on this work in some way?

Yes, very much so. I think each novel in verse that I read inspires my thinking in some way and how I write.

In writing verse, I have also learned that children can handle tough topics. When reading *Out of The Dust* by Karen Hesse, I realized the themes of that story are heavy. Yet that story did so well, earned a Newbery, and was so appealing to me as a reader. Hesse's words were compelling, lyrical, and filled with emotion.

I also remember reading *The House on Mango Street* by Sandra Cisneros and even though it's not in verse *per se*, her lyrical language hooked me in. I remember thinking, I wish I could write like that!

I get so excited when I see reviews that say my language is elegant or graceful, because I am not those things in real life! I also get excited when I hear that my story resonated with them and was lyrical. Kirkus gave *Unsettled* a starred review. They thought it was lyrical and hopeful, and that its metaphors and emphasis on feelings would captivate readers.

I hope that readers connect with my verse and recognize that even ordinary, tiny moments can be gorgeous.

I also loved the musical rhythm of Joanne Rossmassler Fritz's words in *Everywhere Blue* and the emotions of *Me (Moth)* captured by Amber McBride. On a side note, I love how even prose by Padma Venkatraman and Lynn Joseph feel like verse to me, so lyrical!

What have you learnt about writing verse novels from the verse novels you have read?

I have read many verse novels and something I have learned is that each verse novel is so different. There are truly no rules in writing verse. Some authors' verse can be sparse, whereas some others can be dense, but each done in their own way can be unique and effective. For example, I love how Thanhhà Lại's verse consists of a few words for a verse; K. A. Holt's too. I also love the simplicity of Sharon Creech's verse. I think my style leans toward sparser verse.

I love telling you what a character wants in just a few words.

But I also love verse by Chris Baron where he describes the settings with more detail and words, and in doing so paints a poignant picture. I also loved how Jasmine Warga, Lisa Fipps, Safia Elhillo, and Rajani LaRocca use emotion in their verse novels.

I think we are so lucky to live in a world where right now there are plenty of amazing verse novels to choose from. I hope this is always the case!

CHAPTER 21
SARAH TREGAY

Sarah Tregay by John Rogers

Verse novels are magic! Open one and you'll find beautiful language, abundant imagery, elegant white space, and a character-driven narrative.

Sarah Tregay is the author of *Love and Leftovers* (2012, an ALA Best Fiction for Young Adults title) and *Fan Art* (2014, a Bank Street College of Education Best Children's Books of the Year 2015). *Love and Leftovers* is written in verse whereas *Fan Art* is prose with poems inserted between the chapters and illustrations by Melissa DeJesus. Both books are available from Katherine Tegen Books, an imprint of HarperCollins. "I Love You, Man," the shorter, verse version of *Fan Art*, was the 2011 Katherine Paterson Prize for Young Adults and Children's Writing category winner (young adult) presented by Hunger Mountain, VCFA Journal of the Arts. "Love at First Book" (2014), a short story in verse, was an Honorable Mention in the Young Adult Fiction Category of the Writer's Digest Popular Fiction Awards and selected as a finalist for the Katherine Paterson Prize for Young Adult and Children's Writing by Katherine Applegate. It was published in the VCFA Journal of the Arts *2015 LOVE* issue and is available in print and audiobook. "Rosemary's Apples" (2014) is included in *Tales from the Bully Box*, an anthology edited by Cat Woods and published by Elephant's Bookshelf Press.

Raised without television, Sarah started writing her own middle grade novels after she had read all the ones in the library. She has both a Bachelors and a Master of Fine

Art in Graphic Design and taught graphic design at Boise State University in Boise, Idaho. Her obsession with typography and layout naturally translates into formatting poetry on the page. Sarah has presented at writing conferences hosted by the Society of Children's Book Writers and Illustrators (SCBWI), the Idaho Writers' Guild, and the Idaho Council of Teachers of English. She served as Assistant Regional Advisor for the SCBWI Utah/Southern Idaho Region. She is a collector of verse novels and maintains a list of titles on her website, which can be found at sarahtregay.com. Sarah lives in Michigan with her husband and an appaloosa named Mr. Pots.

Love and Leftovers (2012)

What ideas or influences did you have in mind when creating this work?

Plot-wise, I wanted to write about a protagonist who makes a mistake that hurts her friends' feelings. The challenge for me was to make Marcie likable enough that readers might encourage her on, despite her blunder. I felt that stacking the deck against her was a good place to start—so on the first page I made a list of things she had to face. The catalyst for the list was Marcie's parents' separation, a situation later echoed by her breakup with Linus. Her father is dating a man. Her mother is experiencing an episode of depression. As a result, Marcie is stuck on summer vacation. Marcie has to initiate difficult conversations about sexuality and mental health, take the time to understand, and then forgive her parents for splitting up. At the same time, she has made a mistake of her own, and has to rely on her friends' understanding and forgiveness. I made these choices to jump-start the story, add depth, and because I wanted Marcie to be a likeable character, I needed her mom and dad to be likeable as well.

Having decided that Marcie's circle of friends were students who didn't fit into any one clique—the "Leftovers"—I wanted to incorporate a food theme, and whenever possible, chose food phrases, metaphors, and nicknames. I named the characters in Marcie's friendship circle after those in Charles Schultz's comic *Peanuts* and threaded references to his work into the story.

My choice to represent Marcie's friends as diverse began before the first poem was a scribble in a notebook. It added depth to these secondary characters. I didn't need these for the plot. Katie was adopted. Emily had recently given up her baby for adoption, and Linus was helping raise his niece in a multigenerational household. I borrowed these family structures from my friends in high school. The emotional connection led to some of my favorite poems in the novel.

How did you approach writing this verse novel? What were the various stages in its development?

I approached *Love and Leftovers* with a little more "pantsing" and a little less plotting. With the general plot in mind, I wrote the poems in random order. Writing by hand, I focused on the poems—diving into Marcie's thoughts, capturing the setting, and working with the words themselves. For inspiration, I visited the settings. I wrote on a dock on a warm summer's day and in a park playground 3,000 miles away in the middle of winter.

For my second step, I made a stack of 3×5 cards with a poem title on each one and arranged them so that they told the larger story.

My first draft came together when I typed the poems into a document. At this point, I saw both what I had and what I was missing. From there, I could begin to fill in plot holes. After that, I worked with a critique group to revise the manuscript.

When the manuscript was ready, I began querying agents. After signing with an agent, the revision process started anew. But I wasn't done yet! My agent sold the manuscript to an editor with a great feel for pacing. With her help, I removed a character and zipped up the second half of the novel.

Can you recall problem-solving decisions you had to make in the writing process?

One problem that I should have seen coming was the shift from Word document to book dummy. With the page size and font changing, I had to make some last-minute revisions to the poems. In some cases, there were odd line breaks or page turns. Changing a word or two could affect the length of a line. Removing line breaks from between stanzas could prevent a poem from spanning two pages. Or, inserting one could add a page turn at that perfect moment. These changes helped the poems fit on their final pages.

Which poetic and narrative techniques did you decide to employ, and why?

Love and Leftovers is written in free verse. My approach to writing involved both the look and sound of the poetry.

My background is in graphic design, so I put my training to use when writing. Unlike prose, poetry has a visual component. The space around the words, or white space, is a key element in art and design. For example, line length, line breaks, and indents all play a part in how a poem looks on the page. Careful choices about white space can add structure to the poem, aid reader comprehension, and add meaning.

I also listen to audiobooks and love to hear beautiful writing read out loud. I feel that poetry literally has a voice—the type with pitch and cadence. I read my writing out loud and adjust because of the way it sounds. For example, an angry poem will sound grating, and a contemplative one will sound hesitant. Poetic techniques that involved sounds, such as onomatopoeia, repetition, and assonance, can be found throughout my novel.

When it came to story, I chose to tie the creation of the poems to the narrative by having Marcie write poetry in a notebook that she later misplaces. Like many verse novels, I used first-person point of view. I hoped that the close point of view would nudge readers to side with Marcie, despite her mistakes. If they had a direct line to her heart, they might be more sympathetic.

If there were places in the book where you felt it was best to emphasize the poetic strategies over the narrative strategies, or vice versa—what guided these decisions?

On occasion, my poems took shape on the page, whether it was a line of short words trickling down the page, two poems running in parallel, or lines moving off the right margin. These choices brought attention to the poetry as well as adding variety that broke up the narrative.

Poetic choices helped me differentiate my characters' voices. For example, one of my secondary characters was a musician who expressed himself through song. I emphasized rhythm and rhyme for Linus's songs.

One place where I leaned on the narrative was the titles of my poems. More than once I used a poem title to transition the reader to a new setting ("At the Laundromat") or moved them ahead in the story ("The First Day of School"). I chose to place these setting and timing details in the titles so they wouldn't weigh down the poems.

Another instance of emphasizing narrative was when I needed to provide information to the reader. The resulting poems fell in a numbered list beginning with "Things I Left Behind in Boise, Poem 1: My Best Friend" to "Things I Left Behind in Boise, Poem 6: My Baby Fat."

What poetic or narrative effects were you hoping to achieve?

I hoped my poems had immediacy—as if they were scribbled on lined paper as the events unfolded. I used first-person present tense and kept the poems short, each one focusing on one emotion or one moment in time.

For the narrative, I was looking to achieve an epistolary effect without stating the obvious. Even though the poems did not begin with "Dear Diary," I wanted the reader to feel like they were reading Marcie's private thoughts she kept in her blue notebook as she tried to make sense of her topsy-turvy world.

What are your thoughts on the verse novel as a form?

Verse novels are magic! Open one and you'll find beautiful language, abundant imagery, elegant white space, and a character-driven narrative.

Have verse novels you have read been influential on this work in some way?

I have been a fan of verse novels ever since I had the pleasure of hearing Sonya Sones read from *What My Mother Doesn't Know* at a writing conference. After purchasing a copy, I began a search for similar young adult and children's titles. In fact, I was reading *One of Those Hideous Books Where the Mother Dies* when I began *Love and Leftovers*.

In Sones's verse novel, the character Ruby has a father who's gay. Sones's beautiful writing also influenced my own. I fell in love with how the poems sounded when I read them aloud.

What have you learnt about writing verse novels from the verse novels you have read?

One thing I have learned from my favorite authors is to trust the reader. In my early drafts, my poems would have a little summary at the end—sort of a line that told the reader what the poem was about. These summaries needed to go! Readers are savvy and do not need an author to hold their hands. The white space around the poetry is space for the reader to fill in. The page turns between the poems is time for the reader to process. As an author, I learned to step back and give the reader room—the same space that I treasure when I'm reading a verse novel.

CHAPTER 22
JASMINNE MENDEZ

Jasminne Mendez by Tasha Gorel

I think some of the best writing these days is happening with novels in verse.

Jasminne Mendez is a best-selling Dominican American poet, educator, translator, playwright, and award-winning author of several books for children and adults. She has had poetry and essays published in numerous journals and anthologies and she is the author of two multi-genre collections, including *Island of Dreams* (Floricanto Press, 2013) which won an International Latino Book Award. Her debut poetry collection *City without Altar*, winner of the 2023 Texas Institute of Letters Award for Best Book of Poetry, was released in August 2022 (Noemi Press) and her debut picture book *Josefina's Habichuelas* (Arte Publico Press, 2021) was the Writer's League of Texas Children's Book Discovery Prize Winner. Her debut middle grade novel in verse *Aniana Del Mar Jumps In* (Dial) was a 2024 Pura Belpré Honor Book for children's narration. It has received widespread critical acclaim and numerous starred reviews from *Kirkus Reviews*, *Publishers Weekly*, *The School Library Journal*, and others. Jasminne has translated the work of *New York Times*-best-selling authors Amanda Gorman, Nikole Hannah-Jones, René Watson, and Claribel Ortega. She is an MFA graduate of the Creative Writing program at the Rainier Writing Workshop at Pacific Lutheran University and a University of Houston alumni. She is the Program Director for the literary arts non-profit Tintero Projects and she lives and works in Houston, TX. Her website can be found at jasminnemendez.com.

Aniana Del Mar Jumps In (2023)

What ideas or influences did you have in mind when creating this work?

I've always been interested in writing stories and books that help others feel seen and heard. I want diverse stories to be told and to be shared widely because as a child, adolescent, and even into adulthood I have struggled to find stories that represent me and my experiences. When writing this book, I was hoping to capture the lived experiences of those children living with a chronic illness or disability; children who often don't find their stories or experiences represented in books in a compassionate, holistic way. I was also influenced by my own journey and experience with multiple chronic illnesses and disability.

How did you approach writing this verse novel? What were the various stages in its development?

I wrote this verse novel in the early months of 2020 during lockdown for the Covid-19 pandemic. The words poured out of me in that six-month period. I woke up everyday at 5 a.m. and wrote until my daughter would wake up. She was a toddler at the time so writing when she was awake was impossible. I'd also sneak in an hour or two of writing during her nap time.

The novel started as an idea while I was driving in my car one afternoon, and it grew a few poems at a time. I had a rough idea of what I wanted to have happen in the story and just started writing poems that reflected specific scenes and moments. I ended up taking an online writing workshop on how to write a novel in verse and that really helped me flesh out more of the plot and the structure. During the revision stage, I would print out poems and physically rearrange them on the floor or wall of my office and I created charts with poem titles and themes and plot points to help tighten the story.

Can you recall problem-solving decisions you had to make in the writing process?

I think one of the major issues with the first draft of the book was portraying Mami (Aniana's mother) as one dimensional. I had to find ways to make Mami more complex and more whole. I had to dig into her character more so that readers could better understand her and where her fears and PTSD were coming from. I needed to show her softer kinder side and I think in the end, after many revisions, I was able to do that.

This is my first fiction novel, so I was learning a lot about how to write a novel while I was writing and revising it with my editor. I honestly didn't know if I even knew how to do it! But because I had read so many novels and novels in verse, I felt confident that I would figure it out.

Logistically and technically speaking there was the endless problem of formatting the concrete/shape poems on the page. I went through many hours of formatting and reformatting and adjusting text on the page to make it look the way I wanted.

Which poetic and narrative techniques did you decide to employ, and why?

Throughout the book readers will find concrete/shape poems, haikus, tankas, couplets, rhyme, alliteration, assonance, imagery, metaphor and extended metaphor, and a lot of onomatopoeia.

I chose these poetic techniques for a variety of reasons, but one of the main reasons is that I remembered my time as an upper elementary and middle school writing teacher, and the types of poems and literary devices that my students really enjoyed and felt drawn to. While poetry can sometimes feel intimidating for young readers, the poems they often loved were those that were full of sound or were shorter (like the haiku or tanka) or had specific and easy structures they could practice themselves.

The concrete poems are my favorite aspect of the book because I am a very visual person and I think there's something interesting and special about using words to form images and pictures on the page. I also think it's something young readers get really excited about to try on their own and/or read when they see it in a book because it shows them a new way of looking at word and language and what writing can do.

I also used these various techniques because I know that they can create an emotional response in the reader, and it engages the full body of the reader while reading. They hear sounds, see images, read words, and it all helps to bring the story and characters to life in a more visceral way.

One narrative technique I chose to employ that holds the book together is using the metaphor of a hurricane to structure the story. The book is divided into eight sections with a prologue. Most of the middle section of the book is divided into hurricane categories 1–5. I chose this structure and the hurricane metaphor because of where the story is set (Galveston, TX), and to draw parallels and comparisons between the storms the island has faced, and the emotional and physical storms Aniana is experiencing in her life because of her juvenile arthritis, and her mother's trauma. The hurricane metaphor and structure allowed me to use water imagery, storms, and other natural elements throughout the story to help the reader better connect with Aniana's emotional journey and character arc.

If there were places in the book where you felt it was best to emphasize the poetic strategies over the narrative strategies, or vice versa—what guided these decisions?

To me, the places where this was most important was when we go inside what Aniana is thinking or feeling and showing the reader how she's processing her emotions and what's happening to her. It was important to me to ensure that the language and poetry were concise and truly captured her emotional state. I wanted Aniana to be a nuanced and complex character, and for readers to see that as well—using specific poetic strategies like repetition to show how Aniana experienced constant physical pain or fatigue, or how her parents were always on the phone or paying bills after she was diagnosed, helped capture that.

What poetic or narrative effects were you hoping to achieve?

I wanted readers to feel like they were being pushed and pulled in and out of a storm, ideally a hurricane that kept getting progressively worse and worse. I wanted readers to feel a sense of uncertainty and frustration with what was happening to Aniana much like chronic illness patients often feel when first diagnosed.

With some of the concrete poems shaped like waves, I wanted to create a feeling of unsteadiness, the sense of being in the water, or being thrown around by waves.

With shorter poems like the haiku and tanka when Ani was feeling her most vulnerable, sad, or confused I wanted the white space to feel like that looming blank space of nothingness and silence Ani was feeling during this time.

But after the storm, there is the "Rebuilding" section which shows Aniana finding healing with her parents and how they all find a way to move forward and accept Aniana's illness knowing that it has changed her and them as a family.

What are your thoughts on the verse novel as a form?

I think the verse novel is really into its own these days and more and more of them are being written which is great. I think it allows reluctant young readers, English language learner (ELL) students, and others who say they don't like to read, the ability to enter literature in a new way that may feel more accessible and appealing to them. The less text on the page, the focus on the inner life and emotions of the character and the concision of language to tell the story is something that I think a lot of young readers find appealing.

I think the verse novel can do things prose novels can't (or at least don't want to)—like concrete poems, mixing forms (like letters, comics, illustrations, recipes, etc.)—and that is exciting because it seems verse novelists are finding more ways to experiment with the form—and readers like that.

I think some of the best writing these days is happening with novels in verse. Just look at what a lot of the recent National book award finalists and winners and Newbery award winners have been—verse novels!

Have verse novels you have read been influential on this work in some way?

Yes! I read a lot of verse novels (for fun) before diving into this book. I never really thought I would write one myself but when this story idea came, I just knew it had to be in verse. Many of the verse novels I read leading up to writing *Aniana Del Mar Jumps In* had female protagonists looking for their voice or struggling to speak up for themselves. I realized this was a common theme in children's literature right now and knew that a book about a Latina with a chronic illness seeking bodily autonomy and agency didn't exist and I felt like this book could fill that gap.

Some of the most influential books that helped shape *Aniana Del Mar Jumps In* were Elizabeth Acevedo's *The Poet X*, Jasmine Warga's *Other Words for Home*, Jacqueline Woodson's *Brown Girl Dreaming* and *Before the Ever After*, and Aida Salazar's *The Moon Within*.

What have you learnt about writing verse novels from the verse novels you have read?

I think one of the most important things I've learned and that has been re-emphasized by reading verse novels is that you don't have to write *every* scene, moment, or timeline point. You can compress time and jump forward and not every feeling, thought, scene, gesture, or transition must be captured on the page. Rather the writer can create vignettes of scenes and then move on to the next one. What's important is following the emotional journey and character arc of the main character(s).

I've also learned to minimize the amount of sub plots and side characters present to not overwhelm the story with those details. Keep the focus of the narrative simple—only one main conflict versus having multiple.

Lastly, I've learned each poem in a novel in verse should serve the narrative in some way; if it doesn't, then it shouldn't be there.

CHAPTER 23
HOLLY THOMPSON

Holly Thompson by Carter Hasegawa

Everyone who reads a range of YA and middle grade verse novels ... will grasp the emotional power, the storytelling scope and the extraordinary range in the craft ...

Holly Thompson is the author of the poetry picture books *Twilight Chant* (Clarion, 2018), a 2019 NCTE Notable Poetry Book, and *One Wave at a Time* (Albert Whitman, 2018), a SEL story about grief and healing. Her picture book *The Wakame Gatherers* (Shen's, Lee & Low 2007, 2022) was a 2009 NCSS Notable Social Studies Trade Book for Young People and featured in The National Consortium for Teaching about Asia (NCTAsia) programs. Her picture book biography in the haibun form, *Listening to Trees: George Nakashima, Woodworker* (Neal Porter Books), is forthcoming in 2024. Holly Thompson is also the author of the middle grade verse novel *Falling into the Dragon's Mouth* (Henry Holt, 2016), a 2016 NCTAsia Freeman Award Honor book, plus two critically acclaimed YA novels in verse: *The Language Inside* (Delacorte, 2013) and *Orchards* (Delacorte, 2011). *The Language Inside* was a YALSA 2014 Best Fiction for Young Adults title and a Bank Street Books Best Book Selection; *Orchards* was awarded the 2012 APALA Asian/Pacific

American Award for Literature and was a 2012 YALSA Best Fiction for Young Adults title. Holly also compiled and edited the YA anthology *Tomo: Friendship Through Fiction—An Anthology of Japan Teen Stories* (Stone Bridge Press, 2012), and her adult novel *Ash* was published by Stone Bridge Press in 2001. Originally from New England and a longtime resident of Japan, she received her MA in fiction writing from New York University and teaches creative writing and literature at Yokohama City University. Holly Thompson's website can be found at hatbooks.com.

Orchards (2011)
The Language Inside (2013)
Falling into the Dragon's Mouth (2016)

What ideas or influences did you have in mind when creating this work?

One stream of influence for *The Language Inside* was my experience as a student in the New York University Graduate Creative Writing Program, during which I volunteered to assist long-term care residents of the former Goldwater Hospital on Roosevelt Island, New York City, in writing poetry. Besides assisting writers, volunteers also participated with them in poetry workshops led by poet Sharon Olds and guests. One Goldwater Hospital resident I assisted was poet Julia Tavalaro (who ultimately wrote her memoir *Look Up for Yes* together with a subsequent assistant Richard Tayson). Julia was a powerful personality and writer, despite having suffered a brain-stem stroke as a young woman that left her unable to speak or move—except for her fierce lively eyes. With her, I used a letter board, and she would roll her eyes upward when my finger reached the next letter of the word in her poem. Sharon Olds's poetry and her bold, compassionate style of leading those workshops made a huge impression on me, and the entire experience seeded *The Language Inside*.

Instead of setting the story in New York City, I chose Lowell, Massachusetts, with its deep immigrant history and large Asian population. Though I've lived in Japan for most of my adult life, I'd grown up not far from the city of Lowell, which, unlike many Massachusetts towns, had long been a city of many cultures and languages. Key for me in my choice of Lowell, as opposed to other evolving former industrial cities, was that Lowell was one of the US refugee resettlement cities for Cambodians in the 1980s following the 1970s genocide under Pol Pot's rule, and I had decided to have the main character, Emma, raised in Japan, connect with a long-term care center volunteer of Cambodian heritage. I knew that the bilingual character Emma was a dancer, and the Angkor Dance Troupe of Lowell would be a group she would encounter in the novel.

How did you approach writing this verse novel? What were the various stages in its development?

I carry my novels around in my head long before writing. With *The Language Inside*, I could picture the opening migraine scene and had built characters and envisioned moments in the novel years before I began drafting. As I began drafting, I populated detailed charts for plotting, characterization, research, and more.

I knew that in addition to the story being written in narrative verse, poetry would play a key role in the plot: the poetry that main character Emma writes in Massachusetts after being abruptly moved from Japan; the poems that stroke patient Zena writes via a letter board with Emma as volunteer at the long-term care center; the shared poems from the poetry workshop; and poems that represent Emma's aphasia when she suffers through a migraine. Additionally, well known poems would be referenced in the novel, as Emma's volunteer role includes selecting poems to share with Zena for each week she volunteers. So, in addition to writing my chapters in verse, I had to craft Emma's poems, Zena's poems, and volunteer Samnang's poem, and select the poems that Emma would choose to share with Zena.

Obviously, I had to do extensive research on the city of Lowell; Cambodian Americans; Khmer classical and folk dance; Khmer language; Cambodia's complicated history; and more. For me to write a character like Samnang, who has a white American father and a genocide survivor Cambodian mother, I had to dive deep into layers upon layers of research.

Early on, I connected with the Angkor Dance Troupe co-founder and director Tim Thou, who invited me to observe dance classes and eventually to hold a group interview/ listening session with the teen students, some of whom became key expert readers of my novel. I studied the documentary film *Monkey Dance*[1] directed by Linda Mallozzi and met the three featured dancers.

I met with staff at the Lowell Community Health Center to learn more about health care and mental health issues for genocide survivors and their children. I traveled to Cambodia, spent time staying in a rural village to better understand the roots of character Samnang's mother. I observed classical Khmer dance practice at the University of Fine Arts Phnom Penh. And I read Cambodian history, Cambodian American history, and memoirs, novels, and poetry by Cambodian Americans. All of this then had to be understood deeply so that I could weave my story in verse.

Can you recall problem-solving decisions you had to make in the writing process?

For my prior novel *Orchards*, I'd received a two-book publishing deal from Delacorte, so even before *Orchards* was completed, I was at work planning and writing *The Language Inside*. But I was on a very tight deadline.

Without doubt, the most overwhelming problem I faced while writing *The Language Inside* was scrambling to learn and absorb enough knowledge to responsibly write the characters, the settings, and the worlds of the story in time for the deadline set by the publisher. I was determined to do my utmost to create what would feel like an authentic story set in Lowell and Japan, which meant trips back and forth from Japan, where I lived, to Massachusetts, and to Cambodia. Ultimately, I had to ask my editor for another year to complete the novel.

The poetry and dialogue style had to be determined early in the drafting. I opted to write *The Language Inside* in verse with no punctuation except for question marks, dashes, and the occasional exclamation points. Line breaks, stanza breaks, and page breaks create pauses within the rhythm of the language. Hyphens are used for Zena's letter board spellings. Italics are used for dialogue. The aim was to pare away anything except the voice on the page.

Which poetic and narrative techniques did you decide to employ, and why?

My three young adult/middle grade verse novels thus far—*Orchards*; *The Language Inside*; *Falling into the Dragon's Mouth*—are all written in chapter-long poems divided by page breaks into single page, untitled "sub-poems." I employ page breaks and line breaks for breaths, enjambment, and other poetry tools for pacing, and "listen" for what the white space on the page holds. I try to sculpt the poems as much for the words on the page as for the ideas the white space contains, and I consciously utilize page turns. This style has felt organically suited to the voices of these novels and the stories they tell, but with any verse novel, following one's own rules of engagement creates each writer's particular challenges.

The verse chapters of *The Language Inside* carry Emma's thoughts in the present, her recollections of past moments in Japan, her dialogue with other characters, and the various ways of using language and conversing, including letter-board spelling with long-term care center resident Zena. My hope is that this style holds the rhythm and heart of main character Emma.

Emma also suffers from migraine (as do I) with episodes of blindness and numbness on one side of her body, accompanied by aphasia, nausea, and so on. I was keen to use poetry to depict this physical experience of migraine—showing Emma's experience of blindness through missing letters from a signpost's text, for example—and her experience of aphasia, the way a migraine interrupts the ability to process language. Several poems in the book show that disruption to the brain—Emma can hear words but cannot assemble them to make sense.

If there were places in the book where you felt it was best to emphasize the poetic strategies over the narrative strategies, or vice versa—what guided these decisions?

The poems in *The Language Inside* that are written by the characters Emma, Zena, and Samnang for the long-term care center poetry workshops emphasize their individual poetic strategies. Each of these poems, or fragments of poems, was crafted to be true to the character's voice, life experience, and relationship to poetry. Zena's poems, while composed in her head and then spelled to an assistant via letterboard, perhaps reveal a more advanced grasp of poetry; the poem she shares in the workshop is one of the first she's created with a computer that has an eye tracker and thus has short lines and repetition. Samnang's poem is a prose poem on cross cultural use of coins. Emma experiments to find ways to show bilingual thinking in her poems. Finding their poetry voices took time, but the characters guided my choices.

What poetic or narrative effects were you hoping to achieve?

In *The Language Inside*, I was striving to create a story in which the narrative verse reveals the emotional experiences of bilingual, raised-in-Japan Emma struggling to adapt to a new environment in Massachusetts as her mother undergoes a mastectomy, all while she's missing Japan and mourning for Japan post-3/11 earthquake and tsunami. I aimed to stay true to the music of Emma's voice and that of other characters in the story.

I was also striving to deftly weave into this verse novel the concept of poetry as a means of dialogue—between Emma and Zena; between their poems; between Emma and Samnang; between Emma's inner and outer worlds. Via the poems that Emma selects and reads for workshops, I wove in references to sixteen poems by various poets including Lucille Clifton, Garrett Hongo, and Naomi Shihab Nye (all listed in the backmatter of *The Language Inside* and in the novel's Discussion Guide with links provided). In the novel, these poems are selected by Emma, so they had to be poems that would resonate with her and serve to inspire poems crafted by Zena and Emma in the story.

Emma's poems sometimes incorporate *kanji*—the logographic characters used in Japanese writing. In those poems, I wanted English-language readers to be able to sense the dimensionality of *kanji*, gain a glimpse of that visual richness, and quickly see how English and other alphabet languages lack that aspect. A person raised in a language like Japanese will inevitably sense a missing dimension in a language like English. Since my first encounters with the Japanese language in 1983, I have always been interested in bilingual approaches to writing, as well as the challenge of representing bilingualism in novels for English-language readers.

What are your thoughts on the verse novel as a form?

The verse novel form is elastic and has so many possibilities. The category fascinates me because for the writer there is, inevitably, a tension between the poetry and the narrative; there's a bit of a tug-of-war going on. The writer must determine how to make the narration of a story sound organic and natural in verse and consider how far the poetry can go before the storytelling starts to feel contrived, or the poems feel out of voice, or too polished for the characters. The poetry really must serve the narrative to be a "novel." But, that said, there is room for all types of verse novels, and I hope that narrow definitions of verse novels will disappear altogether. I look forward to seeing how diverse linguistic approaches, cultural traditions, experimentation, and voices from around the world will cause the form to stretch and evolve.

Have verse novels you have read been influential on this work in some way?

My shift from writing prose fiction to verse novels was influenced by reading Steven Herrick's *By the River* (2005), which I encountered during a one-month writing residency in Hobart, Tasmania in 2007. My novels *Orchards* and *The Language Inside* are also YA novels that feature teens grappling with forms of grief and loss, and from the outset, I planned these two books in free verse poetry. While I was writing *The Language Inside*, in addition to my novel's research reading, I was reading many verse novels, including *All the Broken Pieces* by Ann E. Burg, *Because I am Furniture* by Thalia Chaltas, *The Poet Slave of Cuba* by Margarita Engle, and others. Poets whose work I read then and continue to read include Gary Soto, Marilyn Nelson, Li-Young Lee, Naomi Shihab Nye, Lucille Clifton, and Richard Blanco.

What have you learnt about writing verse novels from the verse novels you have read?

Truly there are so many ways to craft verse novels—novels with continuous verse chapters; novels in poems; novels as one long poem; novels with compact sequences of poems; novels with narrow poems like a road down a page; novels with slow deliberate pacing; novels with torrents of breathless verse; novels with regular stanzas, irregular stanzas, no stanzas; novels in formal poetry, free verse, original forms; novels with alternating voices, multiple voices, or single narrators ... All the tools of poetry plus fiction are available. There are so many possibilities!

The verse novels that stay with me have the feel of organic craft; the poetry doesn't seem to artificially override the narrative, and the narrative moves in tandem with and via the poetry and is lofted by the poetry. Everyone who reads a range of YA and middle grade verse novels—such as Steven Herrick's *By the River,* Elizabeth Acevedo's *The Poet X,* Dana Walrath's *Like Water on Stone; Marilyn Nelson's American Ace;* David Foenkinos's *Charlotte,* Annie Donwerth Chikamatsu's *Beyond Me;* Helen Frost's *Keesha's House;* Jason Reynolds's *Long Way Down,* Joy McCullough's *Blood, Water, Paint;* Mariko Nagai's *Dust of Eden;* Thanhhà Lại's *Inside Out and Back Again;* Kip Wilson's *White Rose;* Amber McBride's *Me (Moth)* ... to name just a few—will grasp the emotional power, the storytelling scope and the extraordinary range in the craft of the YA and MG verse novel.

CHAPTER 24
CHRIS BARON

Chris Baron copyright Chris Baron

Novels in verse are relevant for all kinds of readers.

Chris Baron is the award-winning author of verse novels for children, *All of Me*, an NCTE Notable Book, *The Magical Imperfect* a Sydney Taylor Book Award Notable Book/a SLJ Best Book of 2021, and *Spark*, from Feiwel & Friends/Macmillan, 2025. His novels are *The Gray* (2023), and *Secret of The Dragon Gems*, a middle grade novel co-authored with Rajani LaRocca from Little Bee Books (2023). He is the editor of *On All Other Nights: A Middle Grade Passover Anthology*, from Abrams (2024), and also the author of *Under the Broom Tree*, part of Lantern Tree which won The San Diego Book Award for Poetry. He is a Professor of English at San Diego City College and the director of the Writing Center. He grew up in New York City, but he completed his MFA in Poetry in 1998 at San Diego State University. He lives in San Diego with his family. His website can be found at chris-baron.com.

All of Me (2019)
The Magical Imperfect (2021)
Spark (2025)

What ideas or influences did you have in mind when creating this work?

I want to write books that I would have wanted when I was a kid—I didn't often see myself in the stories.

The *LA Times* called my first novel in verse, *All of Me,* a fictional retelling. I think this is a perfect way to put it. Almost everywhere I have gone and talked about *All of Me,* someone has asked me if Ari and his adventures are based on my life. The answer is yes. The story is fictional, but so much of it is my heart and soul and a collage of adventures, my Jewish heritage, and experiences from my own middle school years. Most of all, my personal story is embedded deeply in the spirit of the book where Ari, who is put on a diet after a dangerous incident, starts to question whether this diet is really a good thing after all. Fat-shaming is often different than what we think. In *All of Me,* Ari faces real bullies who represent the physical danger of being bullied, but the book also explores the more dangerous microaggressions of subtle comments, quiet words, and indirect actions, even from the ones closest to home, that can bring a compounding shame, impacting lives over the long term. This is why I felt so inspired to write a middle grade novel that has the time and space to explore the story of an overweight, outcast boy who learns what it means to love who he is—as he is.

For *The Magical Imperfect,* my second verse novel, the influences felt even more complex—yet still deeply rooted in my own personal experience. While *The Magical Imperfect* is not a fictional retelling, there are many connections to the life of my family, and the physical and mental health issues the main characters face. For me, suffering from anxiety, and for my wife, her severe eczema. The themes of our experiences are threaded into these stories: both the good and very difficult truth of how hard it can all be.

This book is also deeply rooted in history—so it's often categorized as historical fiction, and a lot of my influence came from research along with experience.

Most of us know about Ellis Island and the approximately 12 million immigrants who arrived at the Port of New York and New Jersey. But not many people know that from 1910 to 1940, the Angel Island Immigration Station in San Francisco served as the processing and detention center for nearly half a million people from China, Japan, South Asia, Korea, Russia, Mexico, Europe (including Jewish people), and the Philippines. There are so many undiscovered stories about these incredible souls. *The Magical Imperfect* finds its heart here. I also need to mention the important book, *Angel Island: Immigrant Gateway to America,* by Erika Lee and Judy Yung.[1]

In addition to all of this, the story takes place during 1989 World Series in the San Francisco Bay area against the backdrop of the Loma Prieta Earthquake.

And of course, I always have my own family in mind when I write anything.

My next novels follow similar ideas and influence, but launch into a different, and in some ways, more personal path. *The Gray,* while not in verse, is very personal—it deals with anxiety, and the challenge of growing up in a world that often seems out of control. I wrote much of the first draft of *The Gray* in verse—but when it was completed it seemed clear that the story was meant to be in prose.

Spark is just the opposite. For this book, I wrote in both genres, but landed squarely in the form of a verse novel. In *Spark*, the influence is much more external, in grappling with kids who experience the destruction of the town and wildlands they love after a terrible wildfire. Is there a way to find normal again?

How did you approach writing this verse novel? What were the various stages in its development?

Imagine the messiest desk possible (that's my brain also) but the good kind with the right image of a steaming mug and just the right placement—maybe a cat curled up near a fireplace (okay maybe not that perfect). I like to start messy—drawing, maps, lines on the page, and then free-writing without any interference. This usually results in a bunch of unfinished poems, but it does help me with the story. I would say that this is the beginning part of the process where writing, research, and the flow of creativity all combine. For *The Magical Imperfect* I had books of Jewish history, folklore, and mythology, wide open on my desk, along with pages of notes from my Filipino family. I try to create an environment full of the themes, characters, and stories of the book— almost like trying to live inside the actual landscape of the book.

This is where the writing process shifts—and I take all the messiness and start to condense the story into verse. I shape the big ideas into concise, imagistic lines. It's this process of taking the huge ideas and then shaping them into more concise, story-telling moments—where the poetry really starts on the page. For me, poetry feels like a native language. Writing in verse is my comfort. I think partly it's because—like reading a novel—it can move fast at times. There is often a feeling of deep accomplishment with every poem/chapter. When I write prose, I feel myself focusing more on organization and detailed outline. In verse novels, the plot unfolds more easily for me, and while I do use outlines to keep track of plot movement, characters, research points, etc., I typically feel the narrative flows much more. In some ways I feel like the verse is a distillation of all the work that came before, and it's the assembling of words in a very specific structure working with all their might to honor the story being told.

Can you recall problem-solving decisions you had to make in the writing process?

Because poems often go very deep internally—I often found myself needing to clarify timelines so readers—especially young readers, don't get lost. I work hard on this in my process. This was especially true in *The Magical Imperfect*. I knew the storyline would end with the Earthquake and the World Series, so I crafted a calendar and worked backwards. I filled the days with poem titles making sure there were touchstone poems in each week to help mark the time—a Halloween Poem to show the end of October, Shabbat poems to remind the reader it was the weekend, and on like this—small context clues that help to keep the story, the characters, and the readers on track. I also like physical markers, so my office wall is often filled with poems marking the time from right to left.

Which poetic and narrative techniques did you decide to employ, and why?

Poetic and narrative techniques intertwine beautifully. The use of figurative language, symbolism, voice, and theme are all poetic and narrative techniques that flow together.

When writing books for young readers, I also try to think of the more traditional elements of a narrative: plot, characters, setting, theme, point of view, and conflict. I think these are important elements of storytelling that connect us to our history. Story is sacred. Story is everywhere. Stories make us human, build empathy, and bring us together. If I know someone's story, I find myself connected with them in a way that transcends my own selfishness and breaks down barriers.

This world is so overwhelmed with information and instant facts, but most of human history is told and remembered through story. With my kids, we end every night by reading a story, and then when the lights go out, we take turns telling stories to each other. Maybe the stories are about space, or giant frogs, or mole people, or a girl at school—and even though we call it fiction, truth is powerfully present in each one. I imagine so many families across so many cultures doing this through the ages—whether they are making their way through the most challenging dangers, tucked away safe and snug in bedrooms, or perhaps even walking along the bay on a crisp San Francisco evening. Stories bring us together.

Once these more traditional elements are identified, I think they can then be broken down and utilized in whatever way best fits the story. This is where the poetics come in.

With verse, I can have more control over the line. While I like to use free verse, I often use syllabic verse and line length to speed things up and slow them down, create more white space on the page, and develop a musicality when I want things to be more lyrical.

I think that poetry speaks to the heart. We see with more than just our eyes, and the music of poetry helps to make words sing directly to us.

If there were places in the book where you felt it was best to emphasize the poetic strategies over the narrative strategies, or vice versa—what guided these decisions?

In *The Magical Imperfect* and *All of Me*, I used the poetics to emphasize the intimacy of the internal life of the characters, sharing their own thoughts on their vulnerabilities, perspectives on experiences, and development of the setting. There are also times in the stories where I wanted to speed things up for the sake of action or slow them down to provide space for reflection.

So, for more reflective poems, the internal voice may sound more like complete thoughts, explained in longer lines. This may read differently than the character's external voice which is much more nuanced and consistent—often using a unique pattern or structure in the poem to create a more recognizable character voice.

What poetic or narrative effects were you hoping to achieve?

There are several narrative techniques I hoped to achieve, but two stand out. The first is the notion that a story told in verse might create something more memorable. By using figurative language, memorable rhythms, and even using more sensory descriptions, the reader will hopefully come away with a more holistic experience of the story.

I think another strength of verse is how fun it can be to utilize poetic elements to form unique voices for the characters. Through verse, I create what I hope are more nuanced character personalities, actions, and emotions, by using line breaks, varying poetic meter, word choices, and syntax to give a character a unique voce that a reader can identify and connect with throughout the narrative. The rhythm of the character's voice and actions can become recognizable for the reader creating a deeper connection.

What are your thoughts on the verse novel as a form?

Novels in verse are my native language. I've always loved the idea of the image being the truth and beauty of a story. I was (and I am now with my own kids) the slowest picture book reader ever because I like to stare at every atom of the image and the words swirling together. To me it's pure poetry—pure story.

I think this is what initially drew me to novels in verse. I love the way verse can shake up our expectations of a story even as traditional story elements—like plot, setting, conflict—are still all present. I think that poetry speaks to the heart. We see with more than just our eyes, and the music of poetry helps to make words sing directly to us. This can be so helpful—especially when dealing with more difficult subject matter. I think young readers see and feel but aren't always good at "talking about" what they experience. Novels in verse can help articulate the internal landscape in a unique way.

Novels in verse are relevant for all kinds of readers. There is space on the page, measured breaks, pacing, music, and movement of lines that a reader at almost any level can find their way into. The structure of verse creates an intimacy with a reader that allows them to hear the tone and cadence of a character's voice. This can create even stronger connections for readers.

Have verse novels you have read been influential on this work in some way?

I love so many verse novels, and I would say they all have been influential for me. I love the way the power of a vast story can be delivered in the one-two punch of a good poem. Like most people of my generation, I encountered poetry such as *Beowulf* or poems by Shakespeare at first, but I was always drawn much more to A. A. Milne and Shel Silverstein for the use of language, and the profound expression of ideas in simple format.

What have you learnt about writing verse novels from the verse novels you have read?

When I read Jacqueline Woodson's *Brown Girl Dreaming*, Nikki Grimes's *Garvey's Choice*, and Thanhhà Lại's Inside *Out and Back Again*, I discovered this incredible form where characters internal and external life could be at the center of the story at the same time.

CHAPTER 25
STEPHANIE HEMPHILL

Stephanie Hemphill by Spicy

… all verse novels, whether they edge closer to poetry, or narrative,
plant their feet in the oral tradition.

Stephanie Hemphill has written seven novels, six of them in verse. Her first book published by Hyperion in 2005, *Things Left Unsaid: A Novel in Poems*, won the 2006 Myra Cohn Livingston Award for Excellence in Poetry. Her second novel, *Your Own, Sylvia: A Verse Portrait of Sylvia Plath* (Random House, Knopf, 2007) received a 2008 Michael J. Printz Honor, the 2008 Myra Cohn Livingston Award for Poetry, made the ALA 2008 Best Books for Young Adults Top Ten, Kirkus Reviews Editor Choice Award, Booklist Books for Youth Editor's Choice, and was a Cybil's Finalist. Her third book *Wicked Girls, A Novel of the Salem Witch Trials* (HarperCollins, Balzer & Bray, 2010) was a finalist for the 2011 Los Angeles Times Book Prize, a School Library Journal Best Book, and an Illinois Reads Best Book of 2015. *Sisters of Glass*, her fourth verse novel, came out in 2012 from Random House, Knopf. *Hideous Love: The Story of the Girl Who Wrote Frankenstein*, published in 2013 by HarperCollins, Balzer & Bray, is Stephanie's fifth verse novel and was a Bank Street Committee's Best Historical Fiction 14+ in 2014. In 2018 Stephanie was a part of *Fatal Throne: The Wives of Henry VIII Tell All* (Random House, Schwartz & Wade) a prose collaboration written in the six voices of the wives of Henry VIII. *Fatal Throne* was an New York Public Library (NYPL) Top 10 Book of the Year, Illinois Reads Best Book 2019, Amelia Bloomer Book for Promoting Feminist Fiction, and ALA Best YA Fiction. Most recently, HarperCollins, Balzer & Bray, published her 2019 verse novel, *The Language of Fire: Joan of Arc Reimagined* which is a 2020 NCTE Notable Poetry & Verse Book & an NYPL Best Book of 2019. In 2006, Stephanie chaired the PEN Award's Children's Literature Committee. Every summer she teaches a Young Writer's Workshop at the Iowa History Museum. Stephanie lives in suburban Chicago.

Your Own, Sylvia (2007)
Language of Fire: Joan of Arc Reimagined (2019)

What ideas or influences did you have in mind when creating this work?

With *Your Own, Sylvia* what excited me was to explore not only the hybrid form of the verse novel, but also to add genre into the mix, to write a historical verse novel, and even more specifically, a biographical verse novel. Writing about the life of one of the greatest poets of the twentieth century in poetry seemed like a perfect marriage of form and subject matter. I was grateful for the opportunity, but at the same time I feared my poetry would pale in comparison to Plath's. So, I hedged my bets a little and used multiple viewpoints, but never wrote in first-person *as* Sylvia. Instead, Sylvia's story is told in the voices of people who knew her, with varying degrees of intimacy, at different periods throughout her life. Marilyn Nelson's *Carver: A Life in Poems* hugely influenced the structure of this book.

In my more recent verse novel, *Language of Fire: Joan of Arc Reimagined*, storytelling takes precedence. My focus switched from creating history and biography out of poems to focusing on a more novel approach of making the history and historical figures relevant and appealing to young adult readers in a verse format. And in terms of the form, if I succeed with *Language of Fire*, the reader might almost forget the book they're reading is written in verse. Only upon second or closer examination will the poetry emerge, with a few exceptions which I call stand-alone poems. The reason I chose to write *Language of Fire* as a verse novel rather than as straight-up prose is not at the poem-by-poem level like with *Your Own, Sylvia*, but for the other reasons one might choose this hybrid form to tell their story. Verse novels allow an author to write in first person for more prolonged interior monologues, which are key for Joan of Arc as she hears voices in her head and is often alone. Poetry allows more space for rumination without losing readers, perhaps by paradoxically using fewer words to express a character's innermost thoughts. Further, novels in verse give a writer the ability to collapse or suspend time without the jump shifts feeling quite as jarring as they might in a prose novel, especially for a young adult audience. My historical novels often span long periods of time so the ability to manipulate time and streamline events, for instance have a whole battle occur in one poem, is invaluable. On a totally personal and much less relevant note, I love poetry and began my writing life publishing adult poetry. At the beginning of my writing career (and to this day if I'm being honest), I found writing something novel length but broken down into poem fragments much less daunting of a task.

How did you approach writing this verse novel? What were the various stages in its development?

Many of my books require tricks for me to enter the writing and *Your Own, Sylvia* required more than most. Prior to picking up a pen, I spent about six months devouring everything I could get my hands on that Plath wrote or created: poetry, art, short stories, novels, letters, children's books, and her complete journals. I read tons of biographies about Plath and Hughes, then chose a few of these sources, along with Ted's and Sylvia's work and her journals and letters, from which to create a portrait of Sylvia's life. Every day before I began writing the book, I would take a line from one of Plath's poems and free verse journal about my life to clear away the baggage in my head, remove any insecurities I had about whether I was up for this task, and warm up my poetic muscles. I write all my first drafts of verse novels long hand, pen to paper. Plath avidly wrote letters to her mother throughout her life, so along with the free verse journaling I did, some days I also wrote letters to my mother and snail-mailed them to her. These actions helped settle me into the time-period and mindset of Sylvia.

Can you recall problem-solving decisions you had to make in the writing process?

My original proposal for this book was that each poem would include an addendum with additional information about either the time-period or something mentioned in the poem, kind of like a footnote. The reader could choose to read the footnotes or disregard them. The poems alone would tell the story. My editor didn't want the book to contain any addendums, and so I wrote it entirely in poetry. I did not take copious notes about the source for the voice of each poem. But as soon as I turned in my first draft, I was asked to add addendums to every poem and source them almost like you would a nonfiction book. I burst into tears at the prospect of figuring out how to approach this task and recall from which source the two hundred plus poems derived. I assumed I was looking at a page one rewrite. But they were happy with the poetry I had written and wanted it to remain as it was. I was at a complete loss. Even though this structure is what I imagined would be best for the book at the onset, I had switched gears. I just wasn't prepared. To help me write the addendums, my editor graciously posed questions about each poem and her wonderful assistant aided me with the research. The book grew into something I could never have created on my own, a true collaboration.

Which poetic and narrative techniques did you decide to employ, and why?

I never had a title for this book—my editor and publisher chose *Your Own, Sylvia*—but I knew, early on, that the subtitle would be "A verse portrait of Sylvia Plath." I distinctly wanted to avoid both the word "poem" and the word "novel" as descriptors. My first book I subtitled "a novel in poems," and in 2007 I made a distinction between a novel in poems and a verse novel. All the semantics mattered so dearly to me then. I have since revised that thinking. The lines in this hybrid form are blurry, especially for a Young Adult readership. Authors, publishers, booksellers, and readers can call this format whatever they prefer or best suits their needs. The writing and the story are what matters. The reason I chose the subtitle of *A verse portrait* for *Your Own, Sylvia* is because I pieced together her life using a mosaic of voices, a collage of verse. I wasn't exactly writing a biography or a novel in poems or verse, but the structure of this book was chronological and precise. And apart from a few of the formal poems, the poetry would make little sense out of order or outside the context of the narrative.

If there were places in the book where you felt it was best to emphasize the poetic strategies over the narrative strategies, or vice versa—what guided these decisions?

In general, when this book feels more narrative, I think it's because the voice of the character/narrator/real life person in the poem is a more prosaic voice. Also because of the addendums, *Your Own, Sylvia* contains prose on every page as footnotes designed to speak to the poetry and add further context. As much as possible I did not want to sacrifice poetic strategies for biography or vice versa, but when I had to choose, I leaned into the poetry. I had the luxury of letting the addendums fill in the narrative gaps.

What poetic or narrative effects were you hoping to achieve?

With *Your Own, Sylvia* my original intent was to tell her biography exclusively through people who knew her and who encountered her. There are over seventy different narrators of the first-person poems in *Your Own, Sylvia*. I think the effect I was after was much like a documentary film. However, it became very clear that Plath—or at least Plath's writing, journals, letters, voice—needed to be in this book. The Estate of Ted Hughes owns all Plath's writing, so we could not excerpt her poetry or journals or letters except with extreme limitations, and under no circumstances was I willing to write poetry of my own in first-person *as* Sylvia Plath. I eventually decided to write third-person poems in the same style as poems that Sylvia herself had written. The placement in the book of these third person "Imagining Sylvia poems" correlates with the chronological time that Plath wrote them. The idea was to point readers toward Plath's poetry in a very direct way—with the more straightforward poems placed in the chronology of her life illuminating the poems Plath wrote at that time. Many of these are fixed-form poems such as a villanelle, or a sonnet, or they contain a defined meter and rhyme scheme. The "Imagining Sylvia" poems also use imagery that was in the Plath poem they reference. And like all the other poems the "Imagining Sylvia" poems tell her story.

What are your thoughts on the verse novel as a form?

Some readers love verse novels, others do not. Some people shy away from anything associated with poetry, fearing they won't be able to understand it or won't like a verse novel. If they see white space on the page, they close the book before reading a single word. The verse novel can be a misunderstood form, even by avid readers. The word novel gets obscured by the word verse, even though most Young Adult verse novels tell complete stories with characters and dialogue and a plot just like "regular" novels do. One perk of verse novels is that they read quickly, in an afternoon or a day. On the flipside, if you love poetry, great Young Adult verse novels contain poems that take your breath away.

Have verse novels you have read been influential on this work in some way?

At the time that I wrote *Your Own, Sylvia*, the Young Adult verse novels I remember influencing the book were Marilyn Nelson's *Carver: A Life in Poems*, Karen Hesse's *Out of the Dust*, and the Young Adult verse novels of Sonya Sones. In the early 2000s, Young Adult verse novels flourished. I read and adored so many before I began writing them myself, that the list of authors whom I admire and whose work influenced me, would be extensive. However, for this book I am specifically grateful to Marilyn Nelson and Karen Hesse. Not many Young Adult historical verse novels or biographical novels in verse existed at that time, and these women wrote masterworks. *Your Own, Sylvia* owes so much to them.

What have you learnt about writing verse novels from the verse novels you have read?

Young Adult verse novels run the gamut. Some are written entirely in sonnets; some feel very close to prose. As with all other writing no subject is off-limits.

After reading many verse novels, what became evident to me is that all verse novels, whether they edge closer to poetry, or narrative, plant their feet in the oral tradition. You hear them. You read them at the speed of speech like an audio book inside your head. This is what I love about poetry. You don't skip words or lines or stanzas. With regular novels, sometimes people skim or read faster than they hear. But verse novels are intended to have you read every word, to hear every word—like you do with poetry. The characters speak like a play. Verse novels return stories on the page to storytelling, to their origin as an oral art, to something not just seen, but heard.

CHAPTER 26
CHUN YU

Chun Yu copyright Chun Yu

Any story can be told in verse. Poetry makes stories
stronger and more unforgettable.

Chun Yu is an award-winning, bilingual poet, graphic novelist, scientist, and translator. She is the author of a memoir in verse, *Little Green: Growing Up during the Chinese Cultural Revolution* (Simon & Schuster) and a historical graphic novel in progress (Macmillan). *Little Green* has won many awards and is taught in world history and culture classes. Chun's poetry and translations have appeared or are forthcoming in: *Poetry; Orion; Obsidian; Poem of the Day; Boston Herald; Konch; Catamaran; Xinhua Daily;* and elsewhere, and in the award-winning collection *Veterans of War, Veterans of Peace* edited by Maxine Hong Kingston (Koa Books). She is a recipient of multiple San Francisco Arts Commission grants for her poetry and graphic novel projects. She is a Library Laureate of the San Francisco Public Library (2023) and an honoree of the 2020 YBCA 100 award (Yerba Buena Center for the Arts) for creative changemakers. Her project Two Languages/One Community with poet Michael Warr brings Chinese

American and African American communities together through poetry and storytelling. Chun holds a BS and MS from Peking University and a PhD from Rutgers University in biomaterials. Chun's website can be found at https://chunyu.org/.

Little Green: Growing Up during the
Chinese Cultural Revolution (2005)

What ideas or influences did you have in mind when creating this work?

I began writing poetry when I was a post-doctoral fellow in a Harvard-MIT (Massachusetts Institute of Technology) joint program. Although I had wanted to be a writer and artist since childhood, I studied science instead, due to my parents' concerns following their experiences during the political movements in China. When I started writing poetry, I had no formal training in creative writing and simply followed my intuition. However, for thousands of years, poetry has held a significant place in Chinese culture, and I believe this cultural tradition deeply influenced me.

How did you approach writing this verse novel? What were the various stages in its development?

I simply let the stories come to me each night, writing one story at a time until it was completed and I felt a poetic sense had been achieved. I finished the first draft in a one-semester creative writing class at Harvard Extension School. The draft contained all the key moments of the book which I expanded over the next ten months.

Can you recall problem-solving decisions you had to make in the writing process?

I initially tried to write the book in prose, but it wouldn't flow. When I switched to verse, something magical happened—the book came to me.

There were many real-life events I could have included. I left out the ones that didn't make a deep impression on me, and the rest emerged. The events are seen from a young child's innocent perspective. I returned to the child's state in my mind and somehow saw the events again in that way. The poetic metaphors simply came to me naturally. It was quite an innocent experience writing the book and truly healing in a deep way.

All my training, work, and publications had been in science when I wrote Little Green, and I had no clue about publishing literature. All the people who read the manuscript loved it. I sent it to a few places, but since the book was written in verse, the agents didn't know how to market it to the publishers. I started a writers' group at MIT with the help of the MIT Writing Center. The group read my manuscript, and a woman in the group became enthusiastic about getting the book published. She connected me to someone at Simon & Schuster who brought the manuscript to an editor, and she accepted it right away. It was a miracle.

Which poetic and narrative techniques did you decide to employ, and why?

As few words as possible. Less is more. Free verse. It felt natural for the story.

If there were places in the book where you felt it was best to emphasize the poetic strategies over the narrative strategies, or vice versa—what guided these decisions?

Simply intuition and what the story needed.

What poetic or narrative effects were you hoping to achieve?

I wanted to evoke the feeling that the readers were living these moments through the narrator, seeing the world through her eyes, and growing up with her.

What are your thoughts on the verse novel as a form?

I love it. I think it is a great way to distill our experience and share our stories with the world.

Have verse novels you have read been influential on this work in some way?

Yes, Homer's *Iliad* and *Odyssey*. Goethe's *Faust*. Also, Karen Hesse's *Out of the Dust*.
    The *Iliad* and *Odyssey* showed me that any stories can be written in verse and that's how human beings have told stories since ancient times. *Out of the Dust* demonstrated how a book in verse can be written from a child's point of view and be poetic and effective at the same time.

What have you learnt about writing verse novels from the verse novels you have read?

Any story can be told in verse. Poetry makes stories stronger and more unforgettable.

CHAPTER 27
LEZA LOWITZ

Leza Lowitz by Anna Hastings

I have read verse novels set in the past, present, and the future, and each is unique and wonderful.

Leza Lowitz is a multi-genre writer who has published over twenty books, many of them best-sellers. Her most recent books are a Young Adult novel in verse, *Up from the Sea*, published by Crown Books for Young Readers (Penguin Random House), and a memoir about adopting and adapting in Japan, *In Search of the Sun: One Woman's Quest to Find Family in Japan*. She has received the PEN Josephine Miles Award in Poetry, a PEN Syndicated Fiction Award, grants from the NEA, NEH, and California Arts Council, the Japan-US Friendship Commission Award for the translation of Japanese literature, the Barbara Deming Fiction Award, a Multicultural WOP Grant from SCBWI, and the 2014 APALA Award in Youth Literature from the American Librarian's Association. A graduate of U.C. Berkeley and San Francisco State University, she has taught writing and literature at San Francisco State University, Tokyo University, and Rikkyo University, and has been an invited speaker at literary festivals/schools in Bali, Japan, Hong Kong, New Zealand, Australia, the UAE, and the United States. Lowitz's nonfiction has appeared in the *New York Times*, *Yoga Journal*, the *Huffington Post*, *Shambhala Sun*, *Harpers*, and *Best Buddhist Writing*. In addition to writing, she currently runs a yoga studio (Sun and Moon Yoga, est. 2003) in Tokyo and teaches yoga and mindfulness worldwide.

Up from the Sea (2016)

What ideas or influences did you have in mind when creating this work?

I was living in Tokyo when the 9.1 magnitude earthquake struck on March 11, 2011. The quake was followed by a massive tsunami and devastating nuclear meltdown. I did not plan to write a novel about the triple disaster—and I certainly did not plan to write a verse novel. I had owned a yoga studio in Tokyo for the past twenty years, and Japan was my home. Many of our students were from the stricken area along the Northern coast. As we helplessly watched the disaster unfold on TV, we determined to try to help those in need. The yoga studio organized relief efforts and charity events, becoming the largest non-corporate donor. I wanted to do more. When it was safe, I visited the disaster area as a volunteer, offering massage and healing work. When I was in Tohoku, I met a boy who had lost family members in the tsunami. As we were leaving, he said: "Don't forget about us." These four words broke my heart.

Disasters are so often forgotten once they are out of the headlines. As days turned into weeks, I thought: "What can I do to help make sure these people are not forgotten?" Friends reminded me that I was a writer. They suggested I write about the people I had met, and how the tsunami had affected them. So, I began to think about the characters and story that would eventually become *Up from the Sea*, a novel about seventeen-year-old Kai, a half-Japanese, half-American teenage boy who loves soccer and creates a team to rally his town after the tsunami. Months later, I discovered that exactly this had been done! In the difficult days following the disaster, supporters from all over the world helped strangers in Japan in many moving ways. I started to collect these stories too.

I based the plot on the events of March 11, 2011, and their aftermath, as well as events surrounding the tenth anniversary of 9/11, but the story is fiction. I wanted to write this novel to keep a light shining on the ordinary and in many cases, extremely brave people whose lives were changed by the earthquake and tsunami to humanize it, to teach future generations what happened, and to record what I had witnessed. I hoped that by doing so, I could let the people there know they had not been forgotten.

How did you approach writing this verse novel? What were the various stages in its development?

It was a scary time, with many foreigners leaving Japan due to the hundreds of aftershocks (7.2 magnitude quakes in their own right) and great uncertainty about the nuclear meltdown. With a Japanese husband, son, and a business I had built over many years, I made the decision to stay. As an American living in Japan, I knew I had a unique perspective through which to tell this story, and I knew we were living through a defining moment in Japan's history. So, I forced myself to sit down and write. I began the novel as a conventional narrative, but so many frequent and strong aftershocks sent me diving under my desk for cover. I simply could not focus long enough to write more than a few lines at a time. Eventually, I surrendered, and began to write short pages of poetry. That is how *Up from the Sea* became a novel in verse.

Once the form was set, the first stage was to create a list of the characters and their dreams, desires, obstacles, and motivations. The second stage was to hash out the plot. The third stage was to do research. For me, this was the richest stage of the novel's development. During my research, I learned that a soccer ball belonging to a teenager in hard-hit Rikuzentakata had washed up in Alaska. Amazingly, the ball was found by a man with a Japanese wife, who could read the messages written on it and realized it must have come from the tsunami. What are the chances? The couple traced the owner and traveled to Japan to return the ball. I was very moved by this story and decided to weave it into the novel. My son plays soccer, so I had a lot of experience with the sport and the trials and tribulations of young players.

In June of 2011, I learned that four Japanese high school students who lost family members in the tsunami, and university students whose parents had perished in the 1995 Great Hanshin earthquake in Kobe, Japan, flew to New York to raise awareness and money for the children of Tohoku orphaned in the disaster. Two American students, one who had lost her father in 9/11 and another who had lost his mother in Hurricane Katrina, joined efforts organized by the Ashinaga—"Daddy Long Legs"—NGO.

I was deeply inspired by this story of survivors of tragedies in one country reaching out to survivors in another. So I decided to include this episode in the novel, having Kai go to New York on this trip, with the ulterior objective of searching for his estranged father—his only family member left. I took the liberty of imagining a meeting between children of 3/11 and children of 9/11 culminating in a visit to the National September 11 Memorial on the tenth anniversary of 9/11. I had not planned to link 3/11 to 9/11 but these true stories gave me a basis to do so, and my novel took on a different shape than being a story set only in Japan. Other events, such as the formation of the soccer team in Onagawa, I learned about after I had already created a similar plot point in my novel. I felt I was on the right path.

The fourth stage was to write a first draft. The fifth stage was to edit that draft, many times. The sixth stage was to get this draft in good enough shape to send to my agent, Kelly Falconer of the Asia Literary Agency. The seventh stage was to incorporate her edits into the manuscript. The eighth stage, after we secured a publisher (Crown Books for Young Readers), was to go through many rounds of edits with my wonderful editor, the legendary Phoebe Yeh. The final stages were proofreading and checking the book after it had been laid out. The entire process took around three years.

Can you recall problem-solving decisions you had to make in the writing process?

There were many problems to tackle in the writing of this novel, but the main one was language. Since the novel is set mostly in Japan, there were many cultural references and Japanese words and phrases in the initial drafts. At each stage of the editing, I had to decide which words to keep and which to delete. Then I had to determine how and where to define them. We ended up leaving only the Japanese words my editor and I felt were essential to convey meaning, important cultural aspects, and local history/atmosphere of the story, putting short notes on the pages where these Japanese words appeared.

Which poetic and narrative techniques did you decide to employ, and why?

I wrote in free verse, and the novel is one long poem rather than shorter poems, or one poem per chapter. To me, this continuous style reflected the intensity and drama of the actions, and the wave-like fluctuations of emotion over the course of Kai's journey. Whenever I could, I tried to used onomatopoeia and graphic layouts on the page to echo the fear and panic the people experienced in the moment the tsunami hit. I felt this form best conveyed the emotional intensity of the trauma in the aftermath as well. I played with word placement on the page to best reflect the tone and pace of the events my characters were experiencing as they were unfolding, without overdoing it or being gimmicky. I would have liked to have had even fewer words on the page/more empty space, but then the book would have been around 400 pages and of course an author must respect a publisher's parameters.

If there were places in the book where you felt it was best to emphasize the poetic strategies over the narrative strategies, or vice versa—what guided these decisions?

I tried to balance both. Because I wove in the stories of many characters over the course of the tsunami and its aftermath, it was important to have narrative cohesion. But there were times when I made bolder choices with the poetic strategy, like repeating the words "big black dirt" in capital letters twenty times in a block of text on the page to symbolize the mass and enormity of the thick, oily muddy black water that swept through the town.

What poetic or narrative effects were you hoping to achieve?

The narrative arc of my story is a classic coming-of-age quest, a survival story. Through the verse and poetic imagery, I hoped to capture the sense of tension, emotion, chaos, and life or death choices people make in a disaster with a kind of cinematic realism.

After visiting the stricken area and meeting the people who had survived the tsunami, this pulled-from-the-headline story became very real to me. I felt I had to try to do something for those people who had trusted me with their stories. I found the real-life incidents of people helping each other incredibly inspirational—and motivating. Kai and his friends became real to me, almost like he was my own son and his friends. I wanted this disaster to become real for the reader, too.

Through verse, I could pare down the emotion and magnify it for the reader. I wanted the characters to be human, imperfect, struggling. I wanted the reader to really see them, and to care. Verse allowed me to do this in the same way that poetry tugs at the heartstrings—by homing in on emotion. Less was more.

It was my hope that by telling the story of one kid whose life was forever changed by the disaster but was even more changed by the kindness of strangers, I could help keep a light shining on Tohoku. I also wanted kids to know that one person truly can make a difference. We can help one another, even across vast oceans.

It has been rewarding to visit schools and community groups all over the world to talk about the disaster and to see people moved to take action to help, even though many years have passed. Through this novel, we have helped reconstruction efforts in Tohoku by building a community library, reconstructing an ancient shrine, building a bell tower, bus shelter, playground, providing fisherwoman uniforms, musical instruments, and more. A group of students from Kazakhstan read *Up from the Sea* and decided to help build trees along the coast with The Great Forest Wall NGO as a kind of natural sea wall to slow a tsunami should one hit in the future. This is the kind of effect a writer can only dream their work might have.

What are your thoughts on the verse novel as a form?

I wrote *Up from the Sea* in verse (rather than straight narrative) because the verse form lent immediacy to the events, and many young readers (some with short attention spans) have found this form to be engaging. Over the years, many "reluctant reader" kids or children with learning differences have come up to me and said that this was the first novel they had finished reading. Now they had more confidence to read novels. Kids who had previously "hated poetry" said they wanted to read more poetry now. At one visit, a young boy raised his hand and asked me a question. He said: "How did you feel when you were writing this novel?" I told him it was a great question, and that I had been very emotional when writing this book, and hoped the reader could feel that emotion. He gave me a "thumbs up" sign and smiled. When the auditorium cleared, his teacher came up to me with tears in her eyes. She said the boy was autistic and had never said a word in any assembly before.

I attribute these incidents to the power of the verse novel to engage readers and get to the heart of a story. Verse novels, with each word carefully chosen, can touch readers on a deep and sometimes mysterious level. I think it is a very primal, powerful, and important form, especially meaningful to teenagers and young adults.

Have verse novels you have read been influential on this work in some way?

Years ago, I wrote my master's degree in part on Elizabeth Barrett Browning's *Aurora Leigh*, a nineteenth-century novel written in blank verse. Ever since then, I had been interested in the form, but never imagined I would write a verse novel myself. Then my friend Holly Thompson, Co-Regional Advisor of the Society of Children's Book Writers and Illustrators (SCBWI) Japan chapter, published a Young Adult verse novel called *Orchards*, which is partly set in Japan. It was beautifully written and inspired me to learn more about the form. Through SCBWI, I learned about this growing trend in YA literature. Necessity being the mother of invention, I ended up writing a verse novel because of severe aftershocks, which limited my ability to focus for longer lengths of time. Had I not been introduced to so many great modern and contemporary YA novels, I would not have even attempted to do that.

What have you learnt about writing verse novels from the verse novels you have read?

I have learned that there is no "right way" or "one way" to write a verse novel. I have also learned that a verse novel is

not
a
novel in prose
with
line
breaks,

although some authors seem to think it is. There are so many different approaches to writing a verse novel, in many styles and voices. I have read verse novels set in the past, present, and the future, and each is unique and wonderful. I have learned that verse novels strike a chord with young readers, especially reluctant readers, and readers with learning differences, in a very special way. I am looking forward to reading what the next generation of verse writers creates.

CHAPTER 28
HELEN FROST

Helen Frost by Tim Andersen

*... the poetry allows the narrative to breathe and flow, and
the narrative gives a dramatic heft to the poetry.*

Helen Frost is the author of two collections of poetry, eleven novels-in-poems, eight nature-themed picture books, and a book about teaching writing. Each of her novels-in-poems has received one or more honors. Among them: a Michael L. Printz honor for *Keesha's House* (2003), the Lee Bennett Hopkins Award and the Michigan Mitten Award for *Diamond Willow* (2008), the William Allen White award for *Hidden* (2011), the New York Historical Society Children's History Book Prize for *Salt* (2013), a National Endowment for the Arts Poetry Fellowship, based on *The Braid* (2006), and, for *All He Knew* (2020), the 2021 Scott O'Dell Award for Historical Fiction. Helen lives in Fort Wayne, Indiana.

Keesha's House (2003)
The Braid (2006)
Diamond Willow (2008)
Crossing Stones (2009)
All He Knew (2020)

What ideas or influences did you have in mind when creating this work?

Long before I began the novel that became *All He Knew* I had been thinking about two possible books I might write:

First, the story of my husband's uncle, born in 1904, who was deaf, misdiagnosed as "unteachable," and spent his entire life in an institution, and of the sister who loved him—I was lucky enough to know her as my mother-in-law, and to encourage her in writing poems about her brother.

Second, a biography of William Stafford for young readers. Stafford was a Second World War Conscientious Objector (CO) who later became a wise and beloved poet and teacher. His memoir about his CO service in Civilian Public Service camps is informative and insightful.

After much thought, many conversations, and considerable research, I became interested in the fact that many COs had been assigned work in institutions and were instrumental in bringing about change. At that point, these two ideas came together, evolving as they merged. The original thoughts and ideas took root and grew into the novel, quite different from either initial idea.

How did you approach writing this verse novel? What were the various stages in its development?

I began with handwritten notes in a journal I use to record early thoughts and initial drafts before I know which ideas will ultimately lead to a substantial project. I experimented with different voices, points of view, and verb tenses before settling on present tense, with dates to define movement through time, and multiple points of view, written in third person. Most of my previous books have been told in first-person narrative poems, so this was something new for me.

Initially, I thought the story would be focused on the friendship between Victor and Molly, but it quickly became clear that Henry was the star.

Thorough research for this book was important and demanding. I needed to learn more about the history of d/Deaf education, the history of conscientious objectors, the economic effects of the Second World War on the people at home (especially people living in poverty), life in institutions in the early 40s and beyond, and many other questions that came up as I wrote the book. I have access to several good libraries, and I have friends and relatives who are knowledgeable about different aspects of the story, so I was able to find much information in books, and then talk with people who were willing to share first-hand knowledge.

I wanted to be sure that no children would feel insulted or hurt by anything I wrote, and I was concerned about the depiction of the children in the institution—other than the three whose stories are highlighted (Henry, the main character, and his two friends, Ted/Ned, and Billy/Buddy). I asked parents of children with developmental and intellectual disabilities to read the manuscript in progress and was appreciative of the advice and encouragement they offered.

An important stage in any story involving characters who are in some significant way unlike the author, is a careful and honest reading by a trusted person who has first-hand understanding of the character's specific situation. For *All He Knew*, I was exceptionally lucky to reestablish an old friendship with Willy Conley, a Deaf author, teacher, and photographer, who read the book several times, with careful attention to my depiction of Henry's deafness and with thoughtful attention to how the book would be received by the Deaf community. (As noted in the book, deaf with a lowercase "d" refers to the audiological condition of not hearing; when capitalized Deaf indicates a particular group of deaf people who share a culture and a language—American Sign Language or another signed language.)

Through many drafts, with feedback from a supportive primary editor (Janine O'Malley at FSG), and then from others on the editorial team, *All He Knew* found its form and the story took shape.

Can you recall problem-solving decisions you had to make in the writing process?

Yes, there were many. I'll mention two.

Initially I had imagined Henry as non-speaking, in part because my husband's uncle did not speak; Willy Conley's advice was to give Henry the ability to speak, which would be realistic, since he'd had language before becoming deaf, and would give Henry more agency. Through important conversations with Willy, I came to see that that it could be empowering for Henry to choose when and to whom he would speak. That change led to some of my favorite scenes and to the character of Sadie—I enjoyed writing about the birthday party where she breaks a window with her strong throwing arm.

It was challenging to decide how much of the horror of life in the institution to depict. For example, I chose to delete a sentence describing what Victor does not do to the boys (implying that these things had happened previously): "He hasn't wrapped a wet towel/around anybody's neck/and pulled the ends/until the boy gets quiet." This was something I had learned that attendants would do because the wet towel did not leave a mark. As I kept polishing the manuscript, this detail continued to horrify me in such a way that I ultimately decided to shield my readers from it.

Which poetic and narrative techniques did you decide to employ, and why?

Much of the book is told in lightly structured poems, varied in their appearance on the page and in their metrical language. This worked well in poems from Henry and Molly's point of view, giving their voices room to change and grow. The poems involving Victor's part of the story worked well in a tighter format. The sonnet structure helped me portray his decision to become a conscientious objector and the consequences of that decision, and later, his and Molly's evolving friendship, distinguishing this part of the story from Henry's part of the story, without overshadowing it.

As for narrative techniques, there was something that wasn't a conscious decision on my part, but after publication a reviewer made me aware of it. The reviewer noted, "Determined sister Molly is a splendid reader surrogate as she keeps faith with her brother and jumps at the chance to find a way to bring him home." I can see how this is true: readers will be furious as they learn what happens to Henry and his friends, and Molly expresses that outrage, first about Henry and then about all the children in the institution.

If there were places in the book where you felt it was best to emphasize the poetic strategies over the narrative strategies, or vice versa—what guided these decisions?

More than a decision, or series of decisions, the poetic elements came about through experimentation and re-writing, which in turn helped the narrative evolve in an organic way.

What poetic or narrative effects were you hoping to achieve?

In *All He Knew*, as in all eleven of my novels-in-poems, the poetry and narrative elements are interwoven in a way that allows me to tell a compelling story through a series of poems.

One narrative element is the connection through different books I've written over the past fifteen years or so. It's not exactly a sequence (as in "sequels") but several generations of a family are depicted in four of my books. In *The Braid*, I introduce Jeannie and Sarah, two sisters who live on an island in the Scottish Hebrides in 1852. Jeannie travels to Canada, and from there different generations of the family appear: in *Crossing Stones* (1917), *All He Knew* (1933–45), and *Diamond Willow* (contemporary when it was written in the early 2000s). The connections are subtly expressed, but interesting to tease out—at least they are interesting for me as a writer, and readers have often expressed interest in this aspect of my work once they realize it is there to be found.

As for poetic elements, I'm fascinated by the intricacies of what language can do. In *The Braid*, I created a form so complex that it still amazes me that it worked (last words of the lines in one poem "braided" with the first words of the lines in the next; the number of syllables in each line matched with the age of the character at the time she is speaking—and that is just part of it). In *Diamond Willow*, I embedded an inner message at the heart of each diamond-shaped poem. In *Crossing Stones*, I used a cupped-hand sonnet form, with a rhyme scheme reaching from one poem to another. All these poetic elements are integral to the story and require both the scope of a novel and the precision that poetry allows and demands.

In *All He Knew*, I employed a mix of lightly structured poems and sonnets written in a strict form, hoping that this keeps the story moving, at the same time it engages the emotions of the reader.

What are your thoughts on the verse novel as a form?

When it is done well, the poetry allows the narrative to breathe and flow, and the narrative gives a dramatic heft to the poetry. I often hear from readers that they didn't like poetry before reading my books (other writers have reported similar comments). Sometimes, the white space surrounding the words on the page is attractive to young readers who have felt daunted by long novels with lots of words. Once they are engaged with the story, readers may come to appreciate the poetry and seek out more of it. Equally important, I often hear from teachers that reluctant readers who have come to love verse novels, mine, and others, go on to enjoy all kinds of books.

Have verse novels you have read been influential on this work in some way?

When Karen Hesse won the Newbery for *Out of the Dust* in 1998, it encouraged many authors to consider what we could do with this form. She wasn't the first, but that book was ground-breaking, and in the years since, poetry/verse has helped many poet-novelists discover and tell their stories.

I don't know how many verse novels I have read—well over one hundred, I'm sure. I have a few friends whose work I follow closely, and we all continue to learn from one another. A few examples: Marilyn Nelson's astounding crown of sonnets in *A Wreath for Emmett Till*; Nikki Grimes use of the Golden Shovel form in *One Last Word* and *Legacy*; each of Margarita Engle's historical novels in verse, as well as her memoirs; other verse memoirs by Marilyn Nelson, Nikki Grimes, Laurie Halse Anderson, Jacqueline Woodson; Allan Wolf's skill in using multi-voiced narratives to explore challenging historical subjects; Ron Koertge's ability to combine humor with serious issues, as in *Coaltown Jesus*; the use of poetry to tell a hard, hard story in *My Book of Life by Angel*, by Martine Leavitt; Jeannine Atkins' skill in nonfiction verse narratives; Thanhhà Lại, Mariko Nagai, Carole Boston Weatherford and Melanie Crowder's ability to bring history to life through narrative poetry; Angela Johnson and Naomi Shihab Nye whose beautiful writing blurs the boundary between poetry and prose; Padma Venkatraman, Skila Brown, Elizabeth Acevedo, Sonya Sones, Kwame Alexander, K. A. Holt—to name just a few more of the authors whose work I admire and who have influenced and encouraged me through the years. Engaging with one another's work keeps pushing the form and helping us discover new possibilities. I'm grateful each time one of my books enters the ongoing conversation and delighted to see a new generation of poet-novelists emerging in recent years.

What have you learnt about writing verse novels from the verse novels you have read?

My early training as a writer was primarily in poetry, and my first verse novel, *Keesha's House*, began as a series of poems in the voices of teens. As I was finishing it, I thought, "Oh, I wrote a novel." I'm not sure I could have done it if I'd started out with the intention of writing a novel, because that had seemed so daunting. As I wrote more novels in poems, I continued to read lots of poetry and lots of novels, as well as novels in poems. I had a wonderful editor, Frances Foster, who edited prose novels as well as novels in poems, and she sometimes recommended books for me to read—she never said so, but looking back, I wonder if those recommendations were her way of helping me learn things I needed to know about novel writing. She often said she would defer to me in questions of poetry, but she was gracious in so many ways, and I suspect she knew more about poetry than she claimed. She had an ear for the music of language and an eye for the perfect image.

One thing above all has become beautifully clear: My voice, and my characters' voices, are part of a worldwide chorus. I am grateful to be a part of it.

NOTES

Preface

1. United Nations Office of the High Commissioner Human Rights, *Born Free and Equal: Sexual Orientation and Gender Identity in International Human Rights Law* (New York: OHCHR, 2019), https://www.ohchr.org/sites/default/files/Documents/Publications/Born_Free_and_Equal_WEB.pdf.

2. "Our Mission," The BIPOC Project, accessed December 14, 2023, https://www.thebipocproject.org/.

3. "Tribal Nations & the United States: An Introduction," National Congress of American Indians NCAI, accessed December 14, 2023, https://archive.ncai.org/about-tribes.

4. "A Guide to Race and Ethnicity Terminology and Language," The UK Law Society, last updated November 28, 2023, https://www.lawsociety.org.uk/topics/ethnic-minority-lawyers/a-guide-to-race-and-ethnicity-terminology-and-language.

5. National Education Union, *Framework for Developing an Anti-racist Approach* (London: National Education Union, 2023), https://neu.org.uk/anti-racism-charter.

6. "A Guide to Race and Ethnicity Terminology and Language."

7. National Education Union, *Framework for Developing an Anti-racist Approach*.

Introduction

Reflecting Realities

1. "About Us," Spread the Word, n.d., accessed December 14, 2023, https://www.spreadtheword.org.uk/about-us/.

2. Centre for Literacy in Primary Education, *Reflecting Realities: Survey of Ethnic Representation within UK Children's Literature 2022* (London: Centre for Literacy in Primary Education, 2023), https://clpe.org.uk/research/clpe-reflecting-realities-survey-ethnic-representation-within-uk-childrens-literature-1.

3. Centre for Literacy in Primary Education, *Reflecting Realities: Survey of Ethnic Representation within UK Children's Literature* 2017–2021 (London: Centre for Literacy in Primary Education, 2022), https://clpe.org.uk/research/clpe-reflecting-realities-survey-ethnic-representation-within-uk-childrens-literature-2017.

4. Sarah Jilani, "In the Far from Diverse Publishing Industry, Sensitivity Readers Are Vital," *The Conversation*, Australian Edition, February 20, 2023, https://theconversation.com/in-the-far-from-diverse-publishing-industry-sensitivity-readers-are-vital-199913#:~:text=Sensitivity%20readers%20are%20contracted%20by,about%20people%20from%20marginalised%20groups.

5. Natalie Kon-yu and Emily Booth, "Research Confirms Lack of Cultural Diversity in Published Literature," Victoria University, published Thursday, October 13, 2022, https://

www.vu.edu.au/about-vu/news-events/news/research-confirms-lack-of-cultural-diversity-in-published-literature.

6. Natalie Kon-yu and Emily Booth, *First Nations and People of Colour Count* (*FNPOC Count*): *First Large-Scale Numerical Dataset That Illustrated the Inequity in Australia's Publishing Industry* (Melbourne: Victoria University, 2022), https://content.vu.edu.au/sites/default/files/media/first-nations-and-people-of-colour-count-infographic.pdf.

7. Tom Holman, "Room for Improvement," in *In Full Colour: Cultural Diversity in Publishing Today,* ed. Danuta Kean (London: The Bookseller, 2004), 4–6, https://content.yudu.com/web/1vcls/0A1xp12/InFullColour2004/html/index.html?page=4&origin=reader.

8. Publishers Association, *UK Publishing Workforce 2020: Diversity, Inclusion and Belonging* (London: Publishers Association, 2021), 3, https://www.publishers.org.uk/wp-content/uploads/2021/01/The-UK-Publishing-Workforce-Diversity-Inclusion-and-Belonging-in-2020.pdf.

9. Publishers Association, UK *Publishing Workforce 2022: Diversity, Inclusion and Belonging* (London: Publishers Association, 2023), 3, https://www.publishers.org.uk/wp-content/uploads/2023/01/The-UK-Publishing-Workforce-Diversity-Inclusion-and-Belonging-in-2022.pdf.

10. Publishers Association, *Industry-Wide Statement on the Book & Publishing Industry's Professional Values* (London: Publishers Association, 2023), https://www.publishers.org.uk/publications/an-industry-wide-statement-on-the-book-publishing-industrys-professional-values/.

11. "About Us," Pride in Publishing, accessed December 19, 2023, https://prideinpublishing.co.uk/about-us/.

12. "Lee & Low Books, Where Is the Diversity in Publishing? The 2015 Diversity Baseline Survey Results," *The Open Book Blog. A Blog on Race, Diversity, Education, and Children's Books*, published January 26, 2016, https://blog.leeandlow.com/2016/01/26/where-is-the-diversity-in-publishing-the-2015-diversity-baseline-survey-results/.

13. "Lee & Low Books, Where Is the Diversity in Publishing? The 2019 Diversity Baseline Survey Results," *The Open Book Blog. A Blog on Race, Diversity, Education, and Children's Books*, published January 28, 2020, https://blog.leeandlow.com/2020/01/28/2019diversitybaselinesurvey/.

14. "Lee & Low Books, Where Is the Diversity in Publishing? The 2023 Diversity Baseline Survey Results," *The Open Book Blog. A Blog on Race, Diversity, Education, and Children's Books*, published February 28, 2024, https://blog.leeandlow.com/2024/02/28/2023diversitybaselinesurvey/.

15. Lee & Low Books, "Where Is the Diversity in Publishing? The 2023 Diversity Baseline Survey Results."

16. Lee & Low Books, "Where Is the Diversity in Publishing? The 2023 Diversity Baseline Survey Results."

17. Melanie Ramdarshan Bold, *Representation of People of Colour among Children's Book Creators in the UK* (Leeds: BookTrust, 2022), 11–21, https://www.booktrust.org.uk/globalassets/resources/booktrust-represents/2022/research-reports/booktrust-represents-representation-of-people-of-colour-among-childrens-book-creators-in-the-uk.pdf.

18. Anamik Saha and Sandra van Lente, *Re:Thinking "Diversity" in Publishing* (London: Goldsmiths Press, 2020), 1–44, https://www.spreadtheword.org.uk/wp-content/uploads/2020/06/Rethinking_diversity_in_publishing_WEB.pdf.

19. Anamik Saha, *Re:Thinking "Diversity" in Publishing* (2020), Report Launch, Vimeo, zoom recording June 23, 2020, 4:28–4:52, https://vimeo.com/433566386?embedded=true&source=vimeo_logo&owner=56579006.

20. Diversity Arts Australia, BYP Group and Western Sydney University, *Shifting the Balance: Cultural Diversity in Leadership within the Australian Arts, Screen and Creative Sectors* (Sydney: Diversity Arts Australia, 2019), 2, https://diversityarts.org.au/app/uploads/Shifting-the-Balance-DARTS-small.pdf.

21. Australian Human Rights Commission, *Leading for Change: A Blueprint for Cultural Diversity and Inclusive Leadership Revisited* (Sydney: Australian Human Rights Commission, 2018), https://humanrights.gov.au/sites/default/files/document/publication/Leading%20 for%20Change_Blueprint2018_FINAL_Web.pdf.

22. Diversity Arts Australia, BYP Group and Western Sydney University, *Shifting the Balance*, 2.

23. "About Us," Australian Publishers Association, 2023, https://www.publishers.asn.au/Web/ Web/About-Us/About.aspx?hkey=e6b11061-eef8-44ae-baf5-562ec6e0bed0.

24. "About Us," Australian Publishers Association.

25. Radhiah Chowdhury, *It's Hard to Be What You Can't See: Diversity within Australian Publishing Lessons in Diverse and Inclusive Publishing from the United Kingdom*, The 2019–20 Beatrice Davis Editorial Fellowship Report (Sydney: Australian Publishers Association, 2020), https://www.publishers.asn.au/common/Uploaded%20files/APA%20Resources/ Research/BDEF/BDEF%202019-2020%20Report%20-%20Radhiah%20Chowdhury.pdf.

26. Susannah Bowen and Beth Driscoll, *The Australian Publishing Industry Workforce Survey on Diversity and Inclusion* (Sydney: Australian Publishers Association and The University of Melbourne, 2022), https://publishers.asn.au/Web/Web/Member-Resources/ ResearchReports/Workforce_Survey_2022.aspx.

27. "Workforce D&I Survey Results Published," Australian Publishing Association, published August 31, 2022, https://publishers.asn.au/Web/Web/Latest/APANews/20220831- Workforce-Diversity-Inclusion-Survey-results.aspx.

28. "Banned in the USA: Rising School Book Bans Threaten Free Expression and Students' First Amendment Rights," PEN America, published April 2022, https://pen.org/banned-in-the-usa/#what.

29. "PEN America's Index of School Book Bans" (July 1, 2021–June 30, 2022), PEN America, https://docs.google.com/spreadsheets/d/1hTs_PB7KuTMBtNMESFEGuK-0abzhNxVv4tgpI5-iKe8/edit#gid=1171606318.

30. Jonathan Friedman and Nadine Farid Johnson, "Banned in the USA: The Growing Movement to Censor Books in Schools," PEN America, published September 19, 2023, https://pen.org/report/banned-usa-growing-movement-to-censor-books-in-schools/.

31. "PEN America's Index of School Book Bans" (July 1, 2021–June 30, 2022).

32. American Library Association, *The State of America's Libraries 2023: A Report from the American Library Association* (Chicago, IL: American Library Association, 2023), https:// www.ala.org/news/sites/ala.org.news/files/content/state-of-americas-libraries-report-2023-web-version.pdf.

33. "American Library Association Reports Record Number of Demands to Censor Library Books and Materials in 2022," American Library Association, published March 22, 2023, http://www.ala.org/news/press-releases/2023/03/record-book-bans-2022.

34. "American Library Association Reports Record Number of Demands to Censor Library Books and Materials in 2022."

35. Deborah Caldwell-Stone, "2022: A Year of Unprecedented Challenges," in *The State of America's Libraries 2023: A Report from the American Library Association* (Chicago, IL: American Library Association, 2023), 4, https://www.ala.org/news/sites/ala.org.news/files/ content/state-of-americas-libraries-report-2023-web-version.pdf.

36. "Essential Voices Classroom Libraries Grades K-12," Perfection Learning, 2024, https://www.perfectionlearning.com/elementary/elementary-class-libr/essential-voices.html.

37. Debbie Reese, "Banning of Native Voices/Books," American Indians in Children's Literature 2006–23, Last updated October 16, 2023, https://americanindiansinchildrensliterature.blogspot.com/p/banning-of-native-voicesbooks.html.

38. "PEN America's Index of School Book Bans," (July 1, 2021–June 30, 2022).

39. "Letter to Duval County, FL Schools from PEN America and We Need Diverse Books—Signed by 70 Authors—Calls for Return of 176 Book Titles Pulled from Classroom Libraries," PEN America, December 6, 2022, https://pen.org/press-release/letter-to-duval-county-fl-schools-from-pen-america-and-we-need-diverse-books-signed-by-69-authors-calls-for-return-of-176-book-titles-pulled-from-classroom-libraries/.

40. Caldwell-Stone, "2022," 4.

41. Tracie D. Hall, "From the Executive Director," in *The State of America's Libraries 2023: A Report from the American Library Association* (Chicago, IL: American Library Association, 2023), 2. https://www.ala.org/sites/default/files/news/content/state-of-americas-libraries-report-2023-web-version.pdf.

42. Hall, "From the Executive Director," 2.

43. Congress.gov., "Text—H.R.2889–118th Congress (2023–2024): Right to Read Act of 2023," April 26, 2023, https://www.congress.gov/bill/118th-congress/house-bill/2889?s=1&r=1&q=%7B%22search%22%3A%222889%22%7D.

44. Alaa Elassar, Taylor Romine and Andy Rose, CNN, "Judge Orders Books Removed from Texas Public Libraries Due to LGBTQ and Racial Content Must Be Returned within 24 Hours," *CNN*, Published 12:09 PM EDT, Saturday, April 1, 2023, https://edition.cnn.com/2023/04/01/us/texas-book-ban-removed-library-replaced-judge/index.html.

45. Peter Hancock, Capitol News Illinois, "Bill Blocking Libraries from State Funding if They Ban Books Clears General Assembly," *Chicago ABC7*, State Politics, Thursday, May 4, 2023, 1:5 p.m., https://abc7chicago.com/book-bans-illinois-library-funding-politics/13210227/.

46. The United States District Court for the Northern District of Florida Pensacola Division Case No. 3:23-cv-10385 Pen American Center, Inc., Sarah Brannen, Lindsay Durtschi, on behalf of herself and her minor children, George M. Johnson, David Levithan, Kyle Lukoff, Ann Novakowski, on behalf of herself and her minor child, Penguin Random House LLC, and Ashley Hope Pérez, Plaintiffs, v. Escambia County School District, and the Escambia County School Board, Defendants, https://pen.org/wp-content/uploads/2023/05/1-Complaint.pdf.

Shifting Reception

47. Shannon Maughan, "Trend Watch with Middle Grade Dealmakers," *Publishers Weekly*, September 9, 2022, https://www.publishersweekly.com/pw/by-topic/childrens/childrens-industry-news/article/90276-trend-watch-with-middle-grade-dealmakers.html.

48. Maughan, "Trend Watch."

49. Maughan, "Trend Watch."

50. Maughan, "Trend Watch."

51. "Revising Your Novel in Verse: An Online Course," Presenter Cordelia Jensen, special guest Amber McBride, Highlights Foundation, October 4, 2023–November 15, 2023, https://www.highlightsfoundation.org/workshop/revising-your-novel-in-verse-an-online-course/.

52. "A Strong Start: The First 20 Pages of Your Novel in Verse," Presenter Cordelia Jensen, special guest Andrea Beatriz Arango, Highlights Foundation, February 7, 2024–March 7, 2024, https://www.highlightsfoundation.org/workshop/a-strong-start-the-first-20-pages-of-your-novel-in-verse/.

53. "Novels in Verse Resources from Our Blog," Highlights Foundation, accessed January 6, 2024, https://www.highlightsfoundation.org/topics/novels-in-verse/.

54. "Crafting Novels in Verse: Workshop and Retreat," Presenters Rajani LaRocca and Chris Baron, with special guest Cordelia Jensen, Highlights Foundation, May 21, 2023–May 24, 2023, https://www.highlightsfoundation.org/workshop/crafting-novels-in-verse-workshop-and-retreat/.

55. "Diverse Verse Scholarship," Highlights Foundation, accessed January 6, 2024, https://www.highlightsfoundation.org/diverse-verse-scholarship/.

56. "Writing Poetry to Empower: A Two-Night Mini," Presenters Padma Venkatraman and Aida Salazar, Highlights Foundation, December 11, 2023–December 13, 2023, https://www.highlightsfoundation.org/workshop/writing-poetry-to-empower-a-two-night-mini./.

57. "The Australian Verse Novels Resource for Younger Readers and Young Adult Readers NCACL Verse Novels Resource Flyer 2021," The National Centre for Australian Children's Literature Inc., ncacl.org.au 2023, https://www.ncacl.org.au/wp-content/uploads/2021/10/NCACL-Verse-Novels-Resource-Flyer-20211001-v1-r1-A4.pdf, https://www.ncacl.org.au/resources/bibliographies/australian-verse-novels-resource/.

58. "The NCACL Aboriginal and or Torres Strait Islander Resource," The National Centre for Australian Children's Literature Inc., 2023, https://www.ncacl.org.au/resources/databases/welcome-to-the-aboriginal-and-or-torres-strait-islander-resource/.

59. "The NCACL Cultural Diversity Database," The National Centre for Australian Children's Literature Inc., 2023, https://www.ncacl.org.au/resources/databases/welcome-to-the-ncacl-cultural-diversity-database/.

60. "About the Award," The Yoto Carnegies, 2023, https://yotocarnegies.co.uk/about-the-awards/.

61. Nielsen Book Research Australia, https://www.nielsenbookdataonline.com/bdol/index.jsp;jsessionid=WeMLnjwnZOBNiN0xrcaXf7H0.

62. "Medal for Writing Winners," The Yoto Carnegies, accessed January 6, 2024, https://yotocarnegies.co.uk/archive/writing-winners/.

63. Sarah Crossan, "Top 10 Verse Novels," *The Guardian*, September 30, 2020, https://www.theguardian.com/books/2020/sep/30/top-10-verse-novels-sarah-crossan-homer-kae-tempest.

64. Charlotte Hacking, "Ten of the Best: Verse Novels," Books for Keeps, BfK 256, September 15, 2022, https://booksforkeeps.co.uk/article/ten-of-the-best-verse-novels/.

65. Kat Sarfas, "The Best Novels in Verse to Read Right Now—B&N Reads," Barnes & Noble, March 31, 2021, https://www.barnesandnoble.com/blog/the-best-novels-in-verse-to-read-right-now/.

66. Michael Symmons Roberts, "Michael Symmons Roberts's Top 10 Verse Novels," *The Guardian*, March 20, 2006, https://www.theguardian.com/books/2006/mar/20/top10s.verse.novels.

67. Melissa Thom, "The Joy of Novels in Verse," with Kari Anne Holt, Rajani LaRocca, Reem Faruqi, and Chris Baron, Episodes 10–13, April 2023, in *The Joyful Learning Podcast*, produced by Melissa Thom, https://podcasts.apple.com/us/podcast/the-joyful-learning-podcast/id1637178531.

68. *Run, Rebel*, adapted by Manjeet Mann, creator, dir. by Tessa Walker. Pilot Theatre, Co-production with Mercury Theatre Colchester, Belgrade Theatre Coventry, Derby

Theatre, and York Theatre Royal, touring March–April 2023, https://www.pilot-theatre.com/production/run-rebel/.

69. *The Crossover,* 2023 television series, April 5, *IMDb,* U.S.A. https://www.imdb.com/title/tt14296996/.

70. Rae White, "Story/Verse," with Pip Harry, Kirli Saunders, Rebecca Jessen, Zana Fraillon, Wednesday, April 12, 2023, in Queensland Poetry Festival, YouTube, hosted by Rae White, 1:01:42, https://www.youtube.com/live/LsD5fyrcxMM.

Negotiations in Verse Novel Poetics

71. Kirli Saunders, "Chapter 2 Kirli Saunders," in *DiVERSE: Conversations with YA and Children's Verse Novelists,* ed. Linda Weste (London: Bloomsbury, 2024), 23.

72. Mariko Nagai, "Chapter 14 Mariko Nagai," in *DiVERSE: Conversations with YA and Children's Verse Novelists,* ed. Linda Weste (London: Bloomsbury, 2024), 84.

73. Ishle Yi Park, "Chapter 15 Ishle Yi Park," in *DiVERSE: Conversations with YA and Children's Verse Novelists,* ed. Linda Weste (London: Bloomsbury, 2024), 91.

74. Holly Thompson, "Chapter 23 Holly Thompson," in *DiVERSE: Conversations with YA and Children's Verse Novelists,* ed. Linda Weste (London: Bloomsbury, 2024), 137.

Widening the Lens of Representation

75. Dean Atta, "Chapter 11 Dean Atta," in *DiVERSE: Conversations with YA and Children's Verse Novelists,* ed. Linda Weste (London: Bloomsbury, 2024), 64.

76. Dean Atta, "I'm Writing the Stories I Need to Write: A Conversation with Dean Atta," *bigblackbooks* 2021–2024, n.d., Produced by Jane Link, https://www.bigblackbooks.org/dean-atta/.

77. "The IoS Pink List 2012," *Independent.co.uk.* November 4, 2012.

78. Kaija Langley, email correspondence with editor, September 19, 2023.

79. Langley, email.

80. Stephanie Hemphill, email correspondence with editor, October 30, 2023.

81. Hemphill, email.

82. Melanie Crowder, "Chapter 7 Melanie Crowder," in *DiVERSE: Conversations with YA and Children's Verse Novelists,* ed. Linda Weste (London: Bloomsbury, 2024), 44.

83. Margarita Engle, "Chapter 1 Margarita Engle," in *DiVERSE: Conversations with YA and Children's Verse Novelists,* ed. Linda Weste (London: Bloomsbury, 2024), 20.

84. Verse novels noted in earlier years of the Rise Feminist Book Project List, or on its former Amelia Bloomer List 2002–19, though not featured in this volume, are Tammi Charles's *Muted,* Mahogany L. Browne's *Chlorine Sky,* Elizabeth Acevedo's *The Poet X* and *Clap When You Land,* Candice Iloh's *Every Body Looking,* Joy McCullough's *Blood, Water, Paint, This Impossible Light* by Lily Myers, Andrea Davis Pinkney's *The Red Pencil,* Caroline Starr Rose's *May B.: A Novel,* and Margarita Engle's verse memoir, *The Firefly Letters: A Suffragette's Journey to Cuba.*

Linguistic Diversity in the Genre

85. Leza Lowitz, "Chapter 27 Leza Lowitz," in *DiVERSE: Conversations with YA and Children's Verse Novelists,* ed. Linda Weste (London: Bloomsbury, 2024), 158.

86. Thanhhà Lại, "Chapter 10 Thanhhà Lại," in *DiVERSE: Conversations with YA and Children's Verse Novelists*, ed. Linda Weste (London: Bloomsbury, 2024), 60.

87. Lại, *DiVERSE*, 61.

88. Lại, *DiVERSE*, 60.

89. Safia Elhillo, "Chapter 5 Safia Elhillo," in *DiVERSE: Conversations with YA and Children's Verse Novelists*, ed. Linda Weste (London: Bloomsbury, 2024), 36.

90. Elhillo, *DiVERSE*, 36.

91. Elhillo, *DiVERSE*, 35.

92. Elhillo, *DiVERSE*, 36.

93. Jasmine Warga, 'Chapter 6 Jasmine Warga', in *DiVERSE: Conversations with YA and Children's Verse Novelists*, ed. Linda Weste (London: Bloomsbury, 2024), 39.

94. Warga, *DiVERSE*, 39.

95. Warga, *DiVERSE*, 38.

96. Warga, *DiVERSE*, 39.

97. Tim Shortis, "Poetry by Heart: Ten Years on," *Teaching English* 31, March 2, 2023, Manchester: National Association for the Teaching of English, 42.

98. Bernardine Evaristo, *Manifesto* (London: Penguin General UK, 2022), 142.

Chapter 12

1. Jon Ronson, interview by Adam Buxton, *Adam Buxton* Podcast, Episode 4, Jon Ronson, October 2015, 20:39, Acast, https://play.acast.com/s/adambuxton/ep-4-jon-ronson.

2. Brené Brown, Performer, TED, "Listening to Shame," March 2012, *TED*, Ted.com/talks/brene_brown_listening_to_shame?language=en).

Chapter 18

1. Sylviane A. Diouf, *Slavery's Exiles: The Story of the American Maroons* (New York and London: New York University Press, 2014).

Chapter 23

1. Linda Mallozzi, Dir., *Monkey Dance* (USA: 2004), SD Video.

Chapter 24

1. Erika Lee and Judy Yung, *Angel Island: Immigrant Gateway to America* (Oxford: Oxford University Press, 2010).

BIBLIOGRAPHY

American Library Association. "American Library Association Reports Record Number of Demands to Censor Library Books and Materials in 2022." American Library Association. Published March 22, 2023. http://www.ala.org/news/press-releases/2023/03/record-book-bans-2022.

American Library Association. *The State of America's Libraries 2023: A Report from the American Library Association*. Chicago, IL: American Library Association, 2023, 1–18. https://www.ala.org/news/sites/ala.org.news/files/content/state-of-americas-libraries-report-2023-web-version.pdf.

Atta, Dean. *The Black Flamingo*. New York City: Balzer + Bray, Imprint HarperCollins, 2019.

Atta, Dean. *Only on the Weekends*. New York City: Balzer + Bray, Imprint HarperCollins, 2022.

Atta, Dean. "I'm Writing the Stories I Need to Write: A Conversation with Dean Atta." *bigblackbooks* 2021–2024. Produced by Jane Link, n.d. https://www.bigblackbooks.org/dean-atta/.

Australian Human Rights Commission. *Leading for Change: A Blueprint for Cultural Diversity and Inclusive Leadership Revisited*. Sydney: Australian Human Rights Commission, 2018. https://humanrights.gov.au/sites/default/files/document/publication/Leading%20for%20Change_Blueprint2018_FINAL_Web.pdf.

Australian Publishers Association. "Workforce D&I Survey Results Published." Published August 31, 2022. https://publishers.asn.au/Web/Web/Latest/APANews/20220831-Workforce-Diversity-Inclusion-Survey-results.aspx.

Australian Publishers Association. "About Us." 2023. https://www.publishers.asn.au/Web/Web/About-Us/About.aspx?hkey=e6b11061-eef8-44ae-baf5-562ec6e0bed0.

Baron, Chris. *All of Me*. New York City: Feiwel & Friends/Macmillan, 2019.

Baron, Chris. *The Magical Imperfect*. New York City: Feiwel & Friends/Macmillan, 2021.

Baron, Chris. *Spark*. New York City: Feiwel & Friends/Macmillan, 2025.

The BIPOC Project. "Our Mission." Accessed December 14, 2023. https://www.thebipocproject.org/.

Bowen, Susannah, and Beth Driscoll. *The Australian Publishing Industry Workforce Survey on Diversity and Inclusion*. Sydney: Australian Publishers Association and The University of Melbourne, 2022. https://publishers.asn.au/Web/Web/Member-Resources/ResearchReports/Workforce_Survey_2022.aspx.

Brown, Brené. TED: Listening to Shame. March 2012. Available at: ted.com/talks/brene_brown_listening_to_shame?language=en.

Bruchac, Joseph. *Rez Dogs*. New York City: Dial Books, 2022.

Burg, Ann E. *All the Broken Pieces*. New York City: Scholastic, 2009.

Burg, Ann E. *Serafina's Promise*. New York City: Scholastic, 2013.

Burg, Ann E. *Unbound*. New York City: Scholastic, 2016.

Centre for Literacy in Primary Education. *Reflecting Realities: Survey of Ethnic Representation within UK Children's Literature 2017–2021*. London: Centre for Literacy in Primary Education, 2022. https://clpe.org.uk/research/clpe-reflecting-realities-survey-ethnic-representation-within-uk-childrens-literature-2017.

Centre for Literacy in Primary Education. *Reflecting Realities: Survey of Ethnic Representation within UK Children's Literature 2022*. London: Centre for Literacy in Primary Education,

2023. https://clpe.org.uk/research/clpe-reflecting-realities-survey-ethnic-representation-within-uk-childrens-literature-1.

Chowdhury, Radhiah. *It's Hard to Be What You Can't See: Diversity within Australian Publishing. Lessons in Diverse and Inclusive Publishing from the United Kingdom.* The 2019–2020 Beatrice Davis Editorial Fellowship Report. Sydney: Australian Publishers Association, 2020. https://www.publishers.asn.au/common/Uploaded%20files/APA%20Resources/Research/BDEF/BDEF%202019-2020%20Report%20-%20Radhiah%20Chowdhury.pdf.

Congress.gov. "Text—H.R.2889—118th Congress (2023–2024): Right to Read Act of 2023." April 26, 2023. https://www.congress.gov/bill/118th-congress/house-bill/2889/text.

Crossan, Sarah. "Top 10 Verse Novels." *The Guardian.* September 30, 2020. https://www.theguardian.com/books/2020/sep/30/top-10-verse-novels-sarah-crossan-homer-kae-tempest.

The Crossover. Television series April 5, 2023. *IMDb,* U.S.A. https://www.imdb.com/title/tt14296996/.

Crowder, Melanie. *Audacity.* New York City: Philomel Imprint of Penguin Books, 2015.

Cuthew, Lucy. *Blood Moon.* London: Walker Books, 2020.

Diouf, Sylviane A. *Slavery's Exiles: The Story of the American Maroons.* New York and London: New York University Press, 2014.

Diversity Arts Australia, BYP Group and Western Sydney University. *Shifting the Balance: Cultural Diversity in Leadership within the Australian Arts, Screen and Creative Sectors.* Sydney: Diversity Arts Australia, 2019. https://diversityarts.org.au/app/uploads/Shifting-the-Balance-DARTS-small.pdf.

Elassar, Alaa, Taylor Romine, and Andy Rose, CNN. "Judge Orders Books Removed from Texas Public Libraries Due to LGBTQ and Racial Content Must Be Returned within 24 hours." *CNN.* Published 12:09 PM EDT. Sat April 1, 2023. https://edition.cnn.com/2023/04/01/us/texas-book-ban-removed-library-replaced-judge/index.html.

Elhillo, Safia. *Home Is Not a Country.* New York City: Make Me A World/Penguin Random House, 2021.

Engle, Margarita. *Your Heart, My Sky.* New York City: Simon & Schuster, 2021.

Engle, Margarita. *Rima's Rebellion.* New York City: Simon & Schuster, 2022.

Evaristo, Bernardine. *Manifesto.* London: Penguin General UK, 2022.

Faruqi, Reem. *Unsettled.* New York City: HarperCollins, 2021.

Faruqi, Reem. *Golden Girl.* New York City: HarperCollins, 2022.

Faruqi, Reem. *Call Me Adnan.* New York City: HarperCollins, 2023.

Friedman, Jonathan, and Nadine Farid Johnson. "Banned in the USA: The Growing Movement to Censor Books in Schools." PEN America. Published September 19, 2023. https://pen.org/report/banned-usa-growing-movement-to-censor-books-in-schools/.

Frost, Helen. *Keesha's House.* New York City: Farrar, Straus, and Giroux, 2003.

Frost, Helen. *The Braid.* New York City: Farrar, Straus, and Giroux, 2006.

Frost, Helen. *Diamond Willow.* New York City: Farrar, Straus, and Giroux/Frances Foster Books/Macmillan, 2008.

Frost, Helen. *Crossing Stones.* New York City: Farrar, Straus and Giroux/Frances Foster Books/Macmillan, 2009.

Frost, Helen. *All He Knew.* New York City: Farrar, Straus, and Giroux/Macmillan, 2020.

Hacking, Charlotte. "Ten of the Best: Verse Novels." Books for Keeps 256. September 15, 2022. https://booksforkeeps.co.uk/article/ten-of-the-best-verse-novels/.

Hancock, Peter, Capitol News Illinois. "Bill Blocking Libraries from State Funding if They Ban Books Clears General Assembly." *Chicago ABC7.* State Politics. Thursday, May 4, 2023, 1:51PM. https://abc7chicago.com/book-bans-illinois-library-funding-politics/13210227/.

Hemphill, Stephanie. *Your Own, Sylvia.* New York City: Knopf/ Penguin Random House, 2007.

Hemphill, Stephanie. *Language of Fire: Joan of Arc Reimagined.* New York City: Balzer + Bray / HarperCollins, 2019.

Bibliography

Highlights Foundation. "Crafting Novels in Verse: Workshop and Retreat." Rajani LaRocca and Chris Baron, special guest Cordelia Jensen. May 21, 2023–May 24, 2023. https://www.highlightsfoundation.org/workshop/crafting-novels-in-verse-workshop-and-retreat/.

Highlights Foundation. "Revising Your Novel in Verse: An Online Course." Cordelia Jensen, special guest Amber McBride. October 4, 2023–November 15, 2023. https://www.highlightsfoundation.org/workshop/revising-your-novel-in-verse-an-online-course/.

Highlights Foundation. "Writing Poetry to Empower: A Two-Night Mini." Padma Venkatraman and Aida Salazar. December 11, 2023–December 13, 2023. https://www.highlightsfoundation.org/workshop/writing-poetry-to-empower-a-two-night-mini/.

Highlights Foundation. "Diverse Verse Scholarship." Accessed January 6, 2024. https://www.highlightsfoundation.org/diverse-verse-scholarship/.

Highlights Foundation. "Novels in Verse Resources from Our Blog." Accessed January 6, 2024. https://www.highlightsfoundation.org/topics/novels-in-verse/.

Highlights Foundation. "A Strong Start: The First 20 Pages of Your Novel in Verse." Cordelia Jensen, special guest Andrea Beatriz Arango. February 7, 2024–March 7, 2024. https://www.highlightsfoundation.org/workshop/a-strong-start-the-first-20-pages-of-your-novel-in-verse/.

Hilton, Marilyn. *Full Cicada Moon*. New York City: Dial Books/Penguin Random House, 2015.

Holman, Tom. "Room for Improvement." In *In Full Colour: Cultural Diversity in Publishing Today*. Edited by Danuta Kean, 1–15. London: The Bookseller, 2004. https://content.yudu.com/web/1vcls/0A1xp12/InFullColour2004/html/index.html?page=4&origin=reader.

Holt, Kari Anne, Rajani LaRocca, Reem Faruqi, and Chris Baron. "The Joy of Novels in Verse." Episodes 10–13. April 2023. In *The Joyful Learning Podcast*. Produced by Melissa Thom. https://podcasts.apple.com/us/podcast/the-joyful-learning-podcast/id1637178531.

Independent.co.uk. "The IoS Pink List 2012." Published November 4, 2012.

Jensen, Cordelia. *Skyscraping*. New York City: Philomel/Penguin Random House, 2015.

Jensen, Cordelia. *The Way the Light Bends*. New York City: Philomel/Penguin Random House, 2018.

Jilani, Sarah. "In the Far from Diverse Publishing Industry, Sensitivity Readers Are Vital." *The Conversation*. Australian Edition. February 20, 2023. https://theconversation.com/in-the-far-from-diverse-publishing-industry-sensitivity-readers-are-vital-199913#:~:text=Sensitivity%20readers%20are%20contracted%20by,about%20people%20from%20marginalised%20groups.

Kon-yu, Natalie, and Emily Booth. *First Nations and People of Colour Count (FNPOC Count): First Large-Scale Numerical Dataset That Illustrated the Inequity in Australia's Publishing Industry*. Melbourne: Victoria University, 2022. https://content.vu.edu.au/sites/default/files/media/first-nations-and-people-of-colour-count-infographic.pdf.

Kon-yu, Natalie, and Emily Booth. "Research Confirms Lack of Cultural Diversity in Published Literature." Victoria University. Published Thursday October 13, 2022. https://www.vu.edu.au/about-vu/news-events/news/research-confirms-lack-of-cultural-diversity-in-published-literature.

Lại, Thanhhà. *Inside Out & Back Again*. New York City: HarperCollins, 2011.

Lại, Thanhhà. *When Clouds Touch Us*. New York City: HarperCollins, 2023.

Langley, Kaija. *The Order of Things*. New York City: Nancy Paulsen Books/Penguin 2023.

LaRocca, Rajani. *Red, White, and Whole*. New York City: Quill Tree Books/HarperCollins 2021.

Lowitz, Leza. *Up from the Sea*. New York City: Crown Books for Young Readers/ Penguin Random House, 2016.

Lee, Erika, and Judy Yung. *Angel Island: Immigrant Gateway to America*. Oxford: Oxford University Press, 2010.

Lee & Low Books, with co-authors Sarah Park Dahlen, PhD, St. Catherine University, and Nicole Catlin, graduate student, St. Catherine University. "Where Is the Diversity in Publishing?

The 2015 Diversity Baseline Survey Results." *The Open Book Blog. A Blog on Race, Diversity, Education, and Children's Books*. Published January 26, 2016. https://blog.leeandlow.com/2016/01/26/where-is-the-diversity-in-publishing-the-2015-diversity-baseline-survey-results/.

Lee & Low Books, with co-authors Laura M. Jiménez, PhD, Boston University Wheelock College of Education & Human Development, Language and Literacy Department, and Betsy Beckert, graduate student, Boston University Wheelock College of Education & Human Development, Language and Literacy Department. "Where Is the Diversity in Publishing? The 2019 Diversity Baseline Survey Results." *The Open Book Blog. A Blog on Race, Diversity, Education, and Children's Books*. Published January 28, 2020. https://blog.leeandlow.com/2020/01/28/2019diversitybaselinesurvey/.

Lee & Low Books, with co-authors Laura M. Jiménez, PhD, Boston University Wheelock College of Education & Human Development, Language and Literacy Department; Betsy Beckert, PhD candidate, Boston University Wheelock College of Education & Human Development, Language and Literacy Department; Rory Polera, data analyst; and Jake C. Dietiker, undergraduate, Boston University College of Engineering. "Where Is the Diversity in Publishing? The 2023 Diversity Baseline Survey Results." *The Open Book Blog. A Blog on Race, Diversity, Education, and Children's Books*. Published February 28, 2024. https://blog.leeandlow.com/2024/02/28/2023diversitybaselinesurvey/.

Mallozzi, Linda, dir. *Monkey* Dance. Film. USA: 2004. SD Video.

Maughan, Shannon. "Trend Watch with Middle Grade Dealmakers." *Publishers Weekly*, September 09, 2022. https://www.publishersweekly.com/pw/by-topic/childrens/childrens-industry-news/article/90276-trend-watch-with-middle-grade-dealmakers.html.

Mendez, Jasminne. *Aniana Jumps In*. New York City: Dial Books/Penguin Random House, 2023.

Nagai, Mariko. *Dust of Eden: A Novel*. Park Ridge, IL: Albert Whitman & Company, 2014.

Nagai, Mariko. *Under the Broken Sky*. New York City: Henry Holt, 2019.

Nagai, Mariko. *The Sword of Yesterday* (provisional title). New York City: Christy Ottaviano/Little, Brown/Hachette Book Group, forthcoming.

The National Centre for Australian Children's Literature Inc. "The Australian Verse Novels Resource for Younger Readers and Young Adult Readers. NCACL Verse Novels Resource Flyer." NCACL Inc, 2021. Accessed December 14, 2023. https://www.ncacl.org.au/wp-content/uploads/2021/10/NCACL-Verse-Novels-Resource-Flyer-20211001-v1-r1-A4.pdf

The National Centre for Australian Children's Literature Inc. "Australian Verse Novels for Younger Readers and Young Adults." NCACL Inc, 2021. Accessed December 14, 2023. https://www.ncacl.org.au/resources/bibliographies/australian-verse-novels-resource/.

The National Centre for Australian Children's Literature Inc "The NCACL Aboriginal and or Torres Strait Islander Resource." NCACL Inc, 2024. https://www.ncacl.org.au/resources/databases/welcome-to-the-aboriginal-and-or-torres-strait-islander-resource/.

The National Centre for Australian Children's Literature Inc. "The NCACL Cultural Diversity Database." NCACL Inc, 2023. https://www.ncacl.org.au/resources/databases/welcome-to-the-ncacl-cultural-diversity-database/.

National Congress of American Indians. 2001–2023. "Tribal Nations & the United States: An Introduction." Accessed December 14, 2023. https://archive.ncai.org/about-tribes.

National Education Union. *Framework for Developing an Anti-racist Approach*. London: National Education Union. Accessed December 14, 2023. https://neu.org.uk/anti-racism-charter.

Park, Ishle Yi. *Angel & Hannah*. New York City: One World/Penguin Random House, 2021.

PEN America. "Banned in the USA: Rising School Book Bans Threaten Free Expression and Students' First Amendment Rights." Published April 2022. https://pen.org/banned-in-the-usa/#what.

PEN America. "PEN America's Index of School Book Bans." July 1, 2021–June 30, 2022. https://docs.google.com/spreadsheets/d/1hTs_PB7KuTMBtNMESFEGuK-0abzhNxVv4tgpI5-iKe8/edit#gid=1171606318.

Bibliography

PEN America. "Letter to Duval County, FL Schools from PEN America and We Need Diverse Books— Signed by 70 Authors—Calls for Return of 176 Book Titles Pulled from Classroom Libraries." Published December 6, 2022. https://pen.org/press-release/letter-to-duval-county-fl-schools-from-pen-america-and-we-need-diverse-books-signed-by-69-authors-calls-for-return-of-176-book-titles-pulled-from-classroom-libraries/.

Perfection Learning. "Essential Voices Classroom Libraries Grades K-12." Last updated 2024. https://www.perfectionlearning.com/elementary/elementary-class-libr/essential-voices.html.

Pride in Publishing. "About Us." Accessed December 19, 2023. https://prideinpublishing.co.uk/about-us/.

Publishers Association. *UK Publishing Workforce 2020: Diversity, Inclusion and Belonging*. London: Publishers Association, 2021. https://www.publishers.org.uk/wp-content/uploads/2021/01/The-UK-Publishing-Workforce-Diversity-Inclusion-and-Belonging-in-2020.pdf.

Publishers Association. UK *Publishing Workforce 2022: Diversity, Inclusion and Belonging*. London: Publishers Association, 2023. https://www.publishers.org.uk/wp-content/uploads/2023/01/The-UK-Publishing-Workforce-Diversity-Inclusion-and-Belonging-in-2022.pdf.

Publishers Association. *Industry-Wide Statement on the Book & Publishing Industry's Professional Values*. 2023. https://www.publishers.org.uk/publications/an-industry-wide-statement-on-the-book-publishing-industrys-professional-values/.

Ramdarshan Bold, Melanie. *Representation of People of Colour among Children's Book Creators in the UK*. Leeds: BookTrust, 2022. https://www.booktrust.org.uk/globalassets/resources/booktrust-represents/2022/research-reports/booktrust-represents-representation-of-people-of-colour-among-childrens-book-creators-in-the-uk.pdf.

Reese, Debbie. "Banning of Native Voices/Books." American Indians in Children's Literature 2006–2023. Last updated October 16, 2023. https://americanindiansinchildrensliterature.blogspot.com/p/banning-of-native-voicesbooks.html.

Rise Feminist Book Project List. Rise a Feminist Book Project for Ages 0–18. Last Updated January 2023. https://risefeministbooks.wordpress.com/.

Ronson, Jon. Interview by Adam Buxton. *Adam Buxton Podcast* (Episode 4, Jon Ronson, July 10, 2015, 00:58, Acast).

Run, Rebel. Adapted by Manjeet Mann, creator. Dir. by Tessa Walker. Pilot Theatre Co-production with Mercury Theatre Colchester, Belgrade Theatre Coventry, Derby Theatre and York Theatre Royal. Touring March–April 2023. https://www.pilot-theatre.com/production/run-rebel/.

Saha, Anamik. *Re:Thinking "Diversity" in Publishing* (2020). Report Launch, Vimeo, zoom recording June 23, 2020, 1:18:16. https://vimeo.com/433566386?embedded=true&source=vimeo_logo&owner=56579006.

Saha, Anamik, and Sandra van Lente. *Re:Thinking "Diversity" in Publishing*. London: Goldsmiths Press, 2020. https://www.spreadtheword.org.uk/wp-content/uploads/2020/06/Rethinking_diversity_in-publishing_WEB.pdf.

Salazar, Aida. *The Moon Within*. New York City: Scholastic Gold, 2019.

Salazar, Aida. *Land of the Cranes*. New York City: Scholastic Gold, 2020.

Salazar, Aida. *A Seed in the Sun*. New York City: Penguin Random House, 2022.

Sarfas, Kat. "The Best Novels in Verse to Read Right now—B&N Reads." Barnes & Noble. Published March 31, 2021. https://www.barnesandnoble.com/blog/the-best-novels-in-verse-to-read-right-now/.

Saunders, Kirli. *Bindi*. Broome: Magabala Press, 2020.

Sheibani, Jion. *The Silver Chain*. London: Hot Key Books, 2022.

Shortis, Tim. "Poetry by Heart: Ten Years on." In *Teaching English*, 31, March 2, 2023. Manchester: National Association for the Teaching of English, 42.

Spread the Word. "About Us." n.d. Accessed December 14, 2023. https://www.spreadtheword.org.uk/about-us/.

Symmons Roberts, Michael. "Michael Symmons Roberts's Top 10 Verse Novels." *The Guardian*. Published March 20, 2006. https://www.theguardian.com/books/2006/mar/20/top10s.verse.novels.

Thom, Melissa. "The Joy of Novels in Verse." With K.A. Holt, Rajani LaRocca, Reem Faruqi, and Chris Baron. Episodes 10–13. April 2023. In *The Joyful Learning Podcast*. Produced by Melissa Thom. https://podcasts.apple.com/us/podcast/the-joyful-learning-podcast/id1637178531.

Thompson, Holly. *Orchards*. New York City: Delacorte, 2011.

Thompson, Holly. *The Language Inside*. New York City: Delacorte Imprint PRH, 2013.

Thompson, Holly. *Falling into the Dragon's Mouth*. New York City: Square Fish/Macmillan, 2016.

Tregay, Sarah. *Love and Leftovers*. New York City: Katherine Tegen/HarperCollins, 2012.

The UK Law Society. "A Guide to Race and Ethnicity Terminology and Language." Last updated November 28, 2023. https://www.lawsociety.org.uk/topics/ethnic-minority-lawyers/a-guide-to-race-and-ethnicity-terminology-and-language.

United Nations Office of the High Commissioner Human Rights OHCHR. *Born Free and Equal: Sexual Orientation and Gender Identity in International Human Rights Law*. New York: OHCHR, 2019. https://www.ohchr.org/sites/default/files/Documents/Publications/Born_Free_and_Equal_WEB.pdf.

The United States District Court for the Northern District of Florida Pensacola Division Case No. 3:23-cv-10385 Pen American Center, Inc., Sarah Brannen, Lindsay Durtschi, on behalf of herself and her minor children, George M. Johnson, David Levithan, Kyle Lukoff, Ann Novakowski, on behalf of herself and her minor child, Penguin Random House LLC, and Ashley Hope Pérez, Plaintiffs, v. Escambia County School District, and the Escambia County School Board, Defendants. https://pen.org/wp-content/uploads/2023/05/1-Complaint.pdf.

Warga, Jasmine. *Other Words For Home*. New York City: Balzer + Bray/HarperCollins, 2019.

Weatherford, Carole Boston. *Becoming Billie Holiday*. Honesdale, PA: Wordsong, 2008.

Weatherford, Carole Boston. *Beauty Mark*. Somerville, MA: Candlewick Press, 2020.

White, Rae. "Story/Verse." With Pip Harry, Kirli Saunders, Rebecca Jessen, Zana Fraillon. Wednesday, April 12, 2023. Queensland Poetry Festival Pre-event. Produced by Queensland Poetry Festival. YouTube. Online video, 1:01:42. https://www.youtube.com/live/LsD5fyrcxMM.

The Yoto Carnegies. "About the Award." yotocarnegies.co.uk. 2024. https://yotocarnegies.co.uk/about-the-awards/.

The Yoto Carnegies. "Medal for Writing Winners." Accessed January 6, 2024. https://yotocarnegies.co.uk/archive/writing-winners/.

Yu, Chun. *Little Green: Growing Up during the Chinese Cultural Revolution*. New York City: Simon & Schuster/Paula Wiseman, 2005.

INDEX

Index

Index

Index